To Hear Angels Sing by Ramona Cecil
For Bridget O'Keefe, there is no going back. Leaving behind the familiar comforts of her Chicago classroom, Bridget travels to Pinewood, Texas, in the autumn of 1883 to teach and minister to Indian orphans. Seth Krueger can't forgive the Comanche who orphaned him—or God, whom he feels allowed it to happen. For Bridget and Seth to reconcile their differences and ride off together into the sunset will require a miracle—a Christmas miracle.

The Face Of Mary by Darlene Franklin
Five years ago, Joseph "Joey" Carpenter told Mary "Polly" Jessup that he would marry her when she grew up. She treasures his words in her heart, but he forgets her and instead returns home with a law degree—and a girlfriend, the banker's daughter. When the bank prosecutes Polly's absentminded father for taking the bank's money, she turns to Joey for help. Will Joey recognize the face of his true love in time for Christmas?

The Christmas Chain by Janelle Mowery
Emma Pickett never dreamed her quest for vengeance would lead her into the arms of a man who could cause her to falter in her purpose. Suddenly, forgiving and forgetting sounds sweeter than revenge—until she learns his father is the murderer she seeks. Torn between vengeance and compassion, Emma must face a chain of decisions that will forever change her life and the lives of all those around her.

Love Came Home at Christmas by Tamela Hancock Murray
Gabriella Noell is on a mission—to find her grandfather and reunite her family. The last thing on her mind is romance. Finding an itinerant wood-carver is the last thing R.C. wants to do, especially in the company of his spoiled sister and her friend, who are certain to do nothing but impede his business of acquiring real estate. But a God full of surprises plans a wonderful journey for them—if only they will open their hearts.

A WOODLAND CHRISTMAS

FOUR-IN-ONE COLLECTION

FOUR COUPLES FIND LOVE IN
THE PINEY WOODS OF EAST TEXAS

RAMONA CECIL
DARLENE FRANKLIN
JANELLE MOWERY
TAMELA HANCOCK MURRAY

BARBOUR
PUBLISHING

ISBN 978-1-60260-970-9

All scripture quotations are taken from the King James Version of the Bible.

Cover design: Kirk DouPonce, DogEared Design

Published by Barbour Publishing, Inc., P.O. Box 719, Uhrichsville, OH 44683, www.barbourbooks.com

Our mission is to publish and distribute inspirational products offering exceptional value and biblical encouragement to the masses.

 Member of the
Evangelical Christian
Publishers Association

Printed in the United States of America.

TO HEAR ANGELS SING

by Ramona Cecil

Dedication

To my beloved Texans, both transplanted and Texas born; Jennifer, Galen, Matthew, Gabriella, and Emily.

Chapter 1

Suddenly there was with the angel a multitude of the
heavenly host praising God, and saying, Glory to God in
the highest, and on earth peace, good will toward men.
LUKE 2:13–14

Pinewood, Texas, October 1883

S eth Krueger sat up straighter at the train whistle's
shrill blast. From his seat on the bench in front of the
Pinewood train station, he narrowed his eyes toward the
bend in the tracks.

"I have better things to do than to fetch some schoolmarm,"
he grumbled beneath his breath.

The next moment, the train chugged into view, its earsplitting whistle filling the air. With a loud *hiss* of rolling steam, the
locomotive came to a stop.

Breathing a sigh of resignation, he stood to get a better view of the disembarking passengers. A stream of people flowed down the lowered iron steps. Every female appeared to be either attached to other passengers or hurrying to embrace loved ones waiting on the platform.

Seth yanked off his hat and ran his fingers through his hair. He scanned the milling crowd in an attempt to identify and cut out of the herd the woman Violet Barton had sent him to fetch.

A green velvet hat atop a tumble of bright, copper-colored curls caught his eye. The woman reminded him of the porcelain doll he'd seen in the general store's front window. Dressed in a traveling dress and cape that matched her hat, she struggled to maneuver a trunk half her size down the steps. She seemed alone and glanced around as if lost.

Though the woman didn't fit Seth's notion of a spinster schoolteacher, he ambled toward her. At the bottom step, a heavyset man puffed past her, bumping against the girl so hard she almost toppled. Seth watched her chin quiver and hastened his steps.

Once on the platform, she lifted her face. The most beautiful, big green eyes he'd ever seen met his, and Seth's heart bucked.

He reached up to drag his hat from his head, then realized he had it in his hand. "Miss O'Keefe?" he finally managed, unable to wrest his gaze from her glistening eyes.

"Y—yes," she hesitated, taking a half step backward.

"I'm Seth—Seth Krueger. Mrs. B.—that is, Mrs. Barton, Mrs. Violet Barton—sent me to fetch you." Seth called himself every kind of imbecile for tangling his words like a six-year-old with a lariat.

"But where's Sally and Van Taylor? I thought they would. . ."

Lord, don't let her cry.

Half shocked at the prayer spilling from his desperate heart, Seth cleared his throat. "Reckon you'll have to take that up with Mrs. B. Just supposed to fetch you, that's all." He grasped the leather handles of her trunk and forced himself to look away from her lovely features that were threatening to crumple.

"Sally told me what a wonderful woman Mrs. Barton is, sponsoring our ministry."

Seth's heart lifted with the timbre of the girl's voice, and he smiled. "Yes. Yes, she is."

She rewarded his reply with a smile that melted his heart like butter beneath the Texas sun.

Lifting her to the wagon seat took no more effort than lifting a newborn calf. In the easy motion, an intoxicating scent of lavender caressed his nostrils. His hands ached with regret as they relinquished her tiny waist.

"Is the orphanage far?" The false cheerfulness in her voice could not mask the fear that rendered it breathless.

Seth's heart constricted and he gentled his answer. "No, not far, but we'll be goin' to the Circle B."

"But Sally said we would all be staying at the orphanage—"

"Hope you won't mind, but I need to stop at the general store and pick up a couple bales of barbed wire." What he really needed was to steer her away from asking any more questions—especially now that his mind had plain stopped working.

Don't be an addlepated fool. All right, so she's a right pretty girl. Not like you ain't never seen a pretty girl before.

After riding a short distance, Seth pulled hard on the reins and brought the wagon to a halt in front of the general store.

"What—what is that?" The girl dug a snowy white handkerchief from her black beaded reticule and pressed the cloth over her nose and mouth.

He followed her gaze to the wagon that had pulled up next to them. "Hides. Deer and elk, mostly. Probably some alligator hides from the swamps in the piney woods, and maybe even a buffalo hide or two. Reckon they are a mite ripe."

Although unpleasant, the smell was just one of many distasteful odors Seth had learned to tolerate. But the delicate creature beside him appeared overcome by the stench.

Even worse, One-Eyed Jake, the buffalo skinner, leered at her with his good eye as he climbed down from his wagon.

"Reckon maybe it would be best if you came in with me," Seth mumbled.

She answered with an emphatic nod and pressed the handkerchief harder against her face.

He guided her inside the dark, dusty building.

The moment they stepped inside, Jake entered behind them. In what appeared to be an intentional move, the skinner brushed against the pretty newcomer.

Miss O'Keefe shrank from the foul-smelling man and moved closer to Seth. Her nearness sent a pleasant warmth flooding through him and set his heart pounding like an Indian war drum.

"I suggest you watch where you're goin', Jake." Seth kept his voice low but glared a threat at the man, whose lecherous gaze slid down the young woman's form.

"Beggin' yer pardon, miss. Didn't mean no harm." Jake displayed a yellow-toothed grin and lifted a greasy black felt hat from his sweaty, balding pate.

Jake pushed past them, and Miss O'Keefe's hat shook as if she were shuddering. Perhaps bringing the woman into the store had not been the best idea.

Remorse struck Seth like a punch in the gut. He wished Jake Tuley was the worst the schoolmarm would face today.

Bridget's bottom felt bruised as they bounced along on the wagon that wound through mile after mile of tall grass and groves of pine trees.

Lord, help me. What have I done?

Her heart shook with trepidation. Only weeks ago, the calling had seemed so clear. She should follow her friends Van and Sally Taylor and take the gospel to the Indian orphanage Violet Barton and the Women's Missionary Union established near Pinewood, Texas. But now she doubted the wisdom of leaving her safe, familiar teaching job in Chicago.

Her unsteady fingers found the gold cross pendant hanging at her throat. She caressed it, wishing her mother could send strength and reassurance to her from heaven.

Despite the warm Texas sun, she shivered. Surely, the horrible-smelling, filthy man with the eye patch would visit her in nightmares. Only now, out here in the open country, did she feel safe enough to mention the subject.

"Are there many like him?" She tilted her head toward the man beside her who guided the team of horses through yet another grove of pines.

"Many like who?" Seth Krueger glanced across his right shoulder at her.

"Men like that—that man in the store." Fear gripped her

11

again. She tried to hide it by uselessly brushing at the pine needles the stiff breeze kept depositing in her lap.

"One-Eyed Jake?" Somehow she found the man's smile comforting. "Naw, Jake's pretty much one of a kind. He's an old buffalo hunter from up around the Red River and Wichita Falls. Him and others hunted out the buffalo to deprive the savages of 'em. But with most all the buffalo gone now, and the savages corralled up at Fort Sill, Jake came down here to harvest sundry hides from the piney woods." He gave her a sidelong grin. "Jake brings the hides to Pinewood to ship out on the railroad."

The man's disparaging term for the Indians raised Bridget's righteous ire. "Savages? Is that what you think of the Indians? They are God's children, too, made in His image as surely as you and I." He gave a sarcastic snort and she bristled. Stiffening, she glared at him. "I feel privileged that God has led me on this mission to bring some of the young ones to Christ."

"Well, I couldn't tell you what God looks like, but I'm right certain it ain't no murderin', red-skinned heathen," he drawled with a chuckle. "If you ask me, this whole scheme of Mrs. B.'s is folly. Tryin' to save the redskins' souls." He snorted again. "Way I see it, you can't save somethin' that don't exist."

While Bridget tried to think of a scathing retort, the man nodded.

"Well, here we are—the Circle B." His announcement drove all other thoughts from Bridget's mind.

Two tall poles flanked the gently curving road with a swinging sign suspended between them. Into the sign was burned a capital *B* nestled in the center of a circle.

Bridget could see why Seth Krueger's voice swelled with

pride. A short distance away, an imposing two-story log house crowned a knoll wreathed by stately pines.

They came to a stop in front of the house, and apprehension gripped Bridget's stomach like a cold fist. The man climbed down from the wagon, then came around and helped her to the ground. Her legs wobbled up the porch steps, and she thanked the Lord for the man's strong arm supporting her. She would feel better as soon as she saw Sally and Van again. Her heart pounded with happy anticipation of their warm reunion.

Inside, he led her along a narrow entranceway that opened on the right to a large, bright space. The room, dominated by a gigantic fireplace made from smooth gray stones, exuded an atmosphere of rustic elegance.

A middle-aged woman dressed in black rose from a maroon velvet chair near the fireplace. She wore her salt-and-pepper hair parted down the middle of her head and pulled severely back in a bun. A sad smile graced her kind face.

"My dear Miss O'Keefe." She walked toward Bridget with one hand outstretched. With her other hand, she dabbed a lace handkerchief at her tear-filled blue eyes.

A sense of foreboding filled Bridget. "Where are the Taylors? Where are Sally and Van?"

"My dear girl. I'm so sorry." The woman's warm fingers curled gently around Bridget's trembling hand. "They are gone. The Lord has taken them."

Chapter 2

The large log room beyond Violet Barton's distraught face swirled around Bridget. What the woman had just told Bridget was impossible.

It has to be impossible.

As Bridget's legs buckled beneath her, Seth Krueger reached an arm around her waist, preventing her from collapsing to the knotty pine floor. He helped her to the horsehair sofa.

"Oh, I was afraid of this." The woman fretted, anxiously rubbing Bridget's hands. "Seth, go to the kitchen and tell Sadie you need to fetch a glass of cool water for Miss O'Keefe."

Seth seemed reluctant to leave but finally released his firm grip on Bridget's waist.

Bridget was vaguely aware of Violet Barton rubbing her hand and whispering unintelligible laments.

The next moment, she felt the warm strength of Seth's arm supporting her shoulders and helping her to sit up. He held a glass of water to her lips. When the cool liquid hit her shock-constricted throat, she coughed.

"Slow," he whispered, "real slow now."

His warm breath fanned her cheek. She gazed into his pale blue eyes. In her excitement and apprehension, she hadn't noticed until now what an exceptionally handsome man he was. He looked to be only a few years older than she. Blond hair, bleached nearly white by the hot Texas sun, framed his tanned, boyish face. He carried the scent of leather and a faint whiff of smells that reminded her of the Chicago stockyards. Altogether, not unpleasant aromas.

"You don't know how sorry I am that you had to learn this way." Violet Barton's voice sagged with regret. "When it happened, we'd already received your telegraph saying you'd left Chicago."

"How?" Bridget managed to rasp.

"Last Saturday they were on their way to Pinewood for supplies. We think something spooked their horses. We don't really know." Violet shook her head as if still struggling with her own disbelief. "Seth and my husband, Andrew, found the wagon at the bottom of a gulch with the couple beneath it." She stifled a strangled sob and dabbed at her eyes again with the handkerchief.

"Do you think they suffered?" Bridget couldn't bear the thought. She'd grown close to the young, enthusiastic missionary couple who had attended her church in Chicago.

Seth shook his head. "I'm sure it was quick." His kind blue gaze met hers squarely and she believed him. The thought soothed her.

The next moment the broader realization struck, and panic seized her. She now faced an altered future. Would she live at the orphanage and try to do alone the jobs the three of them had planned?

"You will be staying here at the ranch of course," Violet Barton said, as if reading her mind. She turned to Seth Krueger. "Seth, please take Miss O'Keefe's portmanteau up to the yellow room."

"Yes, ma'am."

Bridget's mind raced blindly through a fog of uncertainty, grief, and confusion. What would become of her now? Someone else had her teaching job in Chicago. There was no going back.

"Violet told me what you did. . .for Van and Sally. Thank you." Bridget glanced at Seth as they bounced along on the buckboard. Though Violet had urged her to rest for a few days before visiting the orphanage, Bridget was determined to make the three-mile trek the next morning.

Seth fidgeted and cleared his throat. "I'm sorry. Reckon I shoulda told you what happened when you got here. I—"

"No. You were right to wait. I'm glad I was at the Circle B with you and Violet when I learned." Gratitude filled Bridget's heart as tears filled her eyes. "Violet told me how you stayed with them—Van and Sally—until Andrew could get help." She brushed a tear from her cheek. "She said you sat with them for over two hours, keeping away. . .animals." Her voice snagged on the last word.

Seth's Adam's apple moved with a swallow. "It was the decent thing to do. Anybody would have—"

"I don't think so. I think it took someone very special to do that." In light of what Violet had told her, Bridget's opinion of Seth Krueger had risen greatly since their first meeting in

Pinewood yesterday afternoon. His disparaging words about the Indians notwithstanding, she was beginning to understand why the Bartons held their ranch foreman in such high regard.

He gave her a sad smile that sent her heart tumbling. "I wish I could have done more." He shrugged. "If me and Mr. B. had come along a few minutes earlier. . ."

She touched his arm. "You did all you could. More than most. And the lovely crosses you made to mark their gravesite—you didn't have to do that."

His face turned red, and he cleared his throat again, his gaze sliding to the toes of his dusty boots, perched against the wagon's angled footboard. There was something very sweet and touching about his embarrassment at her praise.

Looking up, he bobbed his head. "House is up yonder."

Bridget followed his gaze, and a broken-down farmhouse soon came into view.

As Seth pulled the buckboard to a stop, Bridget's spirit wilted. Weathered gray boards covered the two-story building. An eave creaked as it swung precariously in the breeze. If the house had ever had a coat of paint, the relentless Texas sun and wind had long since worn it away.

"Hasn't anyone even tried to fix it up?" she asked.

"Violet said the Taylors planned to before. . ." Allowing the unfinished thought to dangle, he wound the reins around the wagon brake and jumped to the ground.

He helped Bridget down then climbed back onto the wagon.

"You're not coming in with me?" Surprised and hurt, she looked up at Seth, who looked everywhere but at her face.

He dragged off his stained gray hat and studied the sweat-band lining its bowl for a moment before slapping the hat back on his head. "Naw. I'd rather stay out here. Maybe catch forty winks." The muscles worked in his jaw.

Bridget's stomach twisted in a nervous knot. Irritation buzzed inside her like the flies tormenting the pair of horses hitched to the wagon. Even a cowboy unschooled in social graces should know enough to not leave a woman alone.

She grasped the dark leather reins sagging against the nearest horse's rump. "You promised to escort me. You can't just leave me alone in an unfamiliar place."

He blushed but still didn't meet her eyes. "Old Ming Li won't hurt ya," he said gruffly. He jerked his head toward the ramshackle house. "I've got no business in there."

From his derisive comments yesterday, Bridget took Seth to mean he'd rather not go near Indians.

"Have a nice nap!" She couldn't keep the sharp edge from her voice. How was it that a man who'd otherwise shown him-self to be kind and caring could, at the same time, hold orphan children in disdain simply because they were Indians?

Heaving a sigh, Bridget headed for the house. Seth Krueger was an enigma.

She felt ridiculous shoving open the rusty-hinged gate. A couple of feet away, a great gap in the broken-down picket fence offered easy entrance to the yard strewn with pine needles. Her pounding heart drowned out the sound of her knuckles rapping against the weathered wood of the door.

The door opened to reveal a Chinese woman who smiled and bowed. The knot in Bridget's stomach loosened a bit.

"I am Bridget O'Keefe, the new teacher."

"Ah, yes, Missy Teacher. Come in, come in. I Ming Li." Ming Li's upper torso bobbed her invitation as she backed into the foyer.

The smell of stewed chicken and indiscernible spices welcomed Bridget into the house.

"Missus Violet say you come. Missus Sally, too, and Mr. Van. So sorry. So sorry." The smile vanished as she shook her head.

"Thank you." Bridget could not help staring. She guessed Ming Li's age to be about forty. Strands of gray threaded through the shiny black braid down her back. Instead of a dress, she wore a charcoal gray tunic with voluminous sleeves over baggy pantaloons. Remarkably tiny feet were covered with white cotton socks and tucked into flat black slippers.

According to Violet, the widowed Ming Li's husband had been one of the Chinese immigrants who'd helped to build the railroad.

"I call children." The woman's smile returned, pushing rosy cheeks up to slits twinkling with dark eyes.

"Come! Come now!" Ming Li clapped her hands sharply twice. The sound echoed around the sparsely furnished room. Nothing happened. "Come, come, I say!"

Gradually, little copper faces emerged from side rooms. Bridget lifted her gaze to the old creaking stairway where four more peered down through rickety spindles.

When they had all gathered around Ming Li like chicks around a mother hen, Bridget counted eight. Most were not yet in their teens. A boy, perhaps twelve or thirteen years of age, looked to be the oldest; a girl about seven years of age, the youngest.

"Missy Bridget, new teacher."

The children remained silent and somber-faced at Ming Li's introduction.

Bridget smiled. "I will be coming here soon to teach you English, arithmetic, and all about Jesus. Lots of wonderful stories from the Bible." Her announcement was met with stony stares, and the knot in Bridget's belly tightened. Though the children were undoubtedly grieving the loss of Sally and Van, Bridget hadn't expected them to be so reticent.

A girl who looked to be about ten emerged from behind Ming Li. Her pleasant copper face registered no fear, only curiosity. "They are afraid you will go to heaven like Mrs. Sally and Mr. Van."

Bridget's heart crumbled. She should have thought. These poor children had known so much loss. First their parents, then Sally and Van. She could see why they were reluctant to welcome anyone else into their lives.

Bridget looked into the girl's intelligent dark eyes. "Someday I will go to heaven, but God willing, not for many, many years. So tell me, what is your name?"

"Singing Bird, but my aunt called me *Liebes Mädchen*. She was my second mother when my mother and father died. Then the soldiers came and killed her and my grandfather and all the other grown people of our tribe."

Choking back tears, Bridget gave the girl a hug, overcome by the thought of how much grief this little one had experienced. She asked each child his or her name, then said her farewells, promising to return soon.

A few minutes later, Bridget was still blinking back tears as she and Seth bumped along the dusty road. "Do you know how the children were orphaned?" Perhaps if Seth knew their story, he might be more sympathetic.

He gave an indifferent shrug. "Some kind of a skirmish when the soldiers were roundin' up renegade bands of Comanche back in seventy-seven."

His matter-of-fact tone infuriated Bridget. "Those children's parents were murdered in front of them."

Seth turned steely blue eyes to hers, and the muscles worked in his jaw.

"Miss O'Keefe, Indians were not the only ones killed that day."

"I know. Sally told me there was a gun battle between the soldiers and the Indians." Bridget tempered her voice. Nothing would be accomplished by quarreling with the Bartons' foreman. "I just meant it must have been horrendous for them—the children, I mean."

"You ask me, they should be up at Fort Sill with the rest of the savages. But Mrs. B., well, she got wind of it and was dead set against that."

"Thank the Lord!"

At her pronouncement, a wry grin lifted Seth's lips. When her heart fluttered—a now familiar response to the handsome ranch foreman's smile—Bridget couldn't decide if she was angrier with herself or with Seth.

"Not sure what the Lord had to do with it. What got it done was Mr. B. ridin' ramrod on the Chisholm years back with the Fort Sill commander."

"They've been in that drafty house for six years?" On this one point, Bridget had to agree with Seth. Accommodations at the fort might have been better.

"No. Until last year, they lived in a little house in Pinewood with Ming Li. When the house was torn down to make way for a railroad spur, Mrs. B. moved 'em to that abandoned farmhouse on Barton land." He gave her a lopsided grin and Bridget's heart turned another somersault. "That's when Mrs. B. and her bunch of church women started lookin' for someone like you and the Taylors to teach 'em."

"You mean the Women's Missionary Union."

"If you say so." He snorted. "As if keepin' 'em wasn't enough, now they're determined to educate 'em."

His grin evaporated, replaced by a puzzled look that wrinkled his brow. Alert, he squinted at a cloud of dust in the road ahead.

Bridget followed his gaze and fear slithered down her spine. Out of the rolling dust emerged a mule-drawn wagon, its dirty canvas top billowing against the pale blue sky like a storm cloud.

After the frightening encounter at the general store, Bridget had hoped to avoid the foul animal skinner. So as the wagon rumbled nearer, relief surged through her. The driver was not the repulsive One-Eyed Jake.

Indeed, as the other wagon came up even with theirs, she saw that two pewter gray eyes shone from the man's bewhiskered, grandfatherly face.

He smiled. "Could you kind folks direct me to Mr. Andrew Barton's ranch, the Circle B?"

The pleasant scents of fresh-cut wood, tung oil, and varnish wafting from the wagon's interior tickled Bridget's nose.

"That's where we're headed." Seth rose a few inches off his seat and reached a hand out to the old gentleman. "I'm

Seth Krueger, Circle B foreman." He shot a glancing smile at Bridget. "And this is Miss Bridget O'Keefe, a friend of Mrs. Barton's."

"Gabe Noell. Happy to make your acquaintance." The man tipped his worn brown hat toward Bridget, then clasped Seth's hand. His bare forearm beneath rolled-up sleeves looked remarkably firm and strong for a man of his apparent years.

He eyed Seth and Bridget with what felt like a soul-penetrating gaze that warmed Bridget's face. Did he think them sweethearts? The thought compelled her to clear up any such misconception.

"I'm the new teacher at the Indian orphanage sponsored by the Women's Missionary Union," she blurted. "I've just met my students for the first time, and Mr. Krueger is escorting me back to the ranch."

"Ah." Gabe's bushy dark brows bristled up and he lifted his hat higher this time, giving her a good peek at his salt-and-pepper hair. "A most admirable occupation in the service of our Lord, miss." Merry wrinkles creased the corners of his eyes with his widening smile. "As for myself, my trade is that of carpenter, wood-carver, and some say purveyor of sawdust sermons." His gaze bounced between Bridget and Seth. "I met Mr. Barton in the Pinewood General Store the other day. Said he'd like me to come by, that he had a couple woodworking projects for me."

Seth tensed beside Bridget, and though his smile remained, it looked forced. "You're welcome to follow us to the ranch, Mr. Noell. It's only a couple miles northeast of here."

As they jostled toward the ranch with the wood-carver behind them, sadness gripped Bridget. Seth had acted congenial to the stranger until Gabe Noell spoke of his faith. The wood-carver had just confirmed Bridget's niggling suspicion that Seth remained outside Christ's fold—and was quite content to stay there.

Chapter 3

"Teach me to ride."

At Bridget O'Keefe's bright voice, Seth pushed away from the corral fence he was leaning against and swung around to face her. His heart gave its usual leap when he gazed at the diminutive teacher. The morning sun danced over her russet curls, turning them to burnished copper.

"Is that an order?" He couldn't stop the grin tugging at his lips.

"No, it's a request."

"Sounded like an order to me." He forced his eyes back to the wild mustang colts bucking and prancing in the corral. If the rush of warmth he felt spreading over his face showed, he'd rather she didn't see it.

"If I could ride, you wouldn't have to take me to the orphanage every day."

Confident he had his features under control, Seth turned to her again. "It ain't safe for you to ride out there alone."

The obstinate lift of her chin indicated what she thought

of his concern. "We've been traveling that road for a week now, and the only remarkable animal I've seen was that armor-plated little creature that scurried across the road in front of the wagon yesterday." Her green eyes flashed over her cute turned-up nose, which was sprinkled with golden freckles.

If Seth had ever seen anything more beautiful than Bridget O'Keefe, he couldn't remember when. "Oh yes, the ferocious armadillo," he managed in an almost normal-sounding voice. Try as he might, he could not rein his galloping heart to a walk. He had no interest in looking for reasons to spend less time with her.

His gaze moseyed over her, drinking in her beauty. Her blouse, the color of a green apple, matched her eyes perfectly. Her sturdy-booted stance, along with her outfit—a brown riding skirt and a vest that hugged her curves—told him she wasn't likely to take no for an answer.

"There's plenty of dangers you couldn't begin to imagine. An inexperienced rider has no business out there alone."

"I could ride one of those." She nodded toward the mustang colts. "They are not very big."

Seth chuckled. "And I just might sprout wings and fly! They're mustangs—wild horses. They haven't been saddle-broke yet."

"Well, if you won't teach me, I'm sure Tad will." Giving a huff, she turned and stomped toward the Barton's nephew, who was heading for the corral with a saddle slung over his shoulder. "You'll teach me to ride, won't you, Tad?"

"Now, there's a chore a man wouldn't mind." Tad grinned. Lifting his hat, he pushed dark curls from his forehead with the back of his hand. His bright blue eyes traveled lazily over Bridget.

She flashed her pretty smile at Tad Riedel, and an uncomfortable feeling twisted in Seth's gut. He strode toward the pair, his fists clenched. "No, he won't." He narrowed his eyes at the young cowboy barely out of his teens and as undisciplined as the mustangs in the corral. Seth couldn't abide the thought of Tad lifting Bridget on and off a horse. He had no intention of allowing them to ride out of the paddock together.

"You've got work here to do." Seth glared at the boy, intent on making his meaning plain. "Start lead-breaking that black mustang."

"Right, boss." A heavy sigh followed Tad's reply. "Miss." With a sad smile and a lingering look, Tad lifted his hat toward Bridget before complying with Seth's order.

Bridget spun toward Seth, eyes flashing and fists planted stubbornly on her hips. "If you won't let Tad teach me, then I'll just find someone else!"

"Whoa, there. Don't get yer Irish up. I never said I wouldn't teach you." Grinning, Seth laid his hand on her shoulder. He had to admire the spunk of this slip of a girl who had come halfway across the continent to teach orphan Comanche. "I just said you couldn't ride the mustangs. I'll find one you *can* ride."

He saddled a lady-broke mare and helped Bridget mount it. During the next hour as they rode over the land, Seth's admiration for Bridget grew. Her fear soon turned to confidence, and he never found it necessary to repeat an instruction.

Brains, courage, and beauty, all in one comely little package.

Bridget O'Keefe was more than a man had a right to

dream of. Certainly more than *he* had a right to.

She clicked her tongue and kicked the mare to a quicker pace. At her smile, Seth's heart bolted like a colt at a rifle shot.

"How am I doing?" A happy laugh warbled through her voice.

"Like you were born to ride," he said, unable to budge his gaze from her face as their horses cantered along side by side. A gust of wind blew a bright curl across her forehead. Giggling, she caught it with the crook of a finger. The heart-stopping beauty of the picture took Seth's breath away.

They crested a hill, and Seth reined his horse to a stop. Bridget's horse stopped beside his.

Her eyes widening with wonder, Bridget panned the acres of fescue and johnson grass below them edged by vast pine forests and dotted with several hundred head of cattle. "How far does Circle B land go?"

"Further than the eye can see, includin' five hundred acres of pine forest beyond this pasture." He enjoyed watching her childlike astonishment as she took in the spreading vista. "The Bartons own two thousand acres. About a quarter of that in grazin' land and the rest in loggin' forests and land they share-crop off for corn and cotton farmin'. One day I plan to have a place as big—maybe bigger."

Seth realized with a jolt that he had never shared that dream with anyone. Yet something about this girl caused him to want to open his heart and display his dreams like treasures before her.

"That's what you were buying at the store the day I arrived." She pointed toward a string of barbed wire sagging on the ground between two posts.

At the sight, Seth's anger flared. Dismounting in a leap, he strode to the fence and kicked at the downed wire in disgust.

"What is it?" Before he could caution her not to, Bridget dismounted.

"Poachers." He ground the word through his clenched jaw. "They look for places like this away from the loggin' sites to get access into the woods for game." He cocked his head toward the longhorns grazing in the distance. "Trouble is, it usually don't bother 'em to do some rustlin' on the way in and out. Even a few Caddo Injuns in the next county have been complainin' about poachers."

He walked the fence line, checking for more damage, keenly aware of Bridget's presence behind him. A few yards later, he found another length of cut wire and blew out a long breath in frustration.

"Why do you hate them so?"

Turning, Seth smiled at her. She'd obviously misread his dismay at the vandalism.

"The poachers? They make my job a long sight harder, and Mr. B. ain't gonna like hearin' what I found. But I can't say I downright hate 'em."

"No. Why do you hate the Indians?"

Her question stopped Seth in his tracks. He swallowed hard, resting his hand on the top of a fence post. This sweet, spunky girl he admired—no, more than admired—had just dragged him back to a place he didn't care to revisit.

He allowed his eyes to meet hers and found no hint of reproach, only kind curiosity and a longing for understanding.

"It was a long time ago." He shoved the words through his tightening throat.

"What happened?" The caring touch of her hand on his arm warmed him as if the sun had split the canopy of gray clouds overhead.

"When I was twelve years old, my pa got the notion to sell our land in Pennsylvania and move the family to Texas." Seth marveled at how the story he hadn't recounted for years began to spill out at Bridget's gentle nudging. "So he bought land up by the Red River and started a dairy farm. Right smack in Comanche territory. My folks thought if they were kind to the Indians, the Indians would be kind to them. That's what they believed. They learned different."

The memory of his parents' trusting innocence soured Seth's tone. "I'd gone to the barn to start the mornin' milkin' when I heard the Comanches' whoops. I looked through a knothole in the barn door and saw my pa tryin' to reason with a war party." The picture flashed again before Seth's eyes, and he gripped the fence post until his hand hurt.

"What happened then?" Her kind voice prodded him on.

"I watched one of the painted devils split Pa's head open with a war axe." Seth ignored Bridget's gasp. "They took my mother and my sister."

"What did you do?"

"What *could* I do? I was twelve." Seth regretted the anger in his voice. He didn't want Bridget to think it was directed at her. Tempering his tone, he continued. "I buried my pa, then walked to the next county. An old couple, the Pritcherts, knew my family and took me in. After they died I started ridin' cattle on the Chisholm. That's where I met Mr. B. He took me under his wing. Him and Violet have been like parents to me ever since."

"I'm sorry, Seth." At her sweet compassion, he swallowed hard.

A jagged flash of lightning ripped across dark thunder-clouds along the southern horizon. The cattle in the pasture below set to bawling.

Seth turned his face toward the approaching storm. "Better head back, I reckon." A thunderclap swallowed his words. The wind had picked up, snatching at his hat and blowing the copper curls framing Bridget's face.

He turned toward the horses, glad for a reason to change the subject and leave the painful memories behind.

"Seth, I know how difficult it is to be left alone as a child." She seemed unwilling to let it go. "I was orphaned myself at the age of eleven. My parents died of typhoid fever. I guess being orphans is something we have in common."

Turned up to his, her smiling face looked like delicate pink and white porcelain.

He stood mute, surprised by her revelation and mesmer-ized by her beauty.

The silence exploded with a deafening *crack* followed by bone-jarring thunder, jerking Seth from his trance. The next instant, a vague sensation of tremors worked its way up through the soles of his boots. At a distant rumbling sound, he turned and looked southward.

Barely visible amid a cloud of dust, a brown and white wall of cattle raced straight toward him and Bridget. The animals' long horns stretched out like curved sabers in front of them.

Seth glanced several yards north to where their grazing horses had wandered, now with their heads up, alert. Fear twisted a knot in his stomach.

"What is it?" Though obviously unaware of the approaching danger, Bridget's face reflected the alarm in his.

"Stampede!"

Chapter 4

Bridget stood paralyzed at the sight of the bawling wave of cattle bearing down on them.

"Hurry!" Seth gripped her hand and they raced toward the horses. Before she could catch her breath, he flung her up onto his horse sidesaddle. He mounted behind her and kicked the horse into a gallop toward the sprawling safety of a lone oak tree. Perched between the saddle's pommel and Seth, Bridget twisted and pressed her face against his chest. "God protect us. Please protect us both." Trembling, she murmured her prayer against the coarse wool of his shirtfront.

They sidled up against a gigantic oak tree. Seth clung to the reins with one hand, while his other arm held Bridget tight against him. "Shh, steady now, steady." The soothing words, no doubt meant to calm the snorting and shifting horse beneath them, comforted Bridget's terror-filled heart.

The cattle herd thundered around them. Bridget coughed from the dust and ground her face harder into Seth's chest. His strong arms, wrapped securely around her, offered a sense of security amid the tumult. When the din faded and the earth became quiet again, she lifted her face.

He leaned back so he could see her face but kept his arms clamped around her. "Are you all right?" Beneath pale brows drawn together, his blue eyes were filled with concern.

Bridget realized that she had never been so "all right" in her whole life. "Y–yes. I think so." She knew she could not entirely attribute her hammering heart and breathlessness to fright.

The tension in Seth's arm muscles relaxed a bit. In the long moment of their shared gaze, a silent understanding passed between them.

It happened slowly, as in a dream. His arms tightened around her again, and his eyes closed an instant before she closed her own. When his lips touched hers, the gathering storm, the distant sound of bawling cattle, the whole world around them vanished. Only the two of them existed. Held in his secure embrace, she felt weightless beneath his kiss while his lips caressed hers with a tender urgency.

His lips relinquished hers, and he cleared his throat as if embarrassed. "I'm sorry. I shouldn't have done that."

Bridget opened her eyes and blinked, regretting that the tender moment had passed. She had never known such exquisite joy. It spread through her whole body. Every nerve ending from her scalp to her toes tingled as if she'd taken a direct hit from the lightning bolts slashing across the slate gray sky. "Don't be," she managed in a breathless whisper. "I'm not." She'd never spoken truer words. Of the many emotions surging through her, sorrow was not among them.

For a long while they rode in silence. Bridget's heart

thundered within her like the stampede that had just passed them. What was she feeling? What did it mean? Guilt filled her, squelching her joy. *He's not a Christian. How could you have? How could you feel like this about him?*

A chill wind gusted, nipping at her face. She couldn't resist leaning against the warmth of Seth's chest.

"Are you cold?" He leaned closer as if to shield her from the wind.

"A little." She snuggled against him. "Why do you think they did it?" They were wending their way through a tranquil sea of cattle. The stupid beasts that only a few minutes earlier had been charging in panic now grazed leisurely.

"Stampede?" His chest moved with the chuckle that rumbled up from deep in his throat. The sound sent a ridiculous thrill through her. "The thunder and lightning, I reckon. I should have thought—"

"My horse!" Remembering her abandoned steed, Bridget stiffened in the saddle. She didn't like to think she'd cost the Circle B a horse.

"She knows her way home."

This time she gave in to the rich sound of his throaty laugh and relaxed once more against him.

Sure enough, a few minutes later when they rode into the barn, they found the mare in a stall munching happily on hay.

"See, I told you she'd be here." Seth dismounted and reached up to help Bridget down.

Joy swept through her as his strong hands held her in a secure grip. *You can't. You mustn't allow. . .* If only he were a Christian. If only he were a believer.

A thought struck her with a jolt like the lightning that

had caused the stampede. She could witness to him. She could bring him to Christ. Perhaps God did mean for Seth Krueger to be part of Bridget's mission work here.

"I could. . ." He cleared his throat again, a habit Bridget had begun to notice about Seth whenever he seemed uncomfortable or embarrassed. He looked at the straw-covered dirt floor. His sweet shyness touched her heart as softly as the music of the rain now drumming on the barn roof. "I could ride out with you to the orphan house. . .until you get used to riding." He met her gaze now, hope shining from his eyes.

"I think that would be a wonderful idea." Her words tumbled out in an eager rush. She wasn't nearly as enthused about making the trip without him as she had earlier thought.

He blew out a long breath as if he'd been holding it.

Bridget knew she must crack open the door to the subject of faith if there was ever to be hope of a relationship between them. If he could not accept Christ, she must nip in the bud this blissful feeling in her chest before it bloomed. Her heart ached with the thought. Yet she must not falter.

She laid her hand gently on his arm and mustered her courage with a deep breath that frayed at the edges when she let it out.

"Seth, I know you're not an especially God-fearing man. I hope you don't blame God for what happened to your parents and sister. You shouldn't. And you shouldn't hold it against the Indian children." He drew back, but she forged on. "It wouldn't be fair. Just as it wouldn't be fair for me to hold a grudge against the Polish immigrants who infected my parents with typhoid when my folks helped them move into our tenement." She grasped his hands, which had turned rigid. "Don't you see?

These Indian children are orphans, too, just like us. They need to be taught about God's love—about Christ's commandments that we love our neighbor as ourselves."

He stiffened and pulled away from her, his face reddening. A thunderclap sounded in the distance, as if it were generated by his stormy countenance.

The shift in his demeanor frightened Bridget. Feeling the blood drain from her face, she shrank from his growing anger.

"God? You speak to me of God? God turned His back on my family when they needed His help!" Muscles worked in his taut jaw, and he shook with the fury she'd unleashed. "Yes, I blame God! And maybe I don't want to stop blaming Him, or the Indians." His glare sizzled into her like a branding iron. "And maybe, Miss O'Keefe, thou art just better than me!"

Bridget's heart shredded. Unwilling to let him see the angry tears filling her eyes, she turned and ran from the barn, through the driving rain to the ranch house.

A half hour later she still lay face down on her bed, sobbing.

The howling wind assailed the windowpane with loud splats of rain, interspersed with the crackle of lightning and the deep rumble of thunder.

Bridget gave free rein to her emotions, glad for the noise of the storm drowning out the sound of her anguish. Why had she allowed herself to care for Seth Krueger? She wadded the Texas star quilt in her fists, as angry at her own weakness as with Seth's stubborn rejection of God and his bias against the Indians.

His words—said in a sarcastic tone, which had skated

dangerously close to blasphemy—rang in her ears. He had actually accused her of having a "holier than thou" attitude.

Sniffing, she pushed up to a sitting position and swiped at her wet cheeks with the back of her hand. Seth Krueger was a stiff-necked clod, and she was acting like a silly girl. She would simply squelch her feelings for the man. He wasn't the reason she came here. She came here to teach and minister to the Indian children.

As if mocking her resolve, the memory of Seth's kiss returned, enveloping her in sweet despair. Her heart throbbed with a deep ache. Falling out of love might not be so easily accomplished after all.

Chapter 5

A cool breeze greeted Bridget as she stepped onto the porch that ran across the front of the Bartons' home. With Violet and her cook, Sadie Russell, working on preparations for tomorrow's big meal, the kitchen seemed over-crowded. Besides, the day was far too pleasant to work inside when Bridget could just as easily peel apples in the fresh air.

She set her basket of Jonathan apples on the porch boards. Settling into one of the two rocking chairs, she nestled the empty crockery bowl, complete with paring knife, in her lap. In front of her, the midmorning sunshine poured like molten butter over the bare ground between the house and barn, then reached the porch, splashing across her feet.

The chair creaked softly as Bridget bent and plucked an apple from the basket. She tried to remember a late November day this warm in Chicago but couldn't think of one. She should have utilized these rocking chairs out here on the porch sooner. This would be a perfect place to sew, plan her lessons, or read her Bible.

She knew why she hadn't.

Seth.

The porch was in plain view of the barn and the bunk-house—Seth's domain. They hadn't spoken since their argument last week following her horseback riding lesson. His judgmental words still stung like a lash across her heart, and she was not eager for their next meeting. She'd consciously altered her movements to lessen the chance their paths might cross, and she suspected he was doing the same.

This morning Violet had mentioned that Seth had left early for the piney woods to hunt for their Thanksgiving turkey, so Bridget had felt she could avail herself of the porch without risking an awkward meeting with him. Trouble was, keeping him out of sight hadn't kept him out of her mind. . .or her heart.

Sighing, she sliced the knife's blade into the scarlet-striped skin of the apple, releasing the fruit's fresh, crisp fragrance.

"From the long look on your face, you'd think tomorrow was a day of mourning instead of a day of thanksgiving."

At Gabe Noell's voice, Bridget stopped working the knife around the apple and glanced up. She hadn't seen much of the old wood-carver since his arrival at the Circle B. According to Violet, Andrew had hired him to add decorative pieces around the porch eaves, but so far she'd seen no evidence of his work.

"Sorry, Miss—O'Keefe, is it? I didn't mean to startle you." His gray eyes twinkled as he dragged his battered brown hat off his head.

"You didn't. Well, maybe a little," she said with a laugh. "I must confess I was lost in a muse." The old fellow's kindly demeanor put Bridget at ease. His presence felt almost. . . comforting.

"Ah, muses." He gazed down at her with a grandfatherly smile. "As the apostle Paul tells us in his letter to the Philippians, 'Whatsoever things are lovely, whatsoever things are of good report; if there be any virtue, and if there be any praise, think on these things.'"

Bridget smiled up at him. "That is one of my favorite Bible passages." She wasn't at all sure, though, that her previous thoughts fell within the parameters of the apostle's admonitions.

The crinkles beside his eyes deepened. "Don't let me bother you. I just came to take some measurements." He pulled a folded carpenter's ruler from the pocket of his baggy pants. Unfolding a length of the ruler, he went to work, holding it up to the porch eaves. Then he took a stubby pencil and scrap of brown paper from his shirt pocket and scribbled something.

For the next several minutes, he and Bridget worked on their separate tasks in silence.

"Mmm. I have to say, those apples sure smell wonderful." Gabe ambled toward her from the far end of the porch.

Bridget cut in two the apple she'd just pared and held a half out to him. "Please, have some, Mr. Noell. I have more apples here than I will need for two pies."

He dipped his head in a bow. "Thank you, ma'am. I'm much obliged." He accepted the piece of fruit. "If you don't mind. . ." He nodded at the empty rocking chair beside her.

"Not at all, Mr. Noell, please sit." There was something intriguingly incongruous about this old gent, who dressed like a beggar yet possessed the manners and speech of an educated gentleman.

"But I much prefer Gabe to Mr. Noell." He lowered himself

to the chair with a soft sigh.

"I will call you Gabe if you call me Bridget."

"Deal." He reached his gnarled hand across the chairs' arms, and when she clasped it, Bridget was surprised at the firmness of his grasp.

Settling back in the rocking chair, he took a bite of the apple. "Mmm. I like when the tartness gets me right here." Grinning, he tapped his cheek.

"Then I will be careful not to put too much sugar in the pies for Thanksgiving supper tomorrow."

"Ah, yes, Thanksgiving supper." He gazed beyond the porch with a distant look in his eyes as if remembering something pleasant.

Bridget couldn't help wondering why this obviously educated man had chosen such an itinerant life. But before she could ask, he swung his smiling face back to hers. "I reckon every day is an opportunity for me to thank my Lord."

"Amen, Mr.—Gabe," Bridget amended with a chuckle.

"But I do appreciate the Bartons' kind invitation to tomorrow evening's meal and must admit I'm looking forward to it. Trail fare gets a little monotonous," he said around a bite of apple, "and Mr. Krueger tells me Mrs. Barton sets a. . .how did he put it?. . .'rip-snortin' spread' on Thanksgiving." He rocked the chair back with his laugh.

At the mention of Seth, sadness gripped Bridget and she frowned. If only Seth possessed the faith of this old wood-carver.

Gabe stopped munching his apple and trained a scrutinizing gaze on her. "Did I say something to upset you?"

Avoiding his piercing look, Bridget focused her attention

on peeling the apple in her hand. "I–I'm afraid Mr. Krueger and I are not on the best of terms."

"And why is that?" Bridget never knew her grandfathers, but Gabe's gentle tone sounded exactly as she imagined a grandfather's would.

She shrugged, suddenly feeling like an eight-year-old. Despite his kind coaxing, Bridget wasn't prepared to share her feelings about Seth with Gabe. "There are just some things we don't see eye to eye on, like. . .faith." Sorrow weighted her voice. "Let's just say I doubt Seth will be saying any prayers of thanksgiving at supper tomorrow."

Gabe nimbly plucked a dark seed from beside the apple's core. He held it up to the slice of sunlight that had encroached farther onto the porch. "I've often thought it a great miracle that something so small, if planted and tended, can grow into a tree that bears its own fruit." His voice held wonder as he gazed at the seed.

He dropped the seed in the breast pocket of his faded blue chambray shirt and looked at Bridget. "The Lord tells us that the seed of His Word, if tended with love and watered with prayer, can grow to bear wonderful fruit. Remember that, Miss Bridget O'Keefe. And never forget that with Christ, all things are possible."

He rose slowly with a soft groan, tipped his hat, and ambled down the porch steps and toward the barn.

Watching him disappear behind the barn, Bridget had no doubt Gabe's comments had to do with Seth. . .and her. It was almost as if the old man had read her mind. She realized she'd become the latest recipient of one of the wood-carver's sawdust sermons. She sighed. Though she liked to think her faith was strong, changing Seth's hard heart would require a mighty miracle.

"Miss O'Keefe, I. . ."

At Seth's voice, Bridget jerked around.

He stood in front of the porch gripping the bound feet of two dead turkeys, their featherless gray heads and red wattles dangling past his knees.

Heat flared in her cheeks, and she was sure he must hear her heart pounding.

"I—" He cleared his throat, and his gaze didn't quite meet hers. "I'm sorry for what I said to you last week. You know, in the barn."

Hope rose in Bridget's chest. Maybe, like Gabe had said, the seeds she'd sown in Seth's heart about God had actually taken root. She prayed that was true. Unless he changed his attitude toward God, they could never be more than acquaintances.

"Of course I accept your apology, Mr. Krueger. If you are truly sorry—"

"I just said so, didn't I?" Irritation flashed in his blue eyes, but it disappeared quickly. "I just want you to know that it wasn't you I was angry with." The sharp edge left his voice, replaced by a tone of contrition.

Bridget's hope withered. "So who *were* you angry with, Mr. Krueger?" She forced her hands to go back to peeling the apple she was holding.

He shrugged. "Nobody, I reckon. Just angry about how things are. I don't know."

Bridget swallowed down a knot of tears. "You mean God, don't you?"

He blew out a long breath. "I didn't come here to talk

about God. Listen, I meant no offense to you, that's all." His hard tone smote Bridget's heart, but she had to try again.

She leaned forward over the crock of peeled apples. "I understand your anger, Seth. I was angry at God for a while, too, after my parents died—"

For an instant, his blue eyes turned icy. "I said I don't want to talk about God." He huffed a breath. "I declare, tryin' to say I'm sorry to you is harder'n tyin' down a bobcat with a piece of string!"

How could she get through to him if he wouldn't even listen? Was his heart the hard soil unable to accept the seeds of God's Word Jesus spoke of in the parable? Bridget knew that wasn't true. She'd seen his heart. It was soft and sweet. Beneath his pain, Seth Krueger was a good, kind, and caring man. To someone who had not learned of God's love from childhood as Bridget had, she could see how God might seem a malevolent power, a source of people's pain.

Seth shifted, his feathery burdens swaying. "So no hard feelings?"

"No hard feelings." She gave him a bright smile, and the tense lines on his face relaxed. "Looks like we'll have plenty of turkey." She eyed the two birds he was holding.

Grinning, he glanced down at the turkeys. "I figured we'd need two to feed ten people."

"Eleven people." Bridget slid the knife around another apple, divesting the fruit of its peel in one continuous spiral. "One of my pupils—Singing Bird—will be joining us."

Seth's grin faded and his tanned face went from chalk white to blood red. His Adam's apple moved with a hard swallow.

"Then I won't be there."

Chapter 6

Heat marched up Seth's neck as he entered the Bartons' dining room. He was late.

Mrs. B. had outdone herself. The long table spread with a fancy white cloth sparkled with Violet's finest china, crystal, and silverware. The two turkeys Seth had shot were baked to golden perfection and now lay steaming on silver platters.

He'd almost followed through with his threat to Bridget and stayed in the bunkhouse. But the thought of disappointing Violet and the surety of a tongue-lashing from Andrew had brought him to the dining room dressed in a starched white shirt, broadcloth coat and trousers, and a string tie.

Taking the empty chair beside Tad, he murmured an apology to Violet and Andrew for his tardiness and offered cursory nods and greetings to the two logging bosses, their wives, and the old wood-carver, Noell.

His gaze lit on Bridget, seated directly across the table from him, and his heart bucked hard against his chest. Dressed in a shiny palomino-colored frock, she looked like an angel. Her bright curls piled atop her head sparkled in the candle's glow like a burnished copper halo.

Clearing his tightening throat, he gave her an unsmiling nod but refused to focus on the Indian child beside her. "Miss O'Keefe," he managed in a voice that didn't sound like his.

"Mr. Krueger." She gave him a wobbly smile. "I don't think you've met Singing Bird." She looked down at the girl and back up to him, as if daring him to acknowledge the child.

For one sweet moment yesterday, he'd recaptured the harmony between himself and Bridget—until she'd mentioned this little Comanche. He forced a glance to the doe-eyed girl and bobbed a quick, begrudging nod in her direction. "Miss."

Paying scant attention to Andrew's long prayer of thanks, Seth instead used the opportunity to torture himself by feasting his eyes on Bridget and drinking in her beauty. He had no interest in thanking a God who seemed to enjoy giving just so He could snatch away the gift.

After the prayer, Seth ate in silence, tasting little of the meal as conversations buzzed around him. Making a concerted effort to avoid looking directly at Bridget, he found his gaze drifting to the Comanche child. Apart from an occasional shy glance at those around the table, she, too, ate quietly, despite attempts by Bridget, Violet, and Gabe Noell to coax her into conversation. Her head down, she fidgeted in a too-big blue frock that bunched at the front and shoulders.

Sympathy stabbed at Seth's chest, surprising him. *The kid's probably scared half to death—*

"Well, Seth, have you found any more?" Andrew's voice

barged into Seth's reverie.

He snapped his head around to face Andrew Barton, who sat at the end of the table, wiping gravy from his graying handlebar mustache.

"Sir?"

"Cut fences, man. Haven't you been listening? Ben Shelton here says his loggers found evidence last week of more poaching—field-dressed deer and bear on Barton land. I was just wonderin' if you'd found any more cut fences."

"No, sir. Just those two lengths along the east string of the south pasture." Thoughts of the cut fence brought back other memories of that afternoon—memories of holding Bridget in his arms, the sweet taste of her kiss. . .

Bridget's voice drew Seth's attention to her, leaving Andrew to resume his conversation with the loggers.

Bridget's soft pink lips—Seth knew how soft, he knew how sweet—were smiling at Tad, who was explaining the finer points of breaking mustangs. Her green eyes glistening, she listened in rapt attention to the boy's exaggerated exploits. Once, Tad even had the audacity to wink at her, earning him a kick in the ankle from Seth.

By the time Mrs. B. and Sadie cleared away the supper dishes, Seth had had more than his fill of the Bartons' nephew flirting with Bridget. Afraid he might do something he'd regret, Seth made his excuses and fled the house before dessert was served.

Out on the porch, he hooked an arm around a support post and gazed into the star-flecked indigo sky.

"Fine, Tad's welcome to her."

The only answer to his growled words was the cadence of

a distant barred owl's call.

He inhaled a lungful of cool night air tinged with the scent of pine and slowly blew it out again. Other words flew into his mind, words from another life, another time. Words far truer to how his heart really felt. " 'Thou art all fair, my love—' "

" 'There is no spot in thee.' Song of Solomon, chapter four, verse seven."

Gabe Noell's quiet voice jerked Seth around. Since their first meeting, Seth had tried to avoid the old wood-carver. He didn't want any sermons. Not from Bridget and definitely not from some old tramp.

"Didn't mean to startle you, son." Gabe stepped closer, his footfalls nearly soundless on the porch boards. Folding his arms over his white dress shirt—which appeared to be one of Mr. B.'s—he gazed into the deepening dusk. "It's easy to imagine Solomon writing those words on a night much like this one."

Seth had no interest in getting roped into answering any questions about why he'd quoted words from the Bible—something he didn't even understand himself—so he stretched and yawned. He gave the man a tepid smile. "Well, sir, reckon I'd best say good evenin' and get myself to the bunkhouse. Got a full day of work tomorrow."

"I was hoping you could help me with something." Gabe followed Seth off the porch. "It won't take long."

Seth wished he were immune to the old gent's disappointed tone. "Sure."

They walked together to the old tack shed behind the bunkhouse. Until Gabe arrived, the building hadn't been used for years. Seth had to admit he was curious to see what the wood-carver had been up to.

Gabe pulled a key from his pants pocket and unlocked the padlock securing the door. Inside, the smells of freshly cut pine and varnish greeted Seth. The old man took a kerosene lantern from a nail beside the door and lit it, casting a yellow glow over the space.

Lantern in hand, Gabe walked to a long, canvas-covered object near one wall.

He set the lantern on the floor and pulled back the canvas, revealing what looked like rectangular open box. "Mr. Barton commissioned me to make a breakfront cupboard as a Christmas present for Mrs. Barton. He wants it to be a surprise, so I'd be obliged if you kept this under your hat."

At least now Seth understood the secrecy, but what he saw didn't look like anything he or Andrew couldn't have put together. He shrugged. "Sure." The sooner he accommodated the old coot, the sooner he could climb into his bunk and start contemplating the hardest, nastiest chores to assign to Tad tomorrow.

Gabe lifted the lantern so its light shone directly on the box, and Seth moved closer for a better look. His eyes widened. An intricately carved design of flowers, leaves, and bunches of grapes decorated the top of the cupboard. Seth had never seen better woodworking.

"You do good work, Mr. Noell." Wonder filled Seth's voice as he slowly drew his fingers over the extraordinary carving.

Gabe smiled. " 'Whatsoever thy hand findeth to do, do it with thy might.' Ecclesiastes chapter nine, verse ten."

"I know." The admission escaped Seth's mouth before he could stop it.

Gabe cocked his head at Seth, and one eyebrow shot up. "You surprise me, Mr. Krueger. I'd gotten the idea you were not a man of faith, yet a little while ago I heard you quoting scripture, and you just admitted you're familiar with the verse I quoted from Ecclesiastes."

"I was raised Christian. My pa was Quaker and my ma Lutheran."

"But you're no longer a man of faith?"

"No." Seth barked the word, hoping to discourage any further talk of religion. His tone turned icy. "What can I help you with?"

Gabe nodded at the window on the other wall. "I need to move this under the window so I can get better daylight on my work. That is, if your thigh is not out of joint."

Irritation scampered up Seth's spine. "My leg's just fine, so let's move this thing." He picked up one end of the cupboard while Gabe picked up the other, and together they moved the piece with relative ease to a spot under the window.

Though he wanted to ignore it, curiosity about the man's comment got the better of Seth. "So what made you think I had a bum leg?"

Gabe straightened with a soft groan. "Don't you recall the story of how Jacob wrestled with an angel and the angel put his thigh out of joint?"

"Yes, I remember." When he was a child, it had been one of Seth's favorite Bible stories, but he couldn't see what it had to do with him now. "But I ain't been wrestlin' with anybody— 'specially angels."

"I'm not so sure about that." Gabe picked up a small piece of wood from the floor and settled himself on the head of an empty barrel. A part of Seth wanted to turn and leave the old man to his babblings, but something kept him rooted where he stood.

Gabe took a little folding knife from his pocket and began whittling the wood. "Jacob wrestled with the angel to get God's blessing, but I believe more often, people wrestle with angels to get away from God's blessings. Why, much of the world even rejects God's greatest gift, Christ."

"Like I said, I ain't been wrestlin' with any angels, and anything God's given me with one hand, He's took back with two."

Gabe gave a little shrug and blew shavings from the piece of wood he was whittling. "Sometimes we don't recognize blessings. Or angels." He narrowed a piercing gaze at Seth. "Never wrestle with God when He wants to give you a blessing."

Seth turned to leave. He'd heard enough about angels and blessings and God. He took two steps toward the door before Gabe's next words stopped him.

"I'm just curious. Have you told Miss O'Keefe you were raised Christian?"

Seth stomped back to Gabe. The old man had gone past aggravating to meddling. His fists clenched, he glared down at the wood-carver. "And why do you think I should tell *her*?"

Gabe rose and pressed the piece of whittled wood into Seth's hand, then chuckled and clapped him on the shoulder. "Because you are in love with her, son."

Chapter 7

Bridget lifted her face to the cool wind nipping at her cheeks and tugged at her riding hat. She wouldn't have imagined she could love horseback riding so much.

After that first lesson with Seth, Violet had taken over as Bridget's riding instructor, accompanying her on her daily treks to the orphanage. But this morning Violet was attending a meeting of the Women's Missionary Union in Pinewood and had deemed Bridget accomplished enough to make the trip without her. Violet had assured her, though, that Gabe Noell would be doing some carpentry work on the orphanage today and would accompany Bridget back to the Circle B.

Clad in her brown wool riding skirt, Bridget hugged her knees against the mare's sides. Rocking with the gentle motion, she moved as one with the cantering horse. She thought of her first riding lesson, when Seth said she rode like she was born for it.

Seth.

Her heart throbbed with the familiar ache. No matter how

hard she tried, she couldn't erase him from her heart.

Remembering his terse attitude toward Singing Bird at Thanksgiving, aggravation shimmied up her spine like a gust of the cool December wind. Why couldn't Seth see that by continuing to hate the Indians, he only hurt himself?

The sound of a wagon rumbling behind her broke into Bridget's musings. She smiled. Gabe must have decided to come out early to the orphanage. Did the wood-carver think he was her guardian angel?

As she reined in Rosie and waited for Gabe to catch up, Bridget grinned. Gabriel *was* the name of an angel.

When the wagon came up even with her, she turned toward it, ready to tease the kindly old fellow about taking his name too seriously. But instead of finding Gabe's congenial smile, her gaze met the decayed-tooth grin of the one-eyed buffalo hunter. Her smile vanished as icy fingers of fear gripped her chest.

"Mornin', miss." He lifted his battered black hat. "Member you from the gen'ral store some weeks back, but don't b'lieve we was ever introduced properlike." He raised and lowered his hat again. "I be Jake Tuley. And who might you be?"

Her stomach roiling, Bridget turned her head to the fresh breeze, pretending to get better control of Rosie. The awful smell of the man's unwashed body, fanned by the lifting of his hat, was almost unbearable.

"Bridget O'Keefe. I teach at the Indian orphanage." She immediately regretted the honest answer, fearing he would follow her. Forcing a weak smile, she tried to look everywhere but at his disgusting face.

"The old McCallum place?"

Bridget never answered. Her mind raced, trying to decide if she should kick the mare into a run toward the orphanage, still only a speck in the distance. But before she could make a move, he reached out a grimy hand and grasped Rosie's bridle.

"Whaddaya say we mosey over to that pine grove yonder and get to know each other better?" His mouth twisted in a salacious smirk.

Panic rose in Bridget's chest. She gripped the reins tighter. "Mr. and Mrs. Barton would not appreciate you—"

"Right shame what happened to that Yankee couple." His one bleary gray green eye turned dead cold. "Hate to see somethin' like that happen to Barton and his missus. Or that towheaded foreman of theirs."

"Shouldn't you be workin' on Violet's cupboard?" Seth shot a sidelong glace at Gabe Noell, who was sitting beside him on the buckboard. Resentment rose in Seth's chest. Once again he'd been roped into doing something he didn't want to do, and worse, with the meddling old wood-carving preacher. True, in the two weeks since Thanksgiving, the old man had said nothing more to him about angels, God, or even Bridget. Still, Seth was less than happy when Andrew asked him to help Gabe with some work on the orphan house.

Gabe gave him a bright smile that did nothing to improve Seth's mood. "It's coming right along. Should be done well before Christmas Eve." He winked. "I told Mr. Barton I needed another project to keep Mrs. Barton from getting suspicious."

Seth only grunted and focused on the weathered farmhouse in the distance, partially hidden by a stand of tall pines.

The sooner they got there and got the work done, the sooner they could leave the place.

"Mrs. Barton tells me the staircase railing needs several posts replaced, including the bottom newel." Gabe seemed determined to keep up some kind of conversation.

"Wouldn't know. Never been inside."

"And why is that?"

"Never had any business in there." Seth flicked the reins against the horses' rumps, urging them to a quicker pace.

Out of the corner of Seth's eye, he saw Noell dig into his pants pocket, and he groaned inwardly. He hoped the old man wasn't fixing to carve him another wooden angel like the one he had handed him Thanksgiving evening. A dozen times or more, Seth had thought to pitch the thing into the fire but hadn't been able to bring himself to do it. Even that simple little piece showed the old wood-carver's exceptional talent.

When Seth reined the team to a stop in front of the house, he saw that Gabe held not a knife, but a nail.

"Do you know what this is?" The old man gazed at the object he held between his thumb and forefinger as if he saw something beyond a sliver of pointed iron.

"A nail. Looks to be a horseshoe nail." Seth sighed. He was wearying of the old man's games.

"A broken horseshoe nail," Gabe said. "It came loose from the horseshoe it was holding and caused my brother's horse to stumble. My brother broke his neck. He died the instant he hit the ground."

"I'm sorry. . . ." Amid a rush of sympathy, Seth touched the old fellow's shoulder. He wondered why the man would share such a personal sadness.

"Would you like to know why I kept it?"

"S'pose you kept it to remember your brother."

Gabe shook his head, still gazing at the nail. "No. I kept it to remember the horse."

Seth stared at the old man. Maybe he *was* touched in the head.

A sad smile crept across Gabe's bewhiskered face. "You see, the day we buried my brother, I shot that horse. I was eighteen and grieving. I thought the only way to ease my pain was to make somebody pay for my loss. I've learned better since."

Seth understood what Gabe had felt. He couldn't count the times he'd itched to make a Comanche—any Comanche—pay for taking his family from him.

Gabe rolled the two-inch spike between his thumb and finger. "This nail reminds me that only forgiveness takes away the hurt." He fixed Seth with a knowing gaze. "Nails much like this one, only bigger, pierced our Lord's hands and feet, yet He asked the Father to forgive us, then died to buy us that forgiveness."

Realization of what the wily old coot was up to dawned on Seth. Irritation crawled up the back of his neck. If Gabe Noell thought his horseshoe nail story would make Seth abide the sight of a bunch of Comanche orphans, the crazy old man had another think coming!

Seth shot Gabe a slicing glare and jumped to the ground. "If you want to work in there, go right ahead." He cocked his head toward the house. "I'll stay out here and dig holes for the new fence posts we brought."

The sound of pounding horse's hooves yanked his and Gabe's attention eastward. Seth's eyes popped to see Bridget, atop Violet's old mare, Rosie, galloping at a breakneck clip right toward them.

Fear curled in Seth's belly. If the horse should stumble at that speed. . . It didn't bear thinking. With Gabe's story fresh in his mind, his pulse quickened and sweat broke out on his forehead. But before he could call out for Bridget to rein in her mount, she reached the front fence and did just that.

Seth rushed to her with Gabe at his heels. "Are you all right? Did somethin' spook the horse?" His heart thumping against his chest, Seth reached up to help her down from the mare's heaving sides.

Raw fear shone from Bridget's wide eyes. Her rusty curls tumbled about her face, and her cheeks flamed as crimson as a swamp hibiscus flower. Shaking, she slipped into Seth's arms, and it took all his willpower to not pull her trembling body close against him.

Her breaths came in gasps. "I—I guess I just got her running too fast."

Anger suddenly swamped Seth's fear. Grasping her shoulders, he glared at her. "I thought you were smarter than that, Miss O'Keefe. You could have broke your silly little neck! Don't you ever do anything like that again, you hear?"

She jerked away from his grasp, and her pretty face puckered up in an angry scowl. "I appreciate your concern, Mr. Krueger. But I'm not one of your cowhands and will do as I please!" Turning, she walked to the house, her back stiff as a branding iron.

Gabe clapped Seth on the shoulder. "You should go after her and apologize, son. I know she scared the liver out of you, but it's been my experience that women don't respond well to orders." He grinned. "Proverbs chapter twenty, verse three says,

'It is an honour for a man to cease from strife.'"

" 'But every fool will be meddling.'" Training a glare on the old man, Seth finished the verse, wondering how he remembered that.

To Seth's surprise—and aggravation—Gabe laughed. Smiling, he glanced skyward, then back to Seth. "God does work in mysterious ways, my boy. He does indeed." He went into the house still chuckling and shaking his head.

"Crazy old coot."

Seth strode to the back of the wagon and lifted out the posthole digger. He stomped to the fence line and shoved the twin spades into the moist earth, a tangle of emotions balling up in his gut. "Angels and nails. None of it makes a lick of sense." He gave the handles of the auger a mighty twist. He shouldn't have agreed to come out here when there were at least a dozen other chores he'd rather be doing back at the Circle B. So why did he?

One word: *Bridget.* She'd burrowed deep under his skin and into his heart.

He glanced back at the dingy gray building behind him. Next thing he knew he'd be slapping a paintbrush across that sorry house. And in the bargain, he had to listen to old Noell preach about God's love when right behind him was a passel of Comanche kids, reminding him how God had turned His back on Seth's family.

Seth dug into his coat pocket and pulled out the little wooden figure of an angel Gabe had handed him Thanksgiving evening. The wings were etched to suggest feathers, and he could even see the folds in the robe. The angel's upturned smile seemed to mock him.

With a flick of his wrist, Seth tossed the thing in the dirt at the base of the post oak tree near the corner of the house. If only he could toss away his feelings for Bridget as easily.

Chapter 8

Tad, stop it!" Bridget giggled as Tad dropped a wreath of popcorn on her head. "It belongs on the tree, not me." She raked the fluffy kernels from her hair and tried her best to look perturbed.

A roaring fire popped and crackled in the enormous fireplace, washing the Bartons' parlor in a warm, cheery glow. The scents of pine and popcorn filled the room. Yet Bridget's heart ached, missing the one person who would make the tree decorating festivities complete.

Earlier, when Seth had helped Andrew and Tad carry the ten-foot-tall pine into the Bartons' parlor, he'd avoided Bridget's gaze. They hadn't spoken since last week when he'd scolded her for riding Rosie too fast.

Bridget's heart raced at the memory of Seth's arms around her, holding her safe, chasing away the terror that had gripped her. She'd sensed that if it hadn't been for the presence of Gabe Noell, Seth might have kissed her.

Somehow she'd mustered the courage to kick Rosie into

a gallop and escape Jake Tuley. But the man's veiled threat had prevented her from sharing with Seth and Gabe what had transpired. She had no doubt Seth would have gone after Tuley. It sickened her to think the buffalo skinner might have somehow caused Van's and Sally's deaths. She couldn't chance putting Seth in danger. Feigning anger at Seth's rebuke had given her an excuse to hurry into the house so he wouldn't guess there was more to her fright than Rosie galloping too fast.

"Popcorn angel, that's what I'll call you. You're no bigger'n a kernel of popped corn." Tad laughed and ducked around the Christmas tree's fragrant branches, evading Bridget's swipe at his arm.

Violet Barton stood in the middle of the parlor, shaking her head. "You two are as bad as a couple of children. We'll never get this tree trimmed if you don't stop the silliness." She chuckled. "Now, you both behave while I go look for the tree skirt."

"He started it," Bridget called after Violet, who headed up the stairs chuckling.

"I started it?" Tad pointed at his chest. "Who threw the first piece of popcorn?"

Bridget enjoyed the childish banter with Tad. It reminded her of her growing-up days at the orphanage. Like an overgrown puppy, Tad lived to play, never seeming to take anything seriously.

Without warning, he scooped Bridget up in his arms, and she let out a shriek. "Maybe we should just put you on top of the tree, popcorn angel."

"Tad!"

Seth's stern voice silenced their laughter, and Tad lowered Bridget's feet back to the pine floor.

The muscles of Seth's jaw worked as he trained steely blue eyes on Tad. "Did you replace those broken boards in the south end of the paddock like I asked?"

Heat suffused Bridget's face. She wondered how long he'd been standing in the doorway. Then, indignant anger leaped inside her at his frown. Just because he'd declined Violet's invitation to help decorate the tree didn't give him the right to ruin their fun.

"Not yet, boss." Tad reached down to fetch a shiny red glass ball from an excelsior-filled wooden box. "I'll get to it just as soon as we finish the tree," he said, his voice devoid of concern.

"Reckon I'll have to fix the fence myself while you play Christmas," Seth mumbled as he headed for the doorway.

Tad affixed the ornament to a branch and glanced over his shoulder at Seth. "Hey, boss, before you leave, would you bring me that box from the far end of the fireplace?"

"Get it thyself."

Bridget watched Seth stomp from the room, her jaw dropping at his use of the word "thy."

"Wonder what's put a burr under his saddle?" Tad murmured, seemingly unbothered by Seth's cross reply. He chuckled. "He sure must be mad, though, if he's revertin' to his Quaker talk."

"Quaker?" Stunned, Bridget stared at Tad. Seth Krueger a Quaker? Suddenly she remembered how he'd used the word "thou" in the barn. She'd thought his comment was an attempt to mock her faith.

At the sound of footsteps, she looked up. Violet descended the stairs with a small red, green, and white quilt in her arms.

"Seth is a Quaker?" Bridget asked and watched Violet's smile disappear.

"His pa was. I'm thinking he said his ma was Lutheran. In any event, theirs was a very religious family from what I understand." Violet crossed the room and knelt to spread the material around the base of the pine. "He seems to have turned his back on it all. Blames God for what happened to his family. Lord knows, I've prayed for him and tried to steer him back toward God's grace, but. . ."

Violet stood and raised her hands in a helpless gesture. "Andrew said Mr. Noell was surprised, too, when Seth mentioned his Christian upbringing." She gave Bridget a conspiratorial smile. "I suspect that may be why Andrew is finding little jobs to keep the wood-carver here even though he finished the lovely gingerbread work around the porch weeks ago. I think Andrew is hopeful that Mr. Noell can help in our efforts to nudge Seth back into Christ's fold."

For a moment Bridget's heart sang. Seth had been raised in a Christian home, so he knew of God's love and Christ's salvation. He just needed to be convinced that God still loved him. But why hadn't he told her he was raised in the faith? Everyone else seemed to know, even Gabe Noell.

The intentional omission sent Bridget's heart oscillating between hurt and anger. Seth cared for her. She had no doubt about that. He'd shared the story of his family's tragedy with her, so why had he kept from her something as important as his Christian upbringing—something that could draw them closer?

"Here." Bridget thrust a string of popcorn into Tad's hand. "I'll be back in a bit."

Her legs pumping with purpose, she ran out of the house, down the porch steps, and toward the south side of the paddock.

"Seth!" His name exploded from her lips.

Seth turned from pounding a nail into a new fence board. "You here to scold me for hollerin' at your beau?" His voice sounded as chilly as the December wind whipping at her skirt.

"Tad is not my beau."

"No? You two looked pretty cozy to me." He dug into his jeans pocket and pulled out two nails, sticking the flat end of one in his mouth.

"Why didn't you tell me you're a Christian?"

"Because I'm not anymore." He turned and stabbed a nail into the board, then drove it flush with two solid blows of his hammer.

"You were raised to believe that Jesus is your Savior. How can you turn your back on that?" Bridget couldn't tell if she shook more from cold or anger.

Seth's torso heaved with a deep sigh. He turned to face her. "Look, I'm not sure what I believe anymore. Except that the God I prayed to for the first twelve years of my life allowed the Comanches to take my family from me."

"Seth, this world is not perfect. It's full of sin. Sin causes our troubles and griefs. In the book of Job the scriptures tell us, 'Man that is born of a woman is of few days and full of trouble.' No one is guaranteed a certain number of years on this earth." Bridget could not hold back the tears of frustration stinging her eyes. "Your family, my parents, and Van and Sally Taylor all went home early to God. But they were all Christians and will be celebrating Christmas together in heaven." She swiped at a tear, her fingers trembling across her cheek. "I want that for you, too, one day."

"Why? Why do you even care?" he asked around the nail dangling from his lips.

"Because that's what Christ has commissioned all Christians to do. 'Go ye into all the world, and preach the gospel to every creature,'" she quoted.

"Is that the only reason?" He took the nail from his mouth and pounded it into the board.

"You know it isn't." Shivering, she hugged her arms, rubbing the chill from them.

He turned his attention to the new fence board, pulling at it as if to check its sturdiness. "Stick with Tad. He's a church-goin' boy."

"I like Tad, but I don't feel that way about him." Surely Seth knew how she felt. Surely in that moment when their lips met he'd felt it, too. . . .

He gave her a critical glance. "You should go back into the house. It's too cool for you to be out here without a wrap."

So, that was it. He'd closed the subject. Anger dried her tears and raised her chin. "Why do you care?"

He dropped the hammer with a thud. Two quick strides brought him to her side. "You know why." His voice turned husky, and his smoldering gaze bored into hers.

Bridget gasped as he wrapped her in a canvas-coated embrace, pulling her to him. Hot tears slid down her face.

I mustn't allow this. I mustn't!

He pressed his mouth on hers. His kiss deepened, then gentled to a tender caress that curled Bridget's toes. Her body weakened along with her resolve, and she melted against him, her lips returning the sweet pressure of his.

"I love thee, Bridget O'Keefe," he confessed in a breathless whisper. "I loved thee the moment I first saw thee. And every day, I love thee more." He let her go, and his shoulders slumped as if the strength had drained out of him.

"You still use the words of your father's faith you learned in your childhood. Christ is knocking at your heart, Seth. Just open the door for Him. He still loves you and He never left you."

Glancing from the ranch house to the paddock, she waved her arm in a large circle. "He's given you a home and people who love you, and He can give you peace about what happened to your family. The peace that passes all understanding."

Seth did not answer. He simply turned his back to her, walked to the paddock, and with a savage blow pounded another nail into the fence.

Her heart crumbling, Bridget plodded back to the house. She'd tried to plant the good seed like Gabe Noell said. But tomorrow she'd move out to the orphanage. She couldn't bear to see the man she loved day after day, knowing that unless he came back to Christ, they could never be together.

Chapter 9

"Missy Teacher, man from ranch here!" Ming Li gave two sharp smacks of her hands. The sound echoed like shots around the cramped space inside the orphanage's front door and, Seth assumed, all the way up the stairway where the woman had directed her summons.

Ming Li shuffled away, and left alone, Seth tried to rein in his heart. It bucked like a wild mustang with a belly full of locoweed in anticipation of Bridget's appearance. He must be a fool or a glutton for punishment to put himself through this torture. But when he learned that Bridget had moved to the orphanage, it was as if she'd ripped open his heart and scraped it clean. After what had happened between them yesterday, he couldn't leave things as they were. He grudgingly admitted that Gabe Noell was right—Seth had to try to fix things. At least maybe he and Bridget could part friends. So when Mr. B. asked him to cut a Christmas tree for the orphan kids, Seth had seen a chance to make things right with Bridget.

A sound at the top of the stairs drew his eyes upward,

and the air left his lungs as if he'd been kicked in the gut by a mule. Even in her plain dark wool frock, Bridget's beauty took his breath away. His gaze slid from her lovely features to her unadorned left hand slipping down the banister.

Seth's heart constricted. *She should have my ring on her finger. She should be my wife. This ain't right. This ain't fair.*

God stood between them.

He marked it as but one more cruelty God had visited on his life.

As she neared, the longing inside him tightened his throat. He cleared it, then glanced at the worn floorboards before meeting her questioning gaze.

"Seth." Her voice sounded breathless.

"Andrew said you wanted a tree cut."

"Y–yes." Beyond her obvious surprise, Seth could not interpret the several other emotions flitting across her face. She turned her back just as he thought he glimpsed tears in her eyes.

"I'll gather the children. They will want to help choose the Christmas tree." Her stiff, formal tone smacked painfully against Seth's bruised heart.

Hat in hand, he followed her to a large room awash in sunshine that streamed through three long, narrow windows. Torn and water-stained green paper covered the walls. The scuffed floorboards were bare except for several tattered rag rugs scattered over the floor's center. There, eight children of varying ages sat cross-legged around a blackboard supported by two easels.

Seth found eight pairs of curious dark eyes trained on him. But he felt no anger or unease, just a surprising pang of sympathy.

Bridget walked to the chalkboard. "Children, this is Mr. Krueger. He has come to cut our Christmas tree. So get your wraps, and line up at the kitchen door behind Yellow Feather."

They all obeyed quietly. But the one called Singing Bird, who'd sat across from him at Thanksgiving supper, continued to gaze at him over her shoulder as she followed the others into the next room.

Bridget turned back to Seth. "You didn't have to do this, you know. Andrew could have had one of the loggers cut the tree."

"I don't mind. I've cut Christmas trees since I was a boy." It was a cowardly response, but evading her meaning seemed easier at the moment.

"You know what I mean." Her green eyes studied his, and Seth cleared his drying throat.

"Reckon I do." He fiddled with his hat. "I couldn't leave it like it was. I couldn't leave *us* like we were. . . ."

She clasped her hand over his, sending his heart bucking again. Her eyes glistened and a sad smile curved her lips. "I'm glad you came." Then she cocked her head and gave him a puzzled look. "I thought Quakers didn't have Christmas trees, or even celebrate Christ's birth."

Seth met her bewildered look with a grin. "My pa, bein' a Quaker, was dead set against it. But Ma was raised German Lutheran and was determined to keep her Christmas traditions. Ma, my sister, Elisabeth, and I always decorated a little tree on a corner table while Pa found somethin' he needed to do in the barn." Seth chuckled at the memory. "We got to have our Christmas tree, and Pa just pretended it wasn't there."

For one sweet moment they shared a smile, a fond gaze. If only it could last forever. But the next moment she turned. "Get your axe, and we'll meet you in the backyard."

Seth nodded and headed for the front door with a much lighter heart than when he arrived.

At the wagon, he flipped back the canvas tarp and lifted out the axe. A lump formed in his throat. How odd that something as simple as cutting down a tree could peel away the years, taking him back to a place he'd thought lost to him forever.

He hefted the axe, feeling the soft, worn wood of the handle in his grip and the cold iron axe head against the top of his clenched hand. From the time he was old enough to swing an axe, he'd cut his mother's little Christmas tree. He swallowed hard. How he would love to see his mother's face again, smiling approval at a *Weihnachtsbaum* he cut.

"You're the man from the fancy dinner."

Batting moisture from his eyes, Seth jerked around to find Singing Bird beside him.

"Shouldn't you be with the other kids?" The child had obviously lost some of the shyness she displayed at Thanksgiving.

"Teacher said I could come and tell you we found a good tree to cut." She slipped her hand into his, and Seth's arm stiffened at the unexpected touch then relaxed as her warm little fingers curled around his.

As they made their way around the side of the house through knee-high johnson grass, Seth found himself slowing his steps to match Singing Bird's shorter strides.

She tipped a smile up at him. "Teacher said we could make an angel from wet paper to put on top of the tree."

"Not a star?" Seth grinned down at the girl. He no longer

saw her as a Comanche, or even an Indian. She was just a child. A child who probably longed for a father.

Singing Bird shook her head. "I like angels. Mr. Noell said we each have a special angel that watches over us. Do you have an angel, Mr. Krueger?"

Seth thought of the wooden angel Gabe had given him, the angel he'd thrown away. A pang of guilt struck.

"Not anymore."

Singing Bird frowned. Then seeing Bridget and the other children gathered near Sandy Creek, she let go of Seth's hand and, lifting her calico skirt away from her feet, sprinted toward them.

"I thought Christmas would get here before you two did." Fun sparkled in Bridget's green eyes. She glanced at a little red pine growing along the creek bank. "We've decided that this one is just perfect."

Seth had Bridget keep the children a safe distance away and commenced to fell the evergreen. A few sharp blows severed the little tree from its stump, and Seth enlisted the help of the largest boy—the one Bridget had called Yellow Feather—to help carry the tree back to the house.

Suddenly a scream pierced the winter afternoon, followed by a loud splash.

Chapter 10

Bridget gazed incredulously at the girl flailing in the swollen stream. "Singing Bird!" The child's name tore from her throat on a shriek. She instructed the other children who'd gathered near the bank—some hollering and some crying—to remain calm and stay back. She didn't need any more children in the flooded creek.

Though Bridget had never learned to swim and the swift, muddy water looked daunting, the sight of Singing Bird's tenuous grasp on a protruding dead tree limb eclipsed Bridget's fears for her own safety. She turned to start down the bank, but Seth grasped her arm, stopping her.

"Stay here. I'll get her. You get in that creek, and I'll just have to drag you both out." He pulled off his boots and stockings, as well as his wool shirt, and pitched them onto the bank. A chilly wind gusted, raising gooseflesh on his pale back.

"Be careful." Bridget's anxiety mounted as his bare feet slipped down the muddy bank and into the rushing water. Now two people she cared about were in peril.

He glanced back at her over his shoulder. "No different than pullin' a calf out of a creek, and I've done that a hundred times." The alarm in his eyes belied the false indifference of his tone.

Singing Bird's frightened whimpers squeezed Bridget's heart.

"Hang on, Singing Bird. I'm coming. Just hang on tight." Seth's calm, soothing voice—the same voice he'd used with his horse during the stampede—quieted the girl's heart-wringing pleas. Seth glanced over his shoulder at Bridget. "There's a rope in my wagon. Send the boy. He'll run faster."

Keeping her gaze fixed on Seth and Singing Bird, Bridget sent Yellow Feather for the rope and two other children to the house for blankets.

The brackish water swirled around Seth and Singing Bird as he inched closer to the panicked child. Twice, the girl's head dipped beneath the rushing stream.

Bridget gasped and sent up a desperate prayer. She couldn't imagine how the slight girl, whose fingers must be numb with cold, managed to retain her grip on the slippery branch.

Dear Lord, keep them both safe. And please, hurry Yellow Feather with the rope!

An instant after the prayer formed in her mind, she heard the tall grass whisper behind her. Yellow Feather handed her the coil of rope, and she moved as close to the rushing stream as she dared.

To Bridget's chagrin, Seth moved farther downstream instead of heading directly to Singing Bird. Suddenly the racing water tore the girl's fingers from the tree limb and sucked her beneath its unforgiving torrent.

Bridget gasped, then groaned in dismay. If he'd gone right

to Singing Bird, he might have saved her.

The next moment, Singing Bird's head bobbed up. Seth reached out and snatched her from the water as the swift-flowing stream carried her past him. Now his actions became clear to Bridget.

The chilly wind stung Bridget's cheeks, turning her penitent tears to cold rivulets. *Forgive my uncharitable thoughts, Lord.*

Bridget tossed the rope to Seth. With one arm, he clutched Singing Bird to his chest, and with the other, he grabbed the rope.

Bridget ordered the children to line up behind her. Together they pulled on the rope while walking backward, towing Seth and Singing Bird through the rushing water and up the slippery gray brown mud of the creek bank.

Once on solid land, Seth kept walking while Bridget struggled to wrap him and the half-drowned girl in one of the wool blankets.

Seth glanced down at the drenched girl shivering in his arms and his stride quickened. "We've got to get her in the house and out of these wet clothes as soon as possible."

Back at the house, Ming Li took over. With a series of staccato orders in broken English, she sent the children to their specific tasks. Leaving a kettle whistling shrilly on the stove, she wrapped the blanket closer around Singing Bird. Then, spewing a string of Mandarin, she whisked the child away toward the girls' bedrooms.

"You should change, too." Bridget looked at the water dripping from Seth's soggy pants onto the kitchen floor.

"Reckon it'll have to wait." He cleared his throat as a ruddy hue crept over his face. Turning his back to Bridget, he hurriedly shrugged on his wool shirt that one of the children had retrieved from the creek bank.

"No, it won't." Bridget used her sternest teacher's voice. "Travel three miles with wet pants in forty-degree weather? You'll catch your death!" A grin pulled up the corner of his mouth, and her heart constricted. *Why does he have to be so handsome?*

"Don't see as I've got a choice." He picked up his boots and socks someone had set near the kitchen door.

"Yes, you do." Bridget straightened her back and struggled to maintain a no-nonsense tone. "Van Taylor was about your size. His clothes are still in their bedroom upstairs."

Frowning, Seth fidgeted. "It don't seem right somehow. I—I don't know as I ought to. . . ."

"Nonsense. Van was a very caring person, full of Christian charity. He would want you to." Bridget fought back the tears threatening to fill her eyes. *Lord, he is such a good, decent man, and I love him so much! Please, in Jesus' name, please touch his heart and turn him back to You.*

She watched him start up the stairs, his bare feet padding on the worn treads.

"Seth." Swallowing down a hard knot of tears, she managed a small smile. "Van also would have thanked you for saving Singing Bird, and so do I."

Pausing on the staircase, Seth answered with a sweet smile that ripped at Bridget's heart.

"First door to the left," she murmured before tears drove her to the kitchen.

Bridget pressed her hand hard against her mouth to muffle a sob. Clutching the washstand, she shook in silent agony as the tears that would not be denied flooded down her face.

Chapter 11

Bridget bent over Singing Bird's bed and pressed the back of her hand against the child's hot forehead. At first, the girl had displayed no ill effects from her dunking. But now, two days after the accident, she woke with a sore throat and fever.

"Singing Bird must drink this." With her quick, shuffling steps, Ming Li scooted to the bedside with another cup of aromatic tea.

Frustration rose inside Bridget. Singing Bird needed *real* medicine. Not useless teas made from dried flowers, leaves, and herbs. The vision of an old woman from her tenement placing onions cut in half beneath her parents' sickbed floated before Bridget's eyes.

"Drink, drink." Ming Li slipped her arm behind Singing Bird's back, helping her to sit up. She pressed the rim of the cup against the girl's lips, plying her with the pungent liquid.

A fit of coughing shook Singing Bird's little body until she gasped for breath. Bridget could bear it no longer. Springing up from the chair, she started for the bedroom door. "I'm going to get her some *real* medicine." Pinewood had no doctor, but the general store should have some kind of fever tonic—if the store was open on Christmas Eve, and if the storekeeper agreed to put the medicine on the Bartons' tab.

Ming Li scowled. "This real medicine. This medicine fix!"

Ignoring Ming Li's objections, Bridget headed out of the room. With Singing Bird's life in peril, she couldn't worry about insulting the housemother.

Outside, she squinted at the sun, a yellow smudge hanging low in the pewter sky. It was already late afternoon. *Please, Lord, I need a Christmas miracle.*

Less than a quarter of an hour later, Bridget pulled on the reins, bringing Rosie to a stop in front of the general store. She'd managed to get the bridle on the horse but had decided against trying to lift the heavy saddle. Instead she'd simply thrown the saddle blanket over Rosie's back, climbed to the stall gate, and mounted the placid mare.

As she slid from the horse's back, Bridget sent up a prayer of thanks for her staid, dependable steed, then looked up and down the street, discouraged. She saw no one. Only a couple of other horses stood tethered to hitching posts along Main Street.

Half expecting to find the door to the general store locked, she was surprised when it opened with a jingle. She tentatively stepped a foot inside the dark, dusty store. She hadn't been in the place since her first day in Pinewood with Seth. The scents of leather, wood smoke, and tobacco dominated the dim space.

"Sorry, I'm jist fixin' to lock up." A young man emerged from the back room carrying a broom. Seeing her, he swiped at the lock of greasy brown hair dangling across his left eye.

Bridget made her way toward the counter, maneuvering between the potbellied stove and the pickle barrel. "I need medicine—fever powder. Please, I won't be long." She scanned the shelves behind the boy's head. Her heart lifted. There between the bootblack and a bottle of horse liniment sat several brown paper packets marked DR. JAMES'S FEVER POWDER.

The young man hesitated, scratching at his head with grimy fingernails. "I don't know, my uncle Hiram done tallied up for the day. I'm jist supposed to sweep up and lock up."

Tears of frustration stung Bridget's eyes. "Please, someone is very ill. Can't you just add it on?"

The boy's eyes narrowed. "Hey, ain't you that schoolmarm from the Circle B?"

"Yes." Bridget had no interest in engaging the boy in conversation.

"Somebody sick at the ranch?"

"No, the orphanage."

"You mean them Injun brats at the old McCallum place?"

Bridget dug her fingers into the folds of her wool skirt and fought to keep her voice steady as anger rippled through her. Picking a fight with this ignorant boy would not get Singing Bird her medicine. "Yes. One of the children there is sick. Very sick."

He resumed swiping the broom across the floor, his voice hardening. "Like I said, we're done doin' business for the day."

"Please, have you no charity? It's Christmas!" Bridget hated the tears streaming down her face. She hated, too, having to beg this stupid boy for something no more than four feet in front of her.

He had the grace to look ashamed before he plucked a packet of the medicine from the shelf and plopped it on the counter. "That'll be one dollar."

Bridget expelled a relieved sigh and reached for the packet. "Just put it on the Bartons' tab."

"Can't do that." He snatched the packet away. "Uncle Hiram said I could only do that for the Bartons or Seth Krueger."

Fury pulsed through Bridget. She wanted to go behind the counter, rip the life-saving medicine from his grimy fingers, and run. Her hand went to her throat and she gripped her mother's cross necklace. Suddenly she could hear her mother's voice in her head, whispering God's will.

"You don't carry your faith in the Lord around your neck, Bridget. You carry it in your heart. Let the necklace go and save the child."

Somehow her trembling fingers managed to unhook the clasp, and she held the necklace out toward him. "Here, this is worth more than a dollar."

His eyes widened. "Reckon it is."

Grasping the packet of fever powder, Bridget fled the store. She stuffed the precious medicine into the pocket of her skirt and tried to push from her mind the vision of the boy's dirty fist closing around her mother's necklace.

Outside the store, she mounted Rosie from the top of a horse trough and kicked the mare into a gallop. The blood red sun rode low on the horizon. Bridget's wool shawl did little to fend off the icy wind. She pressed her face closer to Rosie's mane for warmth.

Suddenly she felt a jerk on the reins, and Rosie stopped so

abruptly Bridget almost tumbled off.

"If it ain't Miss Bridget O'Keefe. We're finally gonna get to have that little talk." The sound of Jake Tuley's voice sent terror shooting through Bridget.

He brought his horse close. The stink of whiskey stung her nostrils. "You'll be a right purdy Chris'mas present to unwrap."

"Please, Mr. Tuley, I have to get— Ahh!"

He snatched her from Rosie's back and threw her to the damp grass.

Dear Lord, help me! Please help me!

Sobbing, Bridget pounded her fists against him. She kicked at his shins to no avail. He responded with bawdy laughter. Despair washed over her. She gagged and fought nausea, pushing with all her might against the suffocating weight and stench of his body.

Suddenly the offensive weight lifted off her. Bridget sat up, gratefully inhaling gulps of air as a miracle unfolded before her in the lengthening shadows.

The crack of Seth's fist against Jake's jaw reverberated in the heavy evening air.

"Seth." She breathed his name like a benediction.

Seth jerked Jake Tuley to his feet. "Now, get your filthy hide outta here!" He gave the man a hard shove toward his horse as Jake rubbed his assaulted jaw. "If I ever catch you on Barton land again or near Miss O'Keefe, I'll beat you within an inch of your sorry life!"

Bridget sat trembling as the hoofbeats of Tuley's horse faded in the distance.

Seth helped her to her feet and held her shaking body.

"Shh, it's all right now, my love. Thou art safe."

Wrapped in the sweet sanctuary of Seth's arms, Bridget wept against his chest.

At length, he gently pushed away and looked into her face. "Did—did he hurt you?"

She shook her head. "No, I'm just a little bruised, that's all."

"What are you doin' out here, anyway?"

Bridget told him of Singing Bird's illness and her desperate ride to the store. She reached into her pocket for the fever powder but found it empty. "It's gone!"

"What's gone?"

"The fever powder. Singing Bird's medicine!" Frantic, Bridget beat at the tall grass with her hands, her eyes straining in the advancing darkness.

Seth gripped her shoulder. "You'll never find it in the dark. Shoot, even in the daylight you could look through this grass for days and never find it."

Bridget shrugged off his hand while tears flooded her eyes, further hampering her search. "I *have* to find it! God will help me find it!" She dropped to her knees, groping through the dewy grass. "Lord, *please* help me find it."

"Come away now." Though she batted at his hands, he gently gripped her shoulders, pulling her to her feet.

Exhausted, Bridget finally surrendered to Seth's warm embrace.

He retrieved her wool shawl from the grass and wrapped it around her shoulders. "Let's go back. Maybe the girl is better." He helped her onto his horse, tied Rosie's reins to his horse's bridle, and mounted behind Bridget.

Drained of strength, Bridget lay limp against Seth's strong

chest. As they rode toward the purple, rose, and gold sunset smeared across the western sky, she prayed that Ming Li's teas had finally worked to reduce Singing Bird's fever.

But when they reached Singing Bird's bedside, they found she hadn't improved.

Singing Bird rolled her head on the pillow and faced Bridget, her eyes bright with fever. "Teacher. I dreamed you went away and didn't come back."

Bridget bent over Singing Bird and brushed a lock of hair from her searing face. "I'll stay right here beside you, Liebes Mädchen, I promise."

"What did you call her?"

Bridget turned at the odd tone in Seth's voice.

He stood in the doorway, his chambray blue eyes large in his ashen face.

"Liebes Mädchen," Bridget repeated, wondering at his strange demeanor. "It's the name she said her aunt had called her. I suppose it's Comanche—"

"No, it's German." Seth's voice sounded tight. "It means 'dear girl.' It's what my mother used to call my sister."

He stepped near the bed. "Singing Bird, was your aunt a white woman?"

Singing Bird nodded, and Seth's Adam's apple bobbed.

"What was her name?" He clenched his fists around his hat, crushing it.

"Elisabeth Sky-Eyes," Singing Bird said in a raspy voice.

Seth's eyes glistened in the lantern light.

Bridget touched his arm. "Your sister?"

He nodded. "Must have been."

Ming Li bustled into the midst of the quiet revelation,

carrying a large cup of pungent tea. "Singing Bird need more tea. Tea fix."

Seth plopped his hat on his head. "I'm going to the general store for more medicine."

Bridget stood at his surprising declaration. "But they're closed now, and it's Christmas Eve."

"Hiram will open for me." He bent and kissed Singing Bird's forehead, then turned and brushed a quick kiss across Bridget's lips and disappeared through the bedroom door.

Bridget jerked awake at the sound of quick boot steps echoing through the house, unsure how long she'd slept. The next moment, Seth appeared in the doorway, carrying a drawstring canvas bag.

"How is she?" Worry lines etched his forehead.

Bridget bent forward and touched Singing Bird's face. Her fingertips met cool skin and relief washed through her. "Her fever has broken. She's out of danger, praise God."

Seth blew out a long breath and set the bag down beside Bridget's chair.

Singing Bird stirred and opened her eyes. "Mr. Krueger. You are back."

Seth knelt beside the bed and drew the backs of his curled fingers across the girl's cheek. "Yes, Liebes Mädchen, I'm back. And thee must call me Uncle Seth, because I'm your aunt's brother. Are you feeling better?"

Singing Bird swallowed and touched her throat. "My throat doesn't hurt so much now."

Seth reached for the canvas bag. "I'm glad, because I

brought you a present." He opened the bag and pulled out a red-and-white-striped candy stick. "This was your aunt's favorite Christmas treat when she was a girl." He grinned at Singing Bird and Bridget. "And I bought enough for the other children, too."

Singing Bird's eyes grew big and bright. Bridget's misted as she sent up a grateful prayer, marveling at the change in Seth's heart.

Singing Bird's expression turned serious. "I have a present for you, too, Mr. . . .Uncle Seth." She drew her hand from beneath the covers and held out a little wooden doll to Seth. It had wings and a carved robe that hung in folds. Beneath its smiling face was an impression of little hands steepled in prayer. "You said you didn't have an angel, so you can have this one I found."

For a long moment, Seth remained still, as if paralyzed. He finally took the doll and cleared his throat. "Thank you, Liebes Mädchen." His voice snagged on the endearment. "But I think I was wrong. I think God has given me two angels." He turned a tender look toward Bridget, and she swallowed down a sob.

Seth rose and slipped the angel doll into his pocket, then bent and kissed Singing Bird's forehead. "Thank you for the angel, little one. Now you must rest and get better. Tomorrow is Christmas, and Mr. and Mrs. Barton are coming to visit." He shot a quick grin over his shoulder to Bridget. "And Santa Claus might come, too."

Bridget smiled, knowing Gabe Noell had agreed to don the red wool Santa suit stitched by the Women's Missionary Union. She tucked the quilt under Singing Bird's chin, turned down the lamp, and followed Seth out of the room.

He slipped his arm around her waist as they walked to the front door. "Step out on the porch with me for a while, would thee?"

Still trying to assimilate all that had transpired this evening, she nodded mutely and fetched her shawl from the peg by the door.

The still, cold night met them outside where a full moon bathed the porch in a soft, pale glow. Bridget hugged the shawl around her while Seth leaned a shoulder against a porch post and looked up at the multitude of stars blinking down at them. "You know," he said at length, "my mother used to say if you're really quiet on Christmas Eve, you can hear the angels sing." He turned and drew Bridget to his side. "Because of you, I can hear them again."

"You're not angry at God anymore?"

"No." He reached in his pocket and pulled out the angel doll.

Bridget shook her head. "It's lovely. I wonder where she found it."

"Under the oak tree at the corner of the house, where I threw it."

Stunned, Bridget gaped at him. "But where did you get—"

"It was given to me by a very wise man, who told me to never wrestle with God when He wants to give me a blessing. So I won't." He knelt and took Bridget's hands in his. "I love thee, Bridget O'Keefe," he said, lifting pleading eyes to hers. "Will thee be my wife?"

A flood of joy cascaded down Bridget's cheeks. "Yes." Sobbing, she repeated her answer until he stood and silenced her with his kisses.

"I do have one request," he said at length. "I'd like us to adopt Singing Bird."

Bridget's happiness bubbled out in a giggle. "I'd like that, too."

"I almost forgot." He reached in his shirt pocket and pulled out something shiny. "I bought this back from Hiram."

Bridget gasped. "My necklace! Oh, Seth, thank you." She took the gold chain with trembling fingers and hugged her future husband's neck.

Her heart full to bursting, Bridget clung to her beloved, thanking God for blessings more numerous than stars in the Texas sky, not the least of which was an old wood-carver and his sawdust sermons. She had no doubt that God had used Gabe Noell to bring about this moment. Bridget was sure that for many years to come, Gabe's little wooden angel would remind both Seth and her of God's love and grace. And together, every Christmas Eve, they'd think of the old wood-carver while they listened for the angels' song.

Ramona K. Cecil is a wife, mother, grandmother, freelance poet, and award-winning inspirational romance writer. Now empty nesters, she and her husband make their home in Indiana. A member of American Christian Fiction Writers and American Christian Fiction Writers Indiana Chapter, her work has won awards in a number of inspirational writing contests. Over eighty of her inspirational verses have been published on a wide array of items for the Christian gift market. She enjoys a speaking ministry, sharing her journey to publication while encouraging aspiring writers. When not writing, her hobbies include reading, gardening, and visiting places of historical interest.

THE FACE OF MARY

by Darlene Franklin

Dedication

Seven months ago I moved to a new city and began the difficult process of starting over again. I dedicate *The Face of Mary* to the members of Draper Park Christian Church, who have been the hands and feet of our Lord to me in my hour of need.

Prologue

Breading, Texas, 1880

Polly Jessup eyed the present she had wrapped for Jean Carpenter. Her friend fingered the pink ribbon, looking at Polly with a question in her eyes but didn't say anything.

Yes, it's my hair ribbon. But I wanted something prettier than string. Polly reached up and patted her hair, dressed without adornment. Not that it ever looked nice these days without Mama to help her fix it.

Jean untied the bow and set it to one side before unwrapping the present. When she saw the plain cardboard cover, she wrinkled her nose until she opened the book. "Why, you've copied all the verses we learned in Sunday school this year." She turned a few pages. "And all of Psalm 119, with illustrations." Her fingers traced the letters, and she oohed and aahed over the minuscule drawings Polly had added.

"So you like it?"

"I love it!" Jean read the first verse softly. "'For God so loved the world. . . .'"

"You said you wanted to win the new Bible they're offering for a prize at the scripture memory contest, and anybody who can quote all of Psalm 119 is sure to win."

"Only because you've decided not to enter." Jean flung her arms around Polly and hugged her. "You know so much more of the Bible than I do." Jean started to slip the ribbon into the book but stopped. "You should keep this."

Polly's pride wanted to refuse but she loved that ribbon. It evoked so many memories of her mother dressing her up. "Thanks." To cover her embarrassment, she hurried on. "After I won the adult contest last year, it didn't seem fair to keep competing. I'm practicing with Dolores, hoping she'll place. You and Abe Mott can battle it out for first prize." Polly grinned when Jean turned red at the mention of the young man's name.

"Did I hear something about Abe Mott?" a deep voice boomed behind them.

Polly jumped in her seat. When had Jean's brother Joey come into the room? Heat rushed into her cheeks, and she was sure her face turned the same dark shade as her friend's.

Joey took the book from Jean and opened it at random. "'Let thy mercies come also unto me, O Lord, even thy salvation, according to thy word.' Psalm 119. You even copied the letter *Vau*. I couldn't have done it better myself."

Polly squirmed. Joey had the best penmanship in the school. Everybody knew that, and he could draw anything he wanted.

He smiled at the Liberty Bell she had painted in the margins, tracing the crack with his long index finger. " 'And I will walk at liberty: for I seek thy precepts.' I wrote an essay about that verse once."

"I remember." Jean giggled. "Isn't it beautiful? Polly wants me to memorize the whole psalm for the Bible verse competition this year."

"Now that she's retired from the memory contest, she wants you to win, huh?" Joey handed the book back to Jean and focused his brilliant blue eyes on Polly. "You've always amazed me with your love for God's Word. Any girl who loves the law of the Lord like the psalmist did is a woman after my lawyer's heart. If you don't have a beau when I come home from college, I think I'll marry you myself." He smiled at the girls and left the room.

Speechless, Polly stared after him. Did Jean's handsome brother just say he might marry her someday?

His words engraved themselves on her heart.

Chapter 1

November 1884

Polly dallied longer than usual in the bedroom she shared with her two younger sisters. She wanted to look her best today. Not only was Jean Carpenter celebrating her engagement to Abraham Mott, but also Jean's brother Joey had returned home after four years away.

Polly pulled her dark hair away from her face, but it continued to fall into a center part. Should she wear it up? No, at seventeen she was too young to dress her locks in the style of an old married matron, even if she did feel that way some days. Taking care of four younger brothers and sisters did that to a girl. She teased her fringe across her forehead, hoping it might curl.

Joey Carpenter. *"I think I'll marry you myself."* Her heart beat faster at the memory. How many times had she repeated his words when she learned a new verse from the Bible or studied something new? Even though she had retired from competition, she continued to hide God's Word in her heart. She hungered for it almost as much as she hungered for food, and prayed to walk according to God's law.

Did Joey even remember what he had said to her all those years ago? Would he mention it when he saw her today? She blushed. He had probably forgotten long ago.

"Hurry, Polly." Little Hazel dashed into the room. "Dolores is burning the beans."

Polly swallowed a sigh. Sometimes she wondered if the family would starve if she wasn't there to cook for them. Even when Dolores followed a recipe, things didn't turn out the same. Jean said cooking was a gift, like singing or painting. But Polly didn't think so. Mama hadn't had time to teach the younger girls before she died, that was all.

Polly doubted her cooking ability would impress Joey, however. After all, he'd become a lawyer. He probably hadn't spared her a thought in four years, let alone whether or not she could cook.

But oh, how she hoped he had.

Joseph Carpenter considered the top hat on the shelf of his closet and decided against it. Such finery might have been *de rigueur* among his set in law school, but his Breading friends would laugh him out of town. He fingered the narrow brim, imagining Alice Johnson's reaction to his big-city fashions. She might appreciate it—another reason why he enjoyed her company. With her style and class, she had a sense of life outside the small-town life where he had grown up. Her father, owner of the town's only bank and its richest citizen, had made sure of that. A connection with Breading's leading family wouldn't hurt a man starting out his career.

But he wouldn't worry about that now, although he hoped Alice would enjoy the party. Today was about meeting old friends and celebrating Jean's happiness. As long as their parents focused on marrying off his sister, they wouldn't bother him about finding a suitable wife.

A knock sounded at his door.

"Who is it?" he called.

"Me." Jean opened the door with the word. "Are you ready yet? People are more eager to see you than me."

"I doubt that." He looked his sister up and down. She was dressed in a sage-colored dress with beige lace at the throat. When had she grown up? Of course he had seen her only twice in the past four years: once when the family gathered for his grandfather's funeral, and the second time when he graduated from school this past spring. He had spent the last few months closing his grandfather's affairs and making the difficult decision to return to Breading. "It's your special day." He smiled at her. With her upswept hair, she looked like a fine young lady, not the little sister he used to tease mercilessly. "I'm just the backdrop to your happiness."

"You know the people of Breading. They love an excuse to party. My engagement to Abraham isn't really news. People have been predicting this day since he broke my chalk on purpose back when we were in first grade."

"Including me, I know. But it doesn't matter. They won't see anyone else once you walk into the room." She radiated joy. Abe Mott was a lucky man. How had his sister found the man of her dreams at such a young age while the woman God had chosen for Joseph continued to elude him? His thoughts drifted to Alice Johnson again, and he wondered if she might be the one.

"We're praying our love will be as eternal as the Word of God. 'For ever, O Lord, thy word is settled in heaven.'" Grinning, Jean opened a well-worn book that looked vaguely familiar to a page where the text appeared beneath an artist's rendition of an evening sky. "I've used this little book so much that Mama says I should carry it down the aisle instead of the Bible I won."

The sight of the book triggered a memory in Joseph's brain. A dark-haired girl with bright brown eyes, smart as a whip, who could out-quote anybody when it came to scripture. "Polly Jessup gave that to you." He snapped his fingers. "For your thirteenth birthday."

"And then she helped me memorize every verse. She's the reason I won that year." The grin left Jean's face. "Polly hasn't had an easy time of it since her mother died. Promise me you'll say hello to her today."

"Of course. I'm looking forward to seeing all my old friends."

Jean's mouth opened but she didn't speak right away. "Good. Come down as soon as you're ready." She hugged him and disappeared out the door.

What was Jean about to say? Joseph mused. Give him time, he'd figure it out. After all, he *was* a lawyer.

He headed down the stairs.

"Polly Jessup."

Polly repressed a shudder. Of course Alice Johnson had

come; everyone in Breading was invited. But her derisive tone made Polly's name sound like she was a misbehaving schoolgirl sent to the corner, even though Polly had excelled at her lessons while Alice had struggled. At the teacher's request, Polly had tutored the banker's daughter so she could pass English. But the effort hadn't earned her so much as a thank you.

Polly reminded herself to be pleasant to Alice. After all, the Bible said she showed her love for God by how she loved others. Forcing a smile on her face, she turned around. As she expected, Alice was dressed in a style straight from the latest issue of *Godey's* magazine. The ecru silk and lace that adorned her claret-colored dress and outlined the bodice was not only expensive, it wasn't available locally. She might have had her father order the material all the way from New York.

"Look who's just arrived." Alice spoke to someone behind her.

Eyes as piercing blue as a summer sky, hair the color of hay in the fall. . .all six feet of him. Joey. *Her* Joey. With Alice.

"Joseph, you were asking after the Jessup girls earlier." Alice batted her eyelashes at Joey as boldly as any flirt. "As you can see, they're here." She twined a gloved hand around Joey's arm.

"Polly." Joey eased away from Alice and grasped Polly's hand. "Let me look at you." He looked her up and down, as if committing every detail to memory in case he needed to testify about her in court, and a slow smile spread across his face. "You and Jean grew up while I was gone. Come this way. I know my sister is eager to see you."

He offered Polly his free arm and walked with the two women to the corner of the room where Jean held court. At the sight of Polly, she stood. "Oh, good, you're here. Now we can get started. Mama? Papa?" She nodded at her parents.

Jacob Carpenter, an older, craggier version of Joey, clapped his hands for everyone's attention and motioned for quiet. "Mrs. Carpenter and I have invited you here today to celebrate with us. It gives us great pleasure to announce the engagement of our dear daughter, Jean Louise, to Abraham Mott. They're planning a spring wedding. Mrs. Carpenter insists they cannot do it any sooner."

Applause sprinkled with chuckles greeted the announcement. While Abe's father expressed his delight at the upcoming nuptials, Polly looked around for her father. Noise sometimes bothered him. She scanned the crowd and saw him in the corner. Her little sister was tugging at his arm and pointing at the table, where a specially decorated cake waited.

Maybe Hazel didn't realize she should wait for a piece of the cake. Polly decided she'd better check it out and excused herself from the people around her. Before she reached them, Pa nodded and headed for the table. A sinking feeling formed in Polly's chest, and she pushed through the edge of the crowd.

Mr. Mott was finishing his speech. ". . . you may all enjoy the cake that Mrs. Carpenter has made for the splendid occasion."

Every head turned in time to see Pa placing a corner piece with plenty of icing on a china plate and handing it to Hazel.

A high, piercing laugh floated across the crowd. *Alice.*

A look of panic replaced the pleasure on Pa's face, and he dropped the plate, the china shattering into dozens of pieces.

Chapter 2

One glance at her father's face erased any anger Polly felt. He reminded her of a cat that was unsure why people didn't appreciate the mouse he dragged into the house.

"Let's go find a seat, Pa." She led him toward the kitchen where he could escape the stares. Jean and her mother followed a few steps behind, and Polly scanned the room for the broom closet. As many times as she had visited in their home, she should know where to find it. At last she spied it and grabbed the broom and dustpan.

"Don't you worry with that." Mrs. Carpenter took them out of her hands. "You take care of your father. Are you all right, Mr. Jessup?" She spoke as she might to someone who was hard of hearing—slowly and loudly.

"I'll be fine if people stop screaming." His gaze took in the room and settled on Mrs. Carpenter. "Who are you? You're not my Mary."

A puzzled look crossed her face, and she took a step back.

"No, I'm your neighbor. Rose Carpenter."

Pa blinked. "You're not Mrs. Carpenter. She is." He pointed at Jean.

Please, heavenly Father, not now. Polly had never seen Pa this confused. He clutched his coat close about him and crossed his arms, staring at the floor. "I'm so sorry." At least the kitchen afforded them some privacy, preventing the other guests from seeing him disintegrate before their eyes. She'd known the Carpenters all her life; they were good, decent people.

"How can we help?" Mrs. Carpenter asked, but her gaze shifted to the door.

"I think he just needs peace and quiet. I'll take him home." Polly swallowed her disappointment.

Jean hugged her. "We'll talk later. I'll tell you all about it."

"No need for the rest of your family to leave." Mrs. Carpenter went to the door. "We'll make sure they get home safely."

Polly nodded. "Come on, Pa. Let's go home."

He accepted her arm. "Whatever you say, Mary."

Mary might be her real name, but Polly knew that's not what Pa meant. He thought he was talking to her mother.

What next?

Joseph stared at his mother and sister as they scurried through the door after Polly and her father. He took a half step in their direction before realizing someone had to attend to the rest of the guests. If he could divert people's attention from whatever happened, he would be doing everyone a favor—perhaps Polly most of all. The fathers of the newly affianced couple talked together, and Abe looked lost without Jean by his side. Joseph decided to take charge.

"Please, everyone, help yourselves to a glass of lemonade while we prepare to serve the cake."

Mrs. Mott took her position behind the table with the bowl of lemonade while Joseph headed in the other direction. Chocolate icing stained the carpet like muddy boots after a rainstorm. He grabbed a napkin to pick up the cake crumbs.

"Do you have to do that?" Alice's soft voice tickled his ear. "You'll get the legs of your trousers dirty."

At the touch of her hand, his knee dropped to the floor. As she predicted, chocolate frosting smashed into his dark twill trousers. He brushed at it with the napkin, dropping all the pieces he had managed to pick up in the process.

"Joseph," Alice squeaked and searched around the table for more napkins.

For a fleeting moment, he wondered why Alice wasn't helping clean the floor. Then he reminded himself that she was his guest, not a family member.

Frustrated by his lack of progress, Joseph headed for the kitchen and met Jean at the door, broom in hand. She saw the guests clustered around the punch table and sighed in relief. "Thanks, brother." Within a couple of minutes, she had swept the mess away and cut the remaining cake into pieces.

Joseph took two pieces and joined Alice by the window.

"Poor Polly. Mr. Jessup works at the bank, you know, but after today, I don't see how Father can trust him not to make mistakes." Alice nibbled at the cake like a rabbit, one tiny bite at a time.

Something about Alice's comment set Joseph's teeth on edge. She had no right to make fun of Polly or her family. "Mr.

Jessup is one of the finest men I've ever met. He taught me most of what I know about the Bible."

Alice leveled an indulgent look at him that bade him stay quiet. "You haven't seen him for a long time. He changed after his wife died. Everyone says so."

Joseph was considering the implications of Alice's assertion when a stranger, an older man with salt-and-pepper hair, approached and extended a hand to Joseph. "I was hoping to make your acquaintance today, Mr. Carpenter."

"You have the advantage of me, sir." The men shook hands. "I don't believe we've met."

"Gabe Noell, at your service. The fine folks at Breading Community Church have invited me to carve a life-size nativity scene as part of this year's Christmas celebration. But I've been wanting to meet you to talk over some business. Can we get together on Monday morning?"

Did Mr. Noell represent Joseph's first client in Breading? "I'd love to, but where shall we meet? I confess I don't have an office yet."

The bearded man waved away Joseph's concern. "We can meet at the church if that's all right with you."

Something in the man's gray eyes captured Joseph's attention. "At eleven?"

"Eleven it is." The hand that grasped Joseph's was strong, calloused, the hands of a workman.

"He comes well recommended as a wood-carver," Alice told him. "I wonder why he wants to see you."

Joseph made a noncommittal sound. If the man wanted to discuss business with a lawyer, Joseph wouldn't reveal it to anyone.

"Joseph." Jean approached them next. "You must come. People are anxious to speak with you."

If not Gabe Noell, another person would be Joseph's first client—and that person probably stood in this very room. It was time to celebrate Jean's engagement and reacquaint himself with his friends and neighbors.

Polly packed hay around the gravy boat, turkey platter, and cake plate. She loved sharing Mama's Flow Blue china of royal blue patterns swirling against a white background but at the same time feared something irreplaceable would break. Irreplaceable in terms of both monetary and sentimental value.

But today the Breading Community Church would celebrate the first Sunday of Advent as well as the Sunday after Thanksgiving. People brought whatever leftovers remained from their individual family feasts and enjoyed fellowship together. Polly looked forward first to hearing the pastor's sermon. Every year he preached a special series related to the Christmas season, something that always added to her anticipation of the holiday.

Better to wonder about the pastor's sermon than when she might see Joey again. After the embarrassment at last week's engagement party, she wouldn't blame him if he avoided her. Who would be interested in a young woman who came saddled with a ready-made family and a father given to unpredictable behavior?

Because they were bringing Mama's china, Polly sat in the back of the wagon. She kept the box containing leftover pie, turkey soup, and the Flow Blue as steady as possible. Dolores took Polly's usual place next to Pa on the front seat, while Hazel nestled next to her on the wagon bed. Her twin brothers rode with their legs dangling over the back.

Getting to church was much easier since Pa had sold the farm and moved into town to work at the bank. Polly hoped to arrive early and get Pa settled in, but the Carpenters' surrey already stood beside the building. Joey caught sight of Polly as he assisted Jean from the carriage and waved a greeting. The moment Jean had both feet safely on the ground, he headed in their direction.

"Good morning, Mr. Jessup, Dolores." Joey shook Pa's hand and glanced at the back of the wagon. "Polly."

Polly's heart melted. Joey greeted them as if nothing had gone wrong at his sister's party.

"Joey." Pa's face lit up with pleasure and recognition. "It's good to have you home again."

Joey helped Dolores from her seat, and she giggled. Polly waited for her brothers and Hazel to climb down before she scooted forward, her skirts scrunching beneath her, hampering her progress.

"May I help you with that?"

Amusement gleamed in Joey's blue eyes, and heat rushed to her cheeks. *I must look ridiculous.*

"It's my mother's china. I'm always careful whenever we bring it."

He bent over the side of the wagon and tugged at the box. "Is this it?"

"Yes."

"Let me take it out first so you can be sure it's safe. Then I'll help you down."

Before she could protest, he hefted the heavy box onto his shoulder and, whistling, carried it to the church hall where they would enjoy the fellowship meal. Mrs. Denton, the pastor's wife, met him at the door to let him in.

Why am I sitting here like a lady waiting on her escort? Now that her movements wouldn't jostle the china, she could move about more easily. About the time she reached the end of the wagon bed, Joey trotted back, a frown on his face.

"I asked you to wait for me." He put his hands around her waist and lifted her from the wagon as easily as if she were Hazel's size. His hands lingered on her waist for a moment after her feet touched the ground. "Don't you know I just want to help?" he asked in a low voice.

Unable to look in his face, Polly's eyes sought the ground. Heat poured through her from the inside out, causing her to shiver where the cool air struck her hot skin. Joey tucked her shawl about her shoulders.

"Joseph! There you are!"

At the sound of Alice's voice, Joseph stepped away from Polly. Enough heat to cook an egg rushed into her face.

"Please turn in your Bibles to the first chapter of Luke, verse forty-six," Pastor Denton addressed the congregation.

Beside Joseph, Alice took out her fine-tooled leather Bible and rustled through the pages. His eyes strayed across the row in front of them where Polly put her arm around her little sister's shoulders and helped her find the spot in her Bible.

"Please stand and listen as I read aloud."

By the time Joseph found the passage, the pastor had

started reading. He could see Polly mouthing the words as if recalling them from memory. " 'And Mary said, My soul doth magnify the Lord, and my spirit hath rejoiced in God my Saviour." Polly didn't miss a bit until Pastor Denton concluded his reading of Mary's song.

"This year for Advent we will be considering the character of Mary, the woman God chose to give birth to His Son. We can learn a lot about the person God wants us to be by studying her life. First, we are going to look at her capacity to glorify the Lord. Look at the words she uses in the burst of praise she gave voice to when Elisabeth extra greeted her. She glorified the Lord, she rejoiced in God, she said He had done great things."

For the remainder of the sermon, Pastor Denton outlined many ways Mary lifted up the Lord. "Was Mary having a mountaintop experience when she arrived at Elisabeth's house? No. She had gone to her cousin's home because of the rumors flying around Nazareth about her pregnancy. But she still rejoiced in what God was doing in her and through her and for her, regardless of the difficulties it presented. Can we say the same?"

His words sobered Joseph, and he remained thoughtful after the service. God had led him to return to Breading, although he could have joined a profitable practice near his school. Whatever challenges he faced paled when compared to what Mary endured. He prayed he would praise God whatever the future brought, starting with his meeting with Gabe Noell in the morning.

On Monday morning, Joseph arrived at the church a few minutes before eleven and heard someone whistling. He followed the sound and found Gabe Noell working in a lean-to behind the building. Bundled in a jacket and overalls, the wood-carver was studying a chunk of pinewood in front of him.

"Mr. Noell?"

"Ah! Joseph! You found me. I was about to head inside."

"I followed the music." Joseph smiled. "But we'd probably be warmer inside."

"If it's all right with you, I'd like to stay out here. At least until I show you what I'm working on."

That surprised Joseph. Most artisans he knew preferred to work in private. But the carver laid out several good-sized pieces of pine. The trees grew in abundance near Breading and seemed the logical choice for the manger scene. Perhaps Gabe felt more comfortable telling Joseph his problems if he kept his hands busy.

"Let me tell you about my plans," Gabe said.

His plans? Did he need Joseph to draw up a will?

"The church wants a manger scene that can be displayed outside, to remind all the people of Breading of the reason for Christmas."

Joseph wondered when Gabe would get to the point, but he played along. "How many figures have they asked you to make? Joseph, Mary, and the baby Jesus? Or more as well?"

"Well, that depends partly on you."

What? Did he need Joseph to negotiate a contract for him? "I'm sorry, I don't understand."

"The church wants the figures painted as well as carved. But if I do that, it'll slow me down. Besides, I'm a wood-carver, not a painter. So you see, I thought another artist could help me design their faces." He handed Joseph a piece of paper with rough sketches of the three main figures. "Work together, you see. So. Are you interested?"

Joseph blinked. Had he missed something? "I'm sorry?"

"Are you willing to help me with the manger scene? I would pay you, of course. I understand you're quite an artist."

Joseph almost dropped the paper with the sketches and backed away from Noell. "I thought you wanted to consult me on a legal matter."

A smile creased Noell's face. "Ah. I'm sorry I didn't make myself clear. Just like me—I let my carvings do my speaking for me. No, I'm seeking your help about a different matter. Please say yes."

Joseph studied the sketches Gabe had made. The faces were blank, ready for an artist's brush. He could picture them in his mind. The strong, faithful man. The sweetly slumbering infant. But Mary. . . His mind flew back to the pastor's sermon yesterday. Mary praised God. What else did he know about her? He couldn't picture her in his mind. "I usually paint from real-life models. I don't know. . ." *Am I actually considering the project?*

"You don't know who is worthy of representing the Lord's human family? I understand your dilemma." Gabe chuckled. "Ask God. He'll show you."

Joseph took Gabe to mean he should search for someone who looked like Mary inside and out. *I'm foolish to even consider it. I need to start my business.* But he heard himself say, "I'll give it a try."

Noell shook Joseph's hand. "So it's agreed. I'll meet with you again on Thursday."

On Tuesday morning, Polly headed for church after the children went to school. Was it only last year that Miss Berry, the teacher, had encouraged her to attend normal school? Polly liked the thought of teaching. But Pa and the family needed her too much at home. Leaving to go elsewhere would only indulge her selfish desire to remain in the comfortable confines of the classroom. A part of her had held on to the hope that her Prince Charming, Joey, would sweep in and rescue her, but she knew that was no more than a childish dream.

At least I do get to teach, at Sunday school. At the age of fourteen, she had taken over the little ones at church at the same time Miss Berry had asked her to lead the youngest reading group at school. So when the pastor asked her to help plan the Christmas program, she accepted. This year she had written the script for the play. She clasped the pages of the manuscript in front of her, hoping the committee would be pleased with the result.

Sunday's meeting had been brief. In addition to Pastor and Mrs. Denton, Mr. Post attended to discuss the music they would use. The pastor mentioned that he was looking for another person to help with the rehearsals. He liked for most of the work to be done by church members, to "spread the blessing." Had he found a volunteer?

When she arrived at the church, she heard whistling and followed the sound around the corner to where Gabe Noell worked in his lean-to. Hoping not to disturb him, she watched him studying a block of wood almost as tall as he was, making marks here and there along the length of it. How could someone create things that looked alive out of tree limbs? She had seen samples of his work, forest creatures that looked as though they would jump off the tree branch where they sat. She couldn't wait to see the finished manger scene.

"How's he doing?"

At the sound of the familiar, deep voice, Polly stumbled back a step—and into Joey's broad chest. "I didn't know you were there." Breathy, her voice sounded accusatory.

He put out an arm to steady her. "I'm sorry. I didn't mean to startle you. Are you here for the meeting about the Christmas program?"

Her eyes opened wide. "I am. Are you the new committee member?" *Joey?*

"Don't act so surprised. I guess Pastor Denton figures putting on a play can't be much different than defending people in court." The corners of his eyes crinkled in amusement. "Come to think of it, he might be right."

Polly relaxed. This was the Joey she remembered, even if he was hidden underneath a breasted suit and vest. "Putting on a play is one thing, but what about the twenty children we have to corral to get it together? We need to start rehearsals right away. I'm worried we don't have enough time to get ready before the program."

"I wouldn't worry. People enjoy watching their children— even the mistakes. Maybe especially the mistakes."

Maybe parents did, but what about the children? "That's no excuse for poor preparation." How well she remembered the humiliation of stumbling through her one line in her first Christmas play five times before she gave up and ran, crying, to where her mother sat in the audience. She never forgot her lines again and, in fact, went on to excel in memorizing scripture. She hoped this year's program would spark the same passion in the youngsters who participated.

"Oh, Polly." He tucked her arm beneath his and headed for the door. "I can tell we're going to have fun."

Pastor Denton was arranging a small circle of chairs when they entered the sanctuary. His wife murmured a greeting.

"Here they are." The pastor smiled. "Joseph, I believe you know Mr. Post."

"Very pleased, I'm sure." Mr. Post extended his hand.

"How is your mother faring these days?" Joey asked.

That was Joey all over again, a born politician. Polly would remind herself as often as necessary that he made everyone feel special. Anyone who kept company with Alice Johnson couldn't possibly be interested in someone like her.

Polly became aware that the group had turned quiet.

Pastor Denton cleared his throat. "Miss Jessup, we're all interested in hearing your ideas for the program."

She shuffled the pages in her lap and took a deep breath. "My idea is to let Mary tell the story." She handed out different copies to everyone. "I've used Mary's actual words where they're recorded in the Bible."

"That will tie in nicely with my sermons." The pastor thumbed through his script quickly. "I see that you're covering everything I intend to preach about this month. I like it. A lot."

Joey's face wrinkled as he read and reread the first page. "This is a lot for one person to memorize. Do you have someone in mind?" He smiled, as if to take the sting out of his words. "We're not all as gifted as you are."

Pleased at his compliment, Polly glanced away, hoping to hide her blush. "I was thinking of Jemima Fuller." She caught her breath, waiting for reactions from the others.

"Jemima." Mrs. Denton's voice was thoughtful. "I confess I wouldn't have thought of her, but now that you mention it, I think she'd be perfect. She always studies ahead for Sunday school."

"I hope doing this play will encourage her to keep learning. I'd like to see her in the scripture contest this year. It would mean so much to her if she could win something like that."

"Doesn't Jemima have a pack of brothers?" Joey asked.

"Six of them." Polly nodded. "I hope they'll take part as well. We can never seem to get enough boys interested."

"Are they as rambunctious as I remember?"

"They can be. . .high-spirited," Mrs. Denton said.

"Sounds like fun." Joey chuckled. "I'm glad you asked me to help." He winked at Polly.

Polly drew in her breath. With Joey involved, did the stakes for the Christmas program now include her heart?

Chapter 3

"Alice Johnson has offered to help with the Christmas play," Mrs. Denton told Polly before rehearsal the following Monday.

Her nerves, already stretched, threatened to snap. *Alice?* Alice had never taken part before. Polly could think of only one reason why she had changed her mind this year: Joey. "That's nice," she stammered, her heart protesting against the intrusion. *Be kind,* she reminded herself.

How far she fell short of the biblical Mary. Yesterday Pastor Denton had preached about her obedience and humility. When God called her the most highly favored among women, Mary replied that she was only His servant. *Some servant I am, if I can't accept Alice's help without questioning her motives.*

In spite of her resolution to accept Alice's help, Polly felt relieved when she didn't arrive before they started rehearsal. As Polly hoped, Jemima needed little direction as she rehearsed Mary's response to Gabriel's visit. The pastor's son Peter, as the angel, stumbled over several words.

"Let's try that again," Polly said. "Peter, it's acceptable to read the script for now. Stop and let me know if there are any words you don't understand."

Midway through, Alice swept in with a young woman Polly didn't recognize and marched up to her.

"I understand you've written a little play about Mary for this year's Christmas program."

"That's right." Polly's throat almost closed from the effort to keep her tone pleasant.

"Martha has been the star in several programs at her church in Dallas. I'm sure she would be perfect for the role."

From the look on Martha's face, Polly guessed she hadn't suggested this invasion. The expression on Jemima's face told Polly all the confidence she had displayed could drain out of her more quickly than runoff after a hard storm. She had to speak, now. "But as you see, we already have someone to play the role of Mary. Would Martha be interested in portraying Elisabeth?"

Martha spoke before Alice could protest. "I'd love to be Elisabeth, or even one of the angels." She smiled. "I just love Christmas. As long as I can be in the play, I'll be happy."

Polly's heart warmed toward the girl. "We'll be practicing the part with Elisabeth in a few minutes. Why don't you read the script while we finish running through this scene."

Alice harrumphed and took a seat in the front pew. Polly shifted her attention back to the scene in front of her. "That was good, Jemima. Peter, that was better. It's okay to speak slowly. Just speak up a little louder. Let's start again from the beginning of the scene, and then we'll move on."

Whatever the reason, Jemima didn't do as well the second

time through. Alice whispered in Polly's ear, loud enough for the children to hear, "I thought you said she could act."

Polly chose to ignore both Alice's comment and Jemima's second-rate performance. "That's an excellent start. Martha, are you ready to practice your scene?"

Martha nodded, and Polly held her breath, hoping the girl would do well. To her relief, Martha's reading of the "Who am I, that the mother of my Lord should visit me?" speech sounded genuinely heartfelt. She hugged Jemima, an extra touch not written in the script. Jemima relaxed and hugged her back, and Polly's fears fled. These two girls could work together and be friends, in spite of their elders. *Thank You, Lord.*

"Excellent, girls. Let's take a break while I call in Mr. Carpenter and the boys for the scene with the shepherds."

Going above and beyond his responsibilities on the committee, Joey had taken the boys outside to run off energy. Like Mary, he gave of himself with a servant's heart.

Polly turned toward the door and was surprised to see Joey in the back row with half a dozen boys gathered around him, sitting quietly. He smiled and touched his fingers to his eyebrow in greeting, and her heart flipped.

The Fuller boys had worn out Joseph sooner than he thought possible. Too many years had passed since he played rough-and-tumble with a gang of kids instead of hunkering down with a pile of law books. They had accepted with good grace his suggestion that they end the game and followed him inside.

They slipped through the door as Alice was introducing

Martha to Polly. When he mentioned the play to Alice, he hadn't expected her offer of help. Polly handled the situation with her usual charm and common sense. She would make an excellent lawyer herself, if women did such things. The rehearsal had made good progress under her direction.

"That'un's a keeper." Gabe's soft voice carried only as far as Joseph's ears. A few minutes earlier, he had noticed the wood-carver slip into the sanctuary.

"Polly's got a good head and a good heart," Joseph agreed.

At that moment, Polly turned around and saw him. Her step hitched, and a faint pink blush stained her cheeks. Alice turned her head around then, her wide, fruit-crowned hat looking out of place for a midweek meeting. Polly's plain dress suited the occasion better, but her beauty still shone through.

Beauty. He shook his head. Never before had he thought about Polly in those terms. But already since his return he had seen she was a woman with wisdom and tact who loved God's Word. A woman who found joy in serving others.

He rose to his feet before his thoughts ran too far ahead of him, fighting the nerves that tingled along his arms and hands, the same way he felt when he stood before judge and jury for the first time. "Are you ready for the boys now?" He rubbed his hands together, as if he could rub out his uneasiness with the action.

"Yes, we're about ready to practice the scene with the inn-keeper and the shepherds, and then we're done for the day." Polly smiled at the boys and beckoned them forward.

Entranced, Joseph watched as she worked with the children for another half hour. She encouraged, prompted, assisted, but never scolded. Even shy little Reuben Fuller managed to kneel when the angel appeared. Because of Polly's efforts, these children would understand Christmas on a whole different level.

While they rehearsed, Alice promenaded down the aisle with Martha trailing behind. The girl looked over her shoulder, watching the action at the front. They paused by the pew where Joseph sat, and Alice bent slightly toward him. "I'll see you at dinner tomorrow night, won't I?"

Joseph had forgotten the invitation until that moment. Acceptance meant implying his intention to court Alice Johnson; refusal could create repercussions for his fledgling practice. The banker could direct a lot of business his way. He managed a weak smile. "I wouldn't miss it."

"Wonderful!" She started to clap her hands together and then, with a glance at the children practicing, thought better of it. With a quick look over her shoulder and her hips gently swaying, she left the building with Martha in tow.

"I'm sure you'll do the right thing." Gabe put a hand on Joseph's shoulder and slipped out.

Joseph thought about his commitment to paint the figures the wood-carver was working on. How would he paint Mary's face? He had no more idea now than he had when he started.

The sky had deepened to twilight by the time they finished their afternoon practice and Polly headed home. She considered stopping by the emporium to look for ideas for Christmas presents. Perhaps she would see something she could make at home. The few coins in her reticule might purchase some penny candy but not much more. She bypassed the shop and headed home.

A faint odor of something burning disturbed the crisp cool air, mixing with the scent of pine that was as much a part of Breading as the church steeple. She thought back to the breakfast Dolores had scorched last Saturday and shook her head. Her sister still didn't cook well, but only practice would improve her skills. The scent grew stronger as she approached their house, and her steps sped up. Smoke fogged the kitchen window. She dashed into the room and removed the guilty pan from the stove. Couldn't Dolores fry up a bit of ham without burning it to a crisp? Where *was* her sister, anyhow?

First things first. She removed the pot from stove. Most of the beans seemed unaffected except for a layer stuck to the bottom. Setting them aside, she pulled corn bread from the oven. God had spared them in His goodness. If she hadn't come home when she did, why, the house could have burned down around their ears.

In the silence that descended after her mad dash around the kitchen, she heard Hazel's voice crooning to her baby doll. Out the window, she caught sight of the twins chopping firewood. But she didn't see any sign of Dolores—or Pa. He should have returned from work by now.

Where could she be? Polly pondered what to do next.

The door rattled and Dolores ran in, eyes open wide in panic. Seeing Polly, she sagged against the table in relief. "Oh, Polly, thank goodness you're here. After I left, I realized I had forgotten to take the corn bread out and I was afraid. . ."

Before Polly could utter a word of remonstrance, she heard two other, deeper voices on the front porch.

"Here you are, Mr. Jessup."

Polly recognized that voice. *Joseph.* What was he doing here?

Moments later his broad shoulders filled the doorway as he led Pa inside.

"This isn't my home!" Pa looked bewildered. He saw Polly standing by the stove. "What are you doing here?"

"I, uh, saw Mr. Jessup headed down toward your old farm." Joseph shuffled his feet. "When I was escorting the Fuller children home. He seemed to have forgotten that you have a house in town now. . . ."

"That's where I was headed," Dolores said. "Miss Berry said she saw him going in that direction." She sniffed and seemed to notice the odor permeating the kitchen for the first time. "Did anything burn? I'm so sorry."

Polly wiped the back of her hand across her forehead. How much more would she have to deal with tonight? First the house could have burned down, and then Pa went wandering.

Pa sat down at the table, looking lost and forlorn, and Polly's heart went out to him. She dished out beans and corn bread on a piece of Ma's china and set it in front of him. "This is home, Pa. See? Here's Ma's china. No one else would have it in their house." She held back the tears that flooded her heart.

Pa pushed the beans around the plate, as if the pattern on the china would change if he moved them enough. "This does look like my Mary's china. But I don't recall this house, no, I don't."

"Go ahead and eat. You'll feel better then."

Pa brought a spoonful of beans to his mouth and sighed with pleasure. After refilling his plate, she set out dishes for the rest of the family. She paused with an extra plate. "Do you want to join us for dinner? It's the least we can offer after all your help."

"Another time." Joey beckoned Polly to follow him onto the porch.

What else had Pa done?

"When did your father start to lose his memory?" he asked.

Chapter 4

Joseph walked home, grateful he hadn't chosen to ride on this particular day. Walking and thinking went together like blue skies and sunshine, and he needed to process what he had learned.

According to Polly, her father had been in decline for some time. Her mother's death might have triggered it, although that impression came more from instinct than anything Polly had said. At home they adapted to the imperceptible changes in his behavior, but lately she had worried something was wrong. The first, and so far the only, time he had revealed his weakness in public happened at the engagement party.

Joseph could sense Polly's embarrassment. "People have big hearts. They'll realize he's ill, given time." But she wasn't ready to tell anyone else yet, not until she had no choice.

"I don't know if I should continue working on the Christmas program," she had confided. Joseph insisted she must. She was the heart and soul of the play. Without her, the children would shrivel up on stage. What could he do to make things easier for Polly?

He hadn't found a solution when he arrived at the church for the afternoon's rehearsal the following day. A subdued Polly was already there, as well as Alice, dressed in her almost-Sunday best.

I'm supposed to have supper with her family tonight. The events of the previous twenty-four hours, including an interview with a potential client, had all but driven the appointment from his mind. If it wasn't so late, he would decline to attend. He doubted he would so easily forget an invitation from the woman he loved.

Alice wasted no time in staking her claim on him. She shifted a particularly peculiar hat—complete with velvet ribbons and poinsettia flowers—to a coquettish angle as she looked up at him. "There you are, Joseph! I'm hoping we can leave rehearsal a little early to stop by the emporium. I would appreciate your advice on some Christmas presents I'm buying."

"But I'm needed at the rehearsal."

Their conversation had reached the front. Polly looked composed if somewhat pale. "Go ahead and enjoy yourselves. We'll be fine. Won't we, boys?" She winked with her usual good humor.

They all chorused their agreement. Joseph noticed a platter of cookies waiting for them and sensed a reward for good behavior had been promised. Why he would rather stay and eat cookies with the children before walking Polly home rather than enjoying fine dining with the Johnsons, he couldn't say.

But a commitment was a commitment. He tipped his hat to Polly and offered Alice his arm. "See you tomorrow night, then." They skipped rehearsal on Wednesday afternoons, due to the midweek prayer service.

Joseph turned his mind away from Polly and focused on Alice. "I see Martha didn't come today."

Alice shook her head. "No. Elisabeth is only in one scene, and they're not practicing it today. She wanted to come ahead, but I told her to stay home."

If Martha didn't come to rehearsal, how long would Alice continue? Joseph wasn't a conceited man; otherwise, he might think she wanted him to herself without her niece's interference.

Joseph decided to make the best of it. Being seen on the arm of the daughter of the richest and most powerful man in town wouldn't do his reputation any harm either. He could think of worse ways to spend an evening than in the presence of a lovely, witty woman, even if she was shallow at times.

"Do you mind stopping at the emporium?" Alice asked. "I'm not certain what my brother will like, and I hope you can help." She explained what she had observed of his tastes since his return to Breading as they approached the store.

"I'll help if I can." He stepped forward to open the door.

Before he put his hand on the knob, a man exited. He was piled so high with packages that Joseph couldn't see his face until he passed. *Mr. Jessup*, looking lively and as pleased as Santa Claus's elves on Christmas morning.

"Why, Joseph, I thought you'd be at the church." He juggled his arms so the packages settled more securely and lifted a finger to his lips. "Don't tell Polly my secret. It seems God has answered my prayers and provided a bountiful Christmas for us!" He looked as though he wanted to clap his heels and leap for joy.

A glance at the pile of parcels suggested a stellar Christmas morning for the Jessup household. "God be praised, sir. I am mightily happy for you." If Alice hadn't tugged his arm to enter the store, he would have offered to help carry the packages. He settled for asking, "Are you headed straight home, sir? To Dover Street?" He wanted to be sure the man remembered the location of his house.

"Of course I am! Where else would I go?" Jessup looked surprised at the question. Had the previous evening's events passed out of his mind? "I'll see you later." He traipsed down the sidewalk singing "O Little Town of Bethlehem" off-key.

Alice glanced over her shoulder at his departing figure, her nose wrinkled, before shrugging her shoulders and entering the mercantile. Joseph paused inside the door to breathe in the familiar scents of tobacco and licorice overlaid with the smells that always reminded him of Christmas: pine needles and cinnamon and peppermint. Something more warmed the air, and he turned his head, seeking the source. There it was. In the corner, the merchant's wife was pouring out hot chocolate with peppermint sticks for stirrers.

At the counter, Alice was leafing through the latest catalog from Montgomery Ward. She motioned for him to join her. "I value your opinion. After your years at college, I'm sure you have a better sense of current fashions for men than. . .anyone here in Breading."

The hat she had chosen for her brother had in fact been common back at college, but Joseph feared it might make him look like a dandy here in Breading. "That was a popular style at school. I'm sure whatever you think would be fine."

"Maybe I should ask the milliner to make one." Alice took out a piece of paper and traced the pattern.

Joseph excused himself and headed for the corner where he had seen the children with the hot chocolate. "Is that only for the little ones, or may I have some, too?" He smiled at the young woman, the store owner's daughter.

"Whoever wants it. Christmas, chocolate, and chilly days just naturally go together. But you're only the second adult to indulge." She poured him a cup.

He thanked her but refused the peppermint stick. Cradling the cup in his hands, he blew on the hot liquid. "Oh? Who else imbibed?"

"Mr. Jessup. He was so happy, saying how God had given him a surprise gift so his family could have a good Christmas. He drank the chocolate while Father rang up his purchases."

"I ran into him on the way in. He seemed to be in fine spirits." Joseph sipped the warm drink.

"Are you ready?" Alice returned from the catalog counter.

Joseph gulped down the rest of the chocolate and placed the cup on the table. "I am now."

"Merry Christmas!" Pa called merrily as he entered the kitchen.

Polly turned around from where she was hanging up her coat after returning from church. To her surprise, a half dozen packages weighted down his arms. She took the top bundles and placed them on the table. He looked happier than she had seen him in a long time, almost like. . .back when Ma was alive.

"Where did all this come from?" The family's finances didn't allow for this kind of extravagance, whatever the parcels held.

"God dropped a gift in my lap!" Pa took some coins from his pocket. "I even have some left over. I was on my way to the emporium to buy some nails to fix the front steps. And there was a twenty-dollar bill. I don't remember putting it there, but I must have. After I paid up our account at the mercantile, I still had enough money to buy presents for Christmas."

How *did* the money get there? Maybe Mr. Johnson had given his employees a bonus. He had done that a few times. That must be it. Polly couldn't help thinking the money could have gone for more urgent matters than Christmas presents, but she wouldn't dampen Pa's happiness for anything. "Where do you want to put these?" Polly reached for the top package.

"Oh no, my dear. I must have my little secrets." Pa chuckled and handed her a different bundle. "Carry that one. I'll keep them in my room until Christmas."

Polly followed Pa to his room. She made a note of the nooks and crannies where he stashed the items away, in case he forgot between now and Christmas. Now and again that happened. Pa would wander around the house, looking for his glasses or a missing sock. Polly had become the guardian of Pa's memory.

She looked at the package Pa had grabbed out of her hands. He had included something for her, too. A little piece of her gladdened at the thought. When was the last time she had looked forward to opening presents on Christmas morning?

She told herself she didn't need them. Gifts were for the little ones, and she had everything that mattered in Jesus.

But now she had something to look forward to, like everybody else.

"What can we give to the children in the play?" Polly asked her fellow committee members when they gathered for rehearsal the following afternoon. Pa's shopping trip triggered her thinking. With the gifts Pa had bought, she could contribute the money she had saved for her family.

"Why, I have that all taken care of." Gabe Noell walked in on their discussion. "Don't you worry about it."

"You know the church can't afford to pay you any more," Pastor Denton said.

"No need." The older man waved away the objections. "Consider it my gift to all of you." Whistling, he headed for the front door.

As he went out, Pa came in. What was he doing here in the middle of a workday? Her mind raced with possibilities, none of them good. Had he forgotten to return to the bank after lunch?

Pa paused beside a stained glass window, light illuminating his features and easing away the years. He looked as uncertain and lost as a child. When he saw Polly, his face crumpled like a baby's.

"Polly." He sank onto one of the pews.

"I'll take over here," Joseph said. "You go take care of your father."

She hurried to Pa's side. "What's happened, Pa?" She lowered her voice. "Did you forget where you are?"

He shook his head. "I came to the church. I didn't know what else to do. I knew I would find you here."

Each statement left Polly more confused than the last, but

she kept her composure. "What is it? Is someone hurt?"

Pa sat on the bench, rocking back and forth. Polly heard the door open but didn't look up.

"Shall I go for the doctor?" Pastor Denton had joined them.

"That won't be necessary." Jack Hurd, the town sheriff, had entered the sanctuary, followed by the banker and Alice. "We're here to arrest Mr. Jessup for bank robbery."

Chapter 5

Joseph couldn't have avoided hearing the sheriff's unexpected and unwelcome announcement even if he had wanted to. His voice rang louder than even the pastor's during a heated Sunday sermon.

At the interruption, Jemima and her brothers stopped in the middle of the scene with the shepherds. No one spoke for the span of a second.

"That's enough for now." Joseph broke the silence. "Mrs. Denton has cookies waiting for you at the parsonage." He reached Jessup in three long strides. "The church is usually a sanctuary against arrest."

"He can't use this building to hide out from his crimes," Mr. Johnson scoffed.

Abashed, Sheriff Hurd put away the handcuffs he had ready to clap on Mr. Jessup's wrists. "If you'll just come with me, sir."

Mr. Jessup looked at Polly in bewilderment and sank lower on the pew, looking ready to put his arms over his head and curl up in a ball. She placed herself between her father and his accusers.

"What is all this about?" Joseph refused to let them waltz out with Polly's father without some kind of explanation.

"That's none of your business."

"He stole the bank's money, that's what he did." Mr. Johnson had no qualms about spilling the beans. "Walked out of the bank with twenty dollars of the day's receipts in his pocket."

"That was a gift from God." Mr. Jessup's words were as good as a confession.

Polly's face turned as pale as translucent oilpaper, and Joseph noticed that the arm she had draped around her father's shoulder trembled.

"So you admit you had money in your pocket when you left the bank last night?"

"It was a gift from God," Mr. Jessup repeated. "I didn't steal it."

"I'm afraid you'll have to come with me," the sheriff said. Jessup didn't struggle but shuffled down the center aisle of the church after the law officer and the banker. He glanced about him, almost as if he expected worshippers to arrive and music to begin.

Casting a despairing, pleading glance in Joseph's direction, Polly followed her father. Before he could respond, someone tugged at his elbow. Her face puckered and she turned away.

"Let them go," Alice spoke fiercely. "I knew something was wrong when we saw him with all those packages last night. The Jessups have never had that kind of money. The nerve of that old man."

Joseph straightened his shoulders. "That *old man*, as you call him, is a friend of mine. And he needs my help." He hastened down the aisle.

"But what about my father?" Alice's voice trailed after him. Joseph didn't tarry long enough to hear her complaint.

Polly stumbled out the door only moments after her father. She hesitated in the middle of the street, uncertain which direction to head. Spitting snow, unexpected this early in the season, punched the air. Even as she sped down the street, the snowfall increased in intensity, more like sleet, biting into her hair and skin. She pulled her shawl closer around her and wished she had worn an overcoat. This kind of storm was fine, as long as she was inside beside the fireplace to watch it fall.

Pa won't have a fire. She hated to think of him, confused, cold, and alone, but the family would expect both of them home soon. Since they were old enough to take care of themselves for a little while longer, she decided to go with Pa. How long he could manage on his own in the town jail was uncertain.

Last night Pa had been so pleased with his unexpected windfall, one he thought God had provided. He didn't want it for himself; no, he delighted in providing an extravagant Christmas for the family. What she perceived as Mr. Johnson's generous bonus for his employees had generated genuine goodwill toward the banker in her spirit. She blinked back the tears that threatened to blind her. How had last night's happiness transformed so quickly into today's disaster? Had Pa somehow pocketed money that belonged to the bank?

With all the thoughts circling around Polly's head, she

almost passed the jail. She turned on her heels and her foot slipped on the icy ground. Stumbling forward, she grabbed a lamppost, and her fingers stuck to the cold metal. A few tears spilled, melting the snowflakes that landed on her cheeks. Wiping away the dampness with her hands, she straightened and crossed the boardwalk into the sheriff's office.

Mr. Johnson sat at the sheriff's desk, alternating between dipping his pen into an inkwell and scribbling on a sheet of paper. At the sound of the door opening, he glanced up and his eyes narrowed into a glare. "Miss Jessup." He said her name as if she were guilty by association.

"Mr. Johnson." With quaking heart, she knew she must speak up for her father. "I'm sure this must all be some unfortunate misunderstanding." She glanced over his shoulder, hoping to spot her father or the sheriff, but the door to the cells was closed.

"There's no mistake." The banker infused sympathy into the words, but one look at his face told Polly the truth. He had Pa in a vise, and he intended to take advantage of it. "I've already told the sheriff, and I've written it out here." With his forefinger, he tapped the papers he had been writing on.

Anxious to know the nature of the accusations, Polly reached for the papers, but Mr. Johnson pulled them back. "Now, Miss Jessup. These don't belong to you any more than that twenty-dollar bill belonged to your father, and I can't let you look at them without the sheriff's say-so."

Polly wanted to scream. After a scant five minutes at the jail, she had already antagonized Pa's accuser further. She took a deep breath and walked past the banker to the door. "Sheriff Hurd? It's Polly Jessup."

An anguished cry and clanging bars reached her ears through the thick door, followed by scuffling feet. The sheriff opened the door, his heavy key ring jangling from his belt.

"Miss Jessup. You shouldn't have come down here. There's nothing you can do."

Polly tried to peer around the sheriff without success. The slim line visible through the crack in the door didn't reveal Pa's whereabouts. "Can't I at least see Pa?" Her voice cracked. "Make sure he's warm enough? What are you going to do about his supper? Does he have a blanket?" The questions tumbled out of her as if she were a parent leaving her children with friends overnight.

"No one's going to starve in here. Mrs. Hurd will bring him a sandwich later tonight." He closed the door behind him.

A cold supper wouldn't warm him like the spicy stew simmering on the stove at home. Polly told herself to stay calm. "Thank you kindly. But what about a blanket? He wasn't dressed for the cold."

"Miss Jessup." The sheriff had reached the end of his patience. "No one has ever died of cold in this here jail. And we don't coddle the prisoners. Now you go on home. We'll see about getting your father legal representation. You can come back in the morning with some fresh clothes, seeing as how we'll have a hearing tomorrow, since the judge will be in town."

A hearing. "So soon?" How could she prepare in so little time, when she still didn't know the exact nature of the allegations? "Can't I at least know what the charges are?"

"Your father is the one on trial here, not you. We've advised him of the trouble he's in. Now you get on home and take care of your family."

I should never have come alone, Polly thought bitterly. *The sheriff wouldn't talk to the pastor that way.*

A blast of icy air tore at her throat and announced the arrival of someone in the office.

"Sheriff, I'm here to see my client."

Joey Carpenter stood in front of the door.

Joseph could tell he'd arrived in the nick of time. Polly looked as wilted as a starched apron on a hot summer day. He wanted to pull her close and comfort her, if she would let him. Where did that thought come from? He was here as a longtime friend of the Jessups, nothing more, and he had urgent matters to address.

"You're going to represent Jessup?" Skepticism laced Mr. Johnson's voice.

Joseph straightened his spine, willing away all doubt. "If he'll have me."

"Isn't that—what do they call it?—a conflict of interest with your business with the bank?" Mr. Johnson raised an eyebrow, urging Joseph to abandon this crazy crusade.

"I can't say until I know the nature of the charges." Joseph felt the weight of Mr. Johnson's standing as the town's foremost citizen pressing on him, but he'd learned to face down intimidation in the courtroom. He looked at the man, who had until now been his prospective father-in-law, without blinking.

Mr. Johnson's mouth closed. "It's all here." He thrust the papers at Joseph.

"Thank you." Joseph took them. "May I see my client now?"

Polly took a half step forward. "May I. . . ?"

Joseph almost agreed, to set her heart at rest, but he needed to speak with Jessup in private. "Not now. I'll come by your house after I've spoken with your father." Noticing she wore only a shawl for protection against the elements, he said, "Take my coat with you. I'll pick it up when I see you later."

Polly opened her mouth to protest before demurring and accepting the coat. At the door, she glanced at him over her shoulder, anguish written in her eyes.

"Go ahead," he said, wishing he could do more to make this easier for her. "I'll be there as soon as I can."

Nodding, she opened the door, and a world of white swallowed her. When Joseph returned his attention to the office, Mr. Johnson was speaking.

"When do you think the hearing will be?"

The sheriff shrugged. "It depends on when Judge Heffner gets here. Before noon tomorrow, if we're lucky."

"The judge is coming here? Tomorrow?" So soon? How could he possibly prepare?

"Unless the snow keeps him home."

In either case, Joseph faced a long night of preparation. He doubted he would get much sleep.

Mr. Johnson took his leave. He paused as he brushed past Joseph. "I won't expect you for dinner." Whether he meant it as a statement of Joseph's plans for the evening or a permanent dismissal of his daughter's suitor, Joseph couldn't tell. At the moment, he didn't care. The front door slammed.

"I suppose you want to see Jessup?" the sheriff asked.

"Yes."

Sheriff Hurd unlocked the doors and escorted Joseph into the first of the jail's two cells. Jessup sat on a cot, staring through the bars as if they weren't there. The look on his face reminded Joseph of the day he'd found him heading toward the farm that used to belong to him. When he saw them approach, he stood to his feet, his eyes begging for enlightenment.

"Sheriff. What am I doing here?"

Sheriff Hurd worked his mouth, as if searching for words to explain. Joseph suspected that no answer would penetrate the haze that surrounded the man in the cell, at least not in his present state. "Why don't I let your lawyer here explain it to you? Mrs. Hurd will be here shortly with some grub." He said the latter as much to Joseph as to his client.

Joseph didn't know how much he could explain, even if Jessup could understand. Until he reviewed the documents, he didn't know the details of the charges beyond "bank robbery." He thought back to the previous evening, to the shopping spree Jessup had enjoyed at the mercantile. Could there be any truth to the accusation? He mentally shook himself. Everyone was innocent until proven guilty in a court of law.

Even if his lawyer harbored severe doubts.

Chapter 6

"He doesn't remember taking the money," Joey told Polly. "But there's no doubt it's gone."

Polly sipped her coffee, hoping the fiery liquid would help her take it all in. An air of unreality pervaded the night. Once she'd arrived home, she had fed stew to the rest of the family and only explained that Pa had been detained. When she sent the others to bed, Dolores stayed behind.

"What's happening?" she asked.

Polly struggled with a desire to spill the story to her sister but refrained. She saw no need to burden the young girl with suppositions and possibilities. Tomorrow morning, once she heard what Joey had to say, would come soon enough.

"I don't know," she had said. "Not everything. I promise, I'll tell you when I do. But right now, the little ones need your help. Especially Hazel. Can you do that for me?"

Dolores had agreed and gone to bed with the others. Polly waited for Joseph to come. One hour went by. Then two. The clock had chimed nine times before she heard a knock at the door.

She'd hoped for good news, feared bad. "You think he did it."

"I'm saying money is missing from the bank." Joey paced the kitchen floor, as if in rehearsal for the coming hearing. "And there's more." He bit his lip, the most candid response she had seen from him so far.

"He spent a lot of money at the emporium last night." She said it for him. She didn't know how he knew, but apparently he did. Probably a lot of people did.

A look of resignation replaced a fleeting look of relief on his face. "So you know. I met him leaving the store last night."

"I helped him put away the packages." She thought about the wrapped parcels waiting in her parents' bedroom, thought of the money they cost. That brought another concern to mind. "You know we don't have money to pay you at this time. But we'll take care of it, somehow."

He waved that aside. "I'm not worried about that." He came to a standstill and slid into a chair across from her. "I need to ask you some questions. You might not like what I have to say, but I need to know."

The determined set of his mouth told Polly he believed Pa was guilty. But he still wanted to help. The truth was, Polly didn't know what to believe. "All right."

"Do you know how much money your father makes a week?"

Polly thought back to the chaotic condition their finances had reached before she had convinced Pa to let her manage money matters. From then on, she gave him money to settle their debts—and then checked to make sure the money had reached the intended hands. Sometimes Pa had forgotten, and she had learned to factor that into their expenses. But nothing like this had ever happened.

"I can do better than that. I can show you." She brought out the ledger where she kept track of their income and expenses, as well as her pitiful attempts to save against the day she feared her father would no longer be able to work. "You can see there's not much there." Except a possible motive to take easy money? She shook away the doubts. "Pa might get. . .confused. . .sometimes. But he's as honest as the day is long. I'd stake my life on it."

"Polly." Joey looked at her, a heart-turning half grin on his face. "Or should I say Mary? Anyone grown-up enough to take care of all this"—his gesture took in the books, the house, her life—"deserves to be called by her real name, not a child's nickname."

Heat burned through her, and she felt a moment of giddy relief from the worry weighing down her shoulders.

"I wish I had better news for you."

The heat that stained her cheeks might have come from happiness at the compliment or despair. "What is it?"

Joey tapped his pencil on the pad of paper in front of him. "The bank puts a special mark on each teller's bills. So if there's a discrepancy, they can tell who made the error."

Polly knew what was coming before he said it.

"Everyone else's money tally was complete."

She waited for the final blow.

"And the money he spent at the store—well, it was marked with his initials." He sucked in a deep breath before daring to look at her. "The money he spent at the mercantile was from his till. There's no doubt about it."

Joseph hadn't known how he would break the news to Polly, but he knew he had to. He wished he could take the words back, take back the past twenty-four hours, undo all the burdens placed on her young shoulders.

The least he could do was share the burden with her. He waited through her long silence.

"What will happen at the hearing?" Polly spoke in a low voice. "Will he—go to jail?" Her voice trembled but didn't break.

Joseph frowned. Polly might not approve of his trial strategy. "I think we can avoid that, if you're willing to testify."

"You just said they've proved he's guilty. And I can't prove any different. In fact—" Now a sob shuddered through her. "Oh, Joey, what am I going to do?"

He wanted to get out of his chair and take her in his arms and comfort her, but he settled for taking her hands in his. "I'm going to see you through this. I know it's what God wants me to do." Did that sound cold and uncaring? "It's what I want to do."

"Thank you." Bright wetness shone in her eyes but no tears fell, and she stood. Moving to the sink, she stared out the window at the falling snow. "I don't see how the judge can get here in this weather. Can we discuss this in the morning?" She coughed. "You need to get on home before it gets any worse. You can't spend the night here."

"I already thought of that. The sheriff said I could bring some personal items for your father tonight. After that, I'm going to the boardinghouse where Gabe is staying. He already offered to share his room." Ice crystals had formed on the window, and he, too, wondered how anyone would travel. He sighed. "Let me at least tell you my basic defense strategy, in case the hearing is held tomorrow. Then I'll come back over for breakfast and tell you the rest."

Polly stood as still as an ice statue for a brief moment, eyes closed in prayer. When she finished, she nodded and rejoined him at the table, much calmer.

"Tell me what you need me to do."

Joey had plenty of time to prepare after all. The storm had kept the judge from reaching Breading that day or the next. Of course, that also meant Pa spent the weekend in jail.

By Sunday, the sun was shining and the snow, now a distant memory, had melted into the muddy earth. Polly searched for the Christmas spirit that had danced through her heart over the previous few weeks, but couldn't find it. She didn't know how she would continue, even if Joseph's plan worked and Pa got to come home.

"Polly." Shaking her hand, Pastor Denton greeted her as warmly as ever. His kindness brought tears to her eyes. He was letting the whole congregation know that he stood behind them in their current situation.

"Polly, there you are." Jean came up behind the pastor, Abe at her side and followed by her parents and Joseph. "We are counting on you taking dinner with us." Another public proclamation of friendship.

Polly didn't want to socialize but knew she must accept the invitation, if only for the sake of the children. "We'll accept, gladly."

Gabe walked in next, leading the children's Sunday school class like the Pied Pier of Hamlin.

"He's been working with them on the Christmas program this week," Pastor Denton said. "He's amazing."

He'd what? Before she could think about it further, he'd settled the children with their parents and hurried to her side. "How are you, Miss Jessup?"

"Mr. Noell, I'm so glad you're here." Mrs. Carpenter spoke before Polly could answer. "We wanted to invite you for dinner today, to repay you for your kindness in taking in Joseph the other night."

At that moment, the church doors opened again, and sunlight outlined the members of the Johnson family. Martha waved at Gabe, but the others all turned a stony profile and walked down the aisle to their usual seats at the front on the organ side. They had donated the instrument to the church, after all.

Polly glanced at Joseph, wondering how he took the snub. He rolled his shoulders and smiled in her direction, and relief ran through her.

"I'm afraid I must get to the front," the pastor said. The organist was playing the introduction to "What Child Is This?".

After the singing of the carols, Pastor Denton invited them to turn to the passage in Luke that dealt with Jesus' presentation at the temple. The knowledge God had given to Simeon and Anna about the identity of the baby Jesus amazed Polly yet again.

"Today we'll be looking at the most difficult event Mary had to face, one that would break the heart of every mother.

Her perfect, divine son was born to die. When Simeon held the squirming newborn baby, he saw into His future. He told Mary, 'This child is set for the fall and rising again of many in Israel; and for a sign which shall be spoken against: (Yea, a sword shall pierce through thy own soul also.)'".

Mary couldn't have known what that meant, not then, at the dedication of her miracle baby. But only the blink of an eye later, she stood by His side at the cross, her son condemned to die a criminal's death. How could that be God's will? How could any good come of it?

Polly's personal problems dimmed in comparison. The pastor walked through Mary's life, showing how she always placed her troubles in the Lord's hands, even for something as mundane as running out of wine at a wedding. Polly vowed to do the same.

At the end of the service, the owner of the mercantile, Grant Richards, approached Polly. "Miss Jessup, may I speak with you privately for a few moments? Pastor Denton suggested we use the Sunday school room in the back."

The mercantile. Polly's throat went dry. Did Mr. Richards plan to prosecute Pa as well? His face reflected nothing but kindness and concern. *Remember Mary,* she reminded herself.

"Go ahead and go with the Carpenters," Polly told Dolores. "I'll be along in a few minutes." Out the study window, she looked to the lean-to where the manger scene that Gabe Noell was crafting stood. What would his Mary look like? The roof showed the effects of the snow, and she wondered how the adverse weather had affected his progress. She prayed while she waited for the storekeeper to join her.

A few minutes later, Mr. Richards came in with Pastor

Denton. "I don't ordinarily encourage this kind of business on the Sabbath." Denton held out his hands to Polly. "But these are special circumstances."

Someone knocked at the door, and to Polly's surprise, Joey entered.

"Carpenter. Good, glad you could make it." Mr. Richards rose to his feet and shook Joey's hand. Everyone turned their attention to Polly.

"I feel terrible about what's happened with Mr. Jessup." The merchant took off his hat and turned it around in his hands. "I feel like it's my fault for turning that money over to Mr. Johnson like I did."

Polly couldn't speak past the lump in her throat.

"The truth is, you and your pa have always done right by us. Always made sure you paid your account. I'd be happy to let you keep the things your pa bought. But Joseph here"— Mr. Richards nodded at Joey—"thinks it best if you return the items Mr. Jessup bought. Do you know where they are?"

Polly thought about Pa's bedroom, the joy he had felt in hiding away presents for Christmas morning. "Yes." She couldn't manage any more. "I'll get them back to you first thing in the morning. I should have thought about it before now."

"You've had a lot on your mind," Pastor Denton said.

"And I'll testify to that judge about your pa's character. He's been a little—confused lately, but he's never taken so much as a peppermint. Anybody who knows your pa knows that."

"Thank you, Mr. Richards." Polly held back the sniffle that signaled a desire to give way to weeping—something she refused to do.

"We're behind you," the pastor said. "Everyone's prayers go

with you into the courtroom tomorrow."

Everyone except the Johnsons'. Polly kept that thought to herself.

Joseph accompanied Polly to his parents' house. As they trudged through the icy mud, he studied her appearance. Given the circumstances of helping defend her father and taking care of the family, he feared she would neglect her own needs. But at least she had dressed warmly and put on sensible boots. Her brown hair shone against the dark red of her coat. In her mature dignity, she looked more beautiful than ever. Beauty from the inside outshone Alice's Paris fashions.

"I'm sorry about coming between you and the Johnsons. You didn't have to take Pa's case, but I'm glad you did."

"Think nothing of it." How like Polly. Instead of worrying about her own difficulties, she thought about his.

"But what about Alice?" Polly hesitated, her face turning the same shade as her coat. "You seemed to be courting her."

Why had Joseph ever thought stepping out with the banker's daughter was a good idea? Outward wealth couldn't mask her inward paucity of spirit. "I have no interest in a woman who doesn't understand that it's my duty to represent anyone who gets into trouble with the law."

Polly frowned.

What had he said wrong? He deeply regretted increasing Polly's pain.

He prayed he wouldn't have more to regret after tomorrow's hearing.

Chapter 7

I n view of the fact full restitution has been made to the bank, Jacob Jessup is hereby sentenced to jail time not to exceed thirty days provided he pays a fine of fifty dollars."

Polly slumped back against the hard seat. They hadn't received everything they had hoped for, but it could have been much worse. At least the judge hadn't bowed to the power of the Johnsons.

Whether or not the sentence was reasonable, nothing changed the fact that they had no income and no savings. A five-dollar fine would have been difficult; fifty dollars, impossible.

Pa looked at her, eyes clear and full of understanding, sadness etching more lines onto his forehead, adding years to his age.

I will not cry, not here, not now. Polly summoned the will to smile at him. Once she had regained her composure, she would go to visit him at the jail.

After the deputy escorted Pa back to jail, Joey sought her out. Grinning, he looked as excited as a preacher who had seen a dozen people come forward after a sermon.

"Polly, this calls for quiet conversation over good food. Mrs. Denton said to come over as soon as the hearing finished."

At least he hadn't called it a celebration. Polly didn't feel joyful. "I should tell the children. . . ."

"They'll be there. We can tell them together." He helped her over a mud puddle. The cold temperatures had created a few patches of ice.

Polly accepted his arm. What would they have done without him? Without his help, things could have gone so much worse. Her champion. Her heart flipped. In his presence she rested, quiet and easy. But she wasn't sure she wanted to rehash it all, even with the Dentons. Her steps faltered as they approached the parsonage.

Before they reached the house, Gabe Noell came out of the lean-to. "I heard what happened at court. I'll continue praying for you and your family, Miss Jessup."

"Thank you." Gabe's kind words helped Polly decide. She couldn't handle any more pity. "I'm sorry. But I don't feel like talking with anyone just now. Please give the Dentons my regrets, and ask the children to come home."

She turned and marched in the opposite direction, toward Dover Street, before he could stop her.

Joseph stared after Polly, sensing he shouldn't chase her.

Gabe stopped beside him. "Give her time. She's been hit hard."

Joseph frowned. True, the judge hadn't given them everything they had asked for, but no lawyer expected that—especially when your client insisted on pleading guilty. "I thought she'd be pleased."

Gabe only smiled and shook his head. "Spoken like a lawyer. You're right, you did a good job." He didn't elaborate. "I've nearly finished carving Mary and Joseph. You can paint them whenever you have time—as long as it's before Sunday."

Joseph wondered what he meant while he flexed his fingers. Maybe some time with a paintbrush in his hands would calm his roiling emotions after the turmoil of the past few days. "I've got some unexpected time on my hands this afternoon," he said. "I'll explain the situation to Mrs. Denton and join you a little later."

After the meal—Mrs. Denton said she would package up the leftovers and take them to Polly later in the day—Joseph joined Gabe in his lean-to. In spite of the cool temperatures, a small campfire kept the space cozy and warm.

When Joseph came in, Gabe was carving individual pieces of straw in the manger around the figure of the baby Jesus. As he had many times before, Joseph marveled at the intricacy and beauty of the craftsmanship. Works of art, the simple pine figures didn't need further adornment in his opinion. But the church had requested they be painted, and he had agreed.

He held a precise picture of Joseph in mind—someone a bit like Gabe, with salt-and-pepper hair, kind, peaceful eyes, and gnarled fingers used to working with wood. But he still didn't know how he wanted to paint Mary.

What had Gabe told him? To think about the character of Mary? At first, Joseph thought about using Alice as his model. She was beautiful, and he had fooled himself into thinking she possessed more godly characteristics than she did. The last of his illusions about her fled out the window when she condemned Mr. Jessup without a hearing.

He sighed and studied the figure Gabe had carved. All the things Pastor Denton had preached about were present. The hope and glory of God shone from her face, while the pain that would pierce her soul shadowed her eyes. He only needed to bring what was already there to life. He assembled his paints and brushes before him and set to work, praying all the while.

When the afternoon light faded to the point he could no longer do detailed work, he set aside his brushes. His shoulders ached from bending over the figure, but he felt happy with the results.

Gabe studied his work, a slow smile indicating his pleasure. "Mary, the mother of our Lord. God chose good parents for His Son."

"Yes, He did."

Gabe pulled a tarp over the work to protect it from the elements. As Joseph cleaned his hands at the pump, he realized all his concerns and worries had fled while he worked. Polly had no such release. Guilt assailed him. But what could he do?

"Give her time, Joseph." Gabe seemed to read his mind. "Wait until tomorrow."

Joseph nodded. When he went, he wouldn't go empty-handed. What would Polly take from him that wouldn't offend her pride?

By the next morning, he still hadn't reached a decision. Painting the nativity scene on the previous day proved to be fortunate. Representing Jessup hadn't done his reputation any harm. Three different people stopped by his office, seeking an appointment with Breading's newest lawyer.

Grant Richards expressed the common sentiment. "I want someone who's brave enough to stand up to Albert Johnson representing me." The shop owner asked him to review some shipping contracts.

The morning sped by before Joseph had the opportunity to get to the mercantile. Without a clear idea of how to help the Jessups, he asked God to guide him. He had considered asking Richards's opinion when he came in but refrained. His office was not the place to ask about personal matters.

As Joseph approached the store, he paused, remembering the joy on Jessup's face when he exited with arms laden with presents. Joseph wished he could duplicate his purchases, to give the family the Christmas their father had dreamed of, but Polly would never agree. Besides, neither one of them knew what was in the packages. They had returned them to the store unopened.

Joseph considered other options—perhaps a gift for the family. Strolling through the store, he resisted his usual pull to the books. Only the Bible would benefit the entire family, and they already had one of those. Something for the kitchen? Not food. Mrs. Denton had already spoken with him about a food basket for Christmas.

In the corner he spied a table decorated for Christmas, a cheery red tablecloth adorning the pine wood surface, set with a single setting of blue and white china. A sign announced SERVICE FOR TWELVE AVAILABLE. It looked vaguely familiar. Not the china the Johnsons used. Probably he had seen it at one of the fancy dinners he attended while in law school. He wondered why the store was carrying it. Few people could afford it.

Shaking off the sense of familiarity of the china pattern, Joseph perused the store. Nothing struck the right chord as a gift to give to the Jessups for this season. He'd think about it and come back.

Chapter 8

You shouldn't have done all this." Tears splashed down Polly's face as she unearthed jars of strawberry preserves and green beans and bags of dried apples and potatoes. Not to mention two hams, pumpkin and mincemeat pies, flour, sugar, lard. . .the list was endless. They had enough for Christmas dinner with much more besides.

"Lots of people contributed," Mrs. Carpenter said.

Mrs. Denton nodded. "We were so relieved when we learned that your house was paid for. We hope this tides you over until you figure out what to do."

What to do. Polly didn't know. The fine had been paid, at considerable sacrifice, and Pa would be released from jail in a few weeks. Of course, he had lost his job at the bank and might not get another anytime soon. Mr. Richards had offered to hire Polly at the mercantile. But a clerk's salary wouldn't support a family of six, even with the discount they offered on foodstuffs.

"God will provide, dear. And don't be afraid to ask if you

need help." Mrs. Denton said a prayer and they left.

One look around the well-stocked kitchen confirmed the truth of Mrs. Denton's words. They had everything they needed and more than she hoped for Christmas. God had provided today's daily bread and tomorrow's as well. Thanks to Mr. Richards's generosity, the Lord had even given her a way to pay Pa's fine. How could she doubt God's provision for her future? Humming, she prepared to leave for the final rehearsal for the Christmas program.

"Joy to the world!" Dolores sang along. "I'll have the beans ready when you come home. With some corn cakes?"

Her sweet sister had shouldered more responsibility around the house without grumbling, and the children hadn't complained about the unvarying diet of beans, beans, and more beans. Chili and beans. Beans with salt pork. Sweetened beans. Pinto beans, black-eyed beans, kidney beans. . . Beans with every conceivable spice. "That sounds good. And maybe some of the pumpkin pie? I'm afraid it might spoil before Christmas."

"Oh, can we?" Dolores smiled. "What a treat. I'll see you later, then."

Polly went outside, her shawl the perfect protection against the cool December air, crisp and clear and full of promise. Her heart skipped, and she was glad Joseph and the pastor had insisted she come to the final rehearsal. Spending time in the Lord's house would take her mind off her worries.

Although she expected to arrive early, she opened the door to find everyone already assembled, even Martha Johnson.

"Miss Polly!" Jemima saw her first and ran to her. "You're back!" She was dressed in costume, a delicate blue cloth wrapped around her head and down her gown, a perfect match for her deep blue eyes. "Come on. We can't wait for you to see the play." Her wide smile was infectious, and more of the Christmas spirit seeped into Polly. She let herself be propelled to the front pew.

Jemima came to the middle of the makeshift stage together with Peter. As Polly listened to their well-delivered lines, she wondered who had taken over the rehearsals. Pastor Denton had only told her not to worry; everything was taken care of.

Joey came out from behind the organ and motioned for them to leave the stage. *Joey* had taken over the play? On top of going to trial with Pa and spending so much time with her?

She thought back to her childhood dream that he would come home and claim her as his bride. Such a sweet, considerate, *wonderful* man. Any girl would be blessed to marry him. Since he had stopped keeping company with Alice Johnson, why not her? But he would never look twice at someone like her. What lawyer would marry a woman with a convicted felon for a father and a ready-made family to care for? Friendship, yes. He had proven that. But marriage? Never.

In fact, who would marry her? Maybe no one. One look at Jemima and Martha rehearsing the scene between Mary and Elisabeth, and Polly put that thought aside. If God provided a husband for Mary, unmarried and pregnant, He could do the same for her. Someday. Although it was hard to imagine anyone more wonderful than Joey.

Jemima did a terrific job, as did Martha. When they finished, Martha took a seat next to Polly. "Miss Polly," she whispered as the shepherds prepared for their scene.

Polly faced the young girl, who had all the beauty of her

aunt Alice plus a sweet spirit. She was brave, too, to defy her family. They couldn't approve of her continued participation. "I'm so glad you're taking part in the play."

"You are? You don't mind?" The girl fluttered her hands in a helpless gesture.

"Mind?" Polly smiled. "Of course not. You're *perfect* as Elisabeth. There's no one I would rather have in the play." She hugged the girl, and some of her resentment against the Johnsons and their clan dissipated.

The cast sped through the remainder of the play with scarcely a hitch. Although the church would hold a party after Sunday's church service, complete with luncheon and gift bags for all the children, today the cast of the play threw their own celebration. They traipsed to the parsonage for hot cocoa and sugar cookies.

"I'm sorry I didn't bring any cookies. I had forgotten about the party," Polly apologized to Mrs. Denton.

"Your presence is our gift, dear." The pastor's wife patted her hand. "The children couldn't be happier."

The children held back from starting the party until Jemima and Martha arrived. When they came in, they each carried a package. They stopped in front of Polly.

"We wanted to do something special for you," Martha said.

"You worked so hard to write the play and helped us and all," Jemima said. "Some of the ladies from the church helped so we could get it done in time. Otherwise we couldn't have done it."

Polly teared up as she studied the elaborate packaging. Big white bows sat atop boxes wrapped in shiny red paper. Both boxes looked big enough to hold more food baskets, only they were too light for jars and cans and cuts of meat. She could feel her mouth widening in a smile, using muscles that almost hurt after the heaviness of the past few days. With the children, she didn't mind. She untied the ribbon and worked her finger underneath the wrapping paper of the first parcel, sensing the softness of whatever it covered.

Underneath lay a crazy quilt made of patches of outgrown dresses, torn dungarees, and towels originally destined for shepherd's headgear. She also spotted some material she had lingered over at the mercantile. Altogether it was a beautiful piece of work.

"When. . .how. . ." Polly didn't know what to say.

"Well, it's been cold. And we figured you needed to keep warm. You and Mr. Jessup," Martha said.

"So we all brought things we didn't need anymore." Jemima's words stumbled over each other in her rush to get them out. She probably loved having a chance to give to someone else. Polly had never realized how hard it could be to be on the receiving end until she experienced it herself these past few days.

"I showed them how to cut the squares," Mrs. Denton said. "And we had a quilting bee last weekend."

Last weekend. Before they even knew the outcome of the trial, the children had planned this surprise.

The second parcel—the one Martha carried—held hand-knit scarves in every color imaginable. "Even the boys helped make these." She smiled.

"I cut the fringe." The youngest Fuller boy pointed to bright blue yarn dangling from the end of a lopsided length scarf.

"They're beautiful. Thank you so much." Polly hugged each of the children. Masking the tears that threatened her voice, she said, "Now you'd better drink your cocoa before it gets cold."

Joey smiled at her over the pile of presents in front of her, and she knew who had dreamed up this special surprise.

Friendship, she reminded herself. *Nothing more.* For now, that would be enough.

Joseph studied the manger figures one last time, eyeing them from several angles.

"Never quite satisfied with our work, are we?" Gabe had exchanged his overalls for Sunday clothes. The church had invited him to distribute gift bags to the children—complete with the little toys he had carved for each of them in his spare time. In a plaid shirt red enough for Santa Claus, he looked the part.

Joseph couldn't imagine uncertainty clouding Gabe's mind. His work was so sure, detailed—masterful. "You, too?"

"All artists feel that way." Gabe looked at the figures. "Mary is your best work, in my opinion."

Joseph sucked breath between his teeth. "I tried." Capturing the spirit of the woman God had chosen as the mother of His Son had hovered beyond his reach.

"You had excellent inspiration."

"I wasn't thinking of anyone in particular," Joseph said. He looked at the manger scene without prejudice. "Whatever beauty is there is from your original work."

Gabe shook his head. "There's more to it than that, but you have to figure that out for yourself." He tapped Joseph's shoulder. "Ready or not, today our work is unveiled. It's time to go in to the service."

Joseph spared one last look at the crèche, a sheet shrouding it for now from the congregation's sight. After this morning, the manger scene would be set up in front of the church. The congregation hoped the people of Breading would take a minute to remember that first Christmas morning when they stopped to enjoy the display.

The set for the children's play took up the remainder of the platform. The pulpit had been moved to the front between the aisles. After Mr. Post led rousing renditions of "Joy to the World!" and "O Come All Ye Faithful," the play began.

After the days of practice, Joey could recite each line as well as the children. Polly's play put the familiar story into a new and thought-provoking format. After a few moments' discomfort in front of an audience, Jemima settled in and spoke clearly so that all could hear. Martha, her hair powdered gray, welcomed her into her home. Joseph shook his head. Who would have expected those two girls to become friends?

The other children did well, and Joseph listened as if hearing it for the first time, right to the last lines. Jemima looked straight at the congregation. "What a night it has been. Angels announced the birth of my little baby boy! Shepherds came to visit! The Savior has been born!" She touched the wiggling baby she held in her arms. "What stories I will have to tell You about the night You were born. I will treasure these things always and will think about them often."

A hush spread over the sanctuary as the children sang "Silent Night." Joseph rose to his feet and clapped, and soon the building rang with applause.

Pastor Denton came to the front, and the congregation quieted. "Mr. Noell will have gift bags for all of our children at the end of the service," he told the littlest ones who lingered near the front, looking for the promised treats. Laughter broke out. He looked behind him at the now-empty stage. "I don't know that I need say anything more, do I? They've said it all."

Scattered "amens" and "praise the Lords" arose from the congregation.

"But I did want to talk about one other characteristic of Mary. Jemima has already touched on it during the play. Thoughtful by nature, Mary kept accounts of everything that had happened that first Christmas in her heart for long, long years until Luke interviewed her late in life. Out came the 'treasures,' as she called them. And thank God she shared them." He went on to talk about Mary's ability to hold on to the miracles of God in the midst of the trouble that later came.

Joseph's attention wandered. Soon they would unveil the manger scene. He prayed that his painting complemented Gabe's art and that the visual reminder of the reason for Christmas would lead the congregation in worship. Did the Mary he painted have a thoughtful face? He didn't know; he was too close to the project to tell.

By the time the sermon wound down, the hour had passed noon. Joseph's stomach rumbled from hunger as well as from nervousness.

"And now. . ." Pastor Denton smiled. "The moment has come to unveil our master craftsmen's creation."

Joseph's throat closed; he felt as nervous as he had before the trial.

Grant Richards joined the pastor at the front, and together they pulled back the sheet that hid the manger scene from view.

Spontaneous applause drowned out the initial "oohs" and "aahs." Joseph sagged against the back of his pew.

After the service dismissed, people surged forward to see Gabe's work up close. The wood-carver insisted Joseph stand next to him. Together they greeted each child by name and handed them bags of fruit, candy, and wooden toys.

Her face wreathed in smiles, Polly came forward with her family. He wanted to do everything in his power to keep that joy on her face.

"Why, look!" Little Hazel tugged at her sister's dress and pointed at the figure of Mary. "That's you, Polly!"

Was it true? Joseph looked from the figure to the woman standing before him. *Yes.*

Now what should he do about it?

Chapter 9

The following Thursday, Christmas morning dawned with fresh snow on the ground. As soon as Polly went downstairs to start breakfast, Hazel joined her. Soon all five of them were gathered in the kitchen. This afternoon she would go see Pa in the jail—Joseph had arranged for the special holiday visit. But this morning belonged to the children. Thanks to the generous spirit of the children in the play, they would have a Christmas. Scarves and mittens to warm their bodies and fresh fruit and delicacies of every imaginable kind to delight their palates. If only she could have served the Christmas feast on Ma's china, sold to pay Pa's fine. Polly repressed the thought. Life was about more than fine china. Above all days, today was about faith, love, and the gift of God's Son.

Both the Dentons and the Carpenters had invited them to join their families for Christmas dinner, but Polly had declined. The children needed things as normal as possible, and that meant Christmas at home. Thanks to the Christmas baskets, they would have a feast. She was kneading dough for dinner rolls when Hazel danced into the kitchen. "Someone's at the door."

Who would come calling on Christmas morning? "Dolores, would you find out who it is?" Her sister slipped out of the kitchen while Polly put the dough back into a bowl to rise again.

Dolores returned in a few moments, eyes wide. "You'd better come see."

"Is it Santa Claus?" Polly asked good-humoredly. She rinsed her hands and wiped them dry on her apron before heading to the front room.

Joey waited in the middle of the room, a gigantic box filling his arms.

"He's brought you a present." Hazel giggled.

Santa Claus, indeed. What was in the box? "You shouldn't have done any more. You've already done so much for our family."

"Not enough." His smile suggested a special meaning as he swept past her, into the kitchen, and set the box on the kitchen table.

Polly stared. Surely the carton didn't contain more food; but why else had he brought it into the kitchen? She bit her lower lip.

"Go ahead. Open it." He smiled.

"Let me guess." She lifted a corner to see if it rattled, but she could barely move it. Grabbing scissors, she cut through the string that held the package together and the brown paper covering it. Inside was a plain box.

"It won't bite, I promise." Joey's smile grew wider until it threatened to escape the confines of his face.

Mary opened the top. A delicate blue pattern peeked out between pieces of straw. Could it be. . . ? She dug her hand through the packing material and draped her fingers around the familiar shape of a teacup. Gingerly she lifted it from the box. It was! After that, she scattered straw on the floor, lifting out cups and saucers and plates. Every last piece of Ma's china. She turned her tear-filled gaze on Joey. "How did you know?"

Joey took a step toward her and stopped. "I recognized it in the emporium. Richards confirmed the source. I couldn't let you sell your mother's legacy."

Polly knew how much money Mr. Richards wanted for the china—too much. "But. . .you shouldn't have."

Joey surveyed the kitchen, looking at each child in turn, as if asking their permission for something. Hazel giggled. He closed the distance between them in a single easy step. "Polly, I once told you I would marry you when I came home from college—if you would have me."

Embarrassment toasted her cheeks. "I thought you had forgotten that childish nonsense."

"I had." His voice mellowed, turning warm. "I lost my way. But when I was working on painting Mary's face, Gabe Noell reminded me about what's important."

"Mary looks like our Polly," Hazel piped up. Polly squirmed but Joey grabbed her hands and held her fast.

"She does indeed." Joey winked at Hazel.

Polly wanted to swallow her nervousness, but her throat was too dry. "What else did Gabe say?"

"He said I should model Mary's face after someone who

reminds me of her, the woman highly favored by God. I didn't realize what I had done until Sunday, and I have Hazel to thank for it."

"I knew it." She reached for one of Joey's hands.

"*You* are like Mary, my dearest Polly. Like her, you obey God even in the hard times. Like her, you praise God always in your works and words and deeds. Even through the sadness of your father's situation. *You* are that highly favored woman, Polly. You are virtuous and beautiful and everything a man could want in a wife. You deserve whatever you want—this china is a very small thing. Believe me." He got down on one knee.

Polly put her hand to her mouth. *Can this be happening?*

"Polly Jessup, you will always be the face of Mary to me. Will you allow me to be your Joseph? Will you do me the honor of becoming my wife?"

Polly looked deep into the eyes of the man she had loved since childhood and gave the only possible answer. "Yes, Joey, with all my heart, yes!"

She reached out her hands, and he stood. Taking her in his arms, he twirled her around and kissed her until she lost sight of the children around them.

In her mind, somewhere, she heard Gabe laughing.

Award-winning author and speaker **Darlene Franklin** recently returned to cowboy country—Oklahoma—to be near family. She recently signed the contract for her twelfth book. *Face of Mary* is her third novella. Visit Darlene's blogs at darlenfranklinwrites. blogspot.com and thebookdoctorbd.blogspot.com.

THE CHRISTMAS CHAIN

by Janelle Mowery

Dedication

In loving memory of H. W. Buford, my grandfather-in-law, and to all his loved ones. This story originated from Mr. Buford's handiness with his knife, the joy he recieved from his creations, and in giving them away.

Man looketh on the outward appearance,
but the Lord looketh on the heart.
1 Samuel 16:7

Chapter 1

You've got to move faster. You're losing him.

If Emma Rose Pickett ever found the good-for-nothing man who made her lame, she'd make him regret it for the rest of his life. For now, she had her hands full with another type of worthless animal.

Of all the confounding, rotten critters in this world, why am I stuck with the worst of them?

Emma raced after the stubborn mule as fast as her crippled leg would allow. Tied upon the beast's back was every possession to her name. He'd given her nothing but trouble since they left Irontree two days ago. Now he was dead set on returning home while she was just as determined to go the opposite direction. If she ever got her hands on that lop-eared varmint, she'd give him what for till his hard head was downright soft.

"Stop, Skeeter, you ungrateful old coot. You know Doc would want you to take care of me."

Her chest heaved from the exertion as the mule continued his purposeful trotting pace. The ache in her bad leg urged her to stop, but she was almost close enough to the mule's flicking tail to grab hold and make him drag her till he couldn't go on.

She lunged with every bit of energy in her weary body. Fingers tangled in the wiry hair, she latched on, laughing with pride at her success. The beast bellowed and kicked. Seconds later, she rolled to a stop and sat up, spitting dirt from her mouth while the ornery brute galloped away. Several strands of his tail dangled from her fingers. Her bonnet lay in a filthy heap at her side.

"Thanks for nothing, Skeeter."

Flinging every scathing word she could think of at him, she hoped the very insects he was named after would haunt his steps for years. . .if he lived that long. She swiped her sleeve across her mouth, wishing she could get rid of the gritty particles sticking to her teeth. Her leg throbbed, demanding her attention. She lifted her skirt to rub the scar just below her right knee.

The food and belongings strapped to Skeeter's back would be missed much more than the hideous beast of burden. She scooped up the ugly bonnet her benefactor insisted she own and shoved to her feet, refusing to waste any more time and energy going after that dumb mule. With a huff, she plopped the bonnet on her head, spun around, and continued down the road toward Woodville. Neither man nor willful beast would stop her from her mission. When she found Mr. Charles Little, he'd end up smaller than his name.

The last thought wouldn't shake loose. Doc said she needed to give up her thoughts of revenge and forgive in order to live a long, peaceful life. His gentle voice warned her that only God had the right to vengeance. Maybe Skeeter running off was a sign. Hadn't God used donkeys before to speak to man? She snorted. No way was Skeeter kin to an animal that smart. God would have to be more obvious if He wanted her to turn back.

Over an hour later, the burning in her leg matched the fiery sun beating down on her head. Emma's resolve slipped away like the sweat rolling down her temples. For late October, it sure was hot. Shouldn't it be cooler in East Texas by now? Or maybe fear of being alone had finally set in. A lone woman on a quiet stretch of road couldn't bode well. Even a mangy old mule rendered some amount of security. But he was gone, along with the gun hidden in the bottom of her bag.

As if to validate her fears, the unmistakable rattle of wagon wheels approached. Terror started in her parched throat and slammed to her toes, rendering her feet about as useful as a heavy coat on a sultry day.

Move.

But where?

A thicket beckoned ahead, but her bad leg wouldn't get her there in time. A whistled tune reached her ears. They were close.

Move, you worthless feet.

Like breaking free from a puddle of molasses, she scurried to a small stand of trees to her right. She glimpsed a horse rounding the bend in the road before she ducked out of sight.

The whistling stopped. Surely they didn't see her. No, she didn't even see the wagon before she made it to the trees. She was safe.

She hunkered down low, praying the intruders would hurry

by. She needed to find a town so she wouldn't have to spend the night in the woods. No telling what kind of critters she'd encounter.

The wagon stopped. Right across from her.

Oh, Lord, no. Make it leave.

It didn't move.

At least there was only one man on the seat. An elderly man at that. Maybe she could take him with the element of surprise. She glanced around for a branch big enough to use as a club. Nothing.

"You can come on out of there, little lady."

Dread tingled its way down her spine and pinched her heart. Now what?

"Come on, now. That bonnet may have hidden you from the sun, but it announced your presence louder than a rooster at sunrise."

Her bonnet? She fingered the hideous scrap of cloth. Of all the things to get her in a scrape. She had told Doc she didn't want it, but he had insisted.

"I promise I won't hurt you."

Right, and buzzards didn't swarm on dead meat. Did he take her for a fool? She peered harder at the man. He appeared rather normal. Well-kept even, except for his faded clothing. Reminded her a bit of Doc.

"I've got water."

He held up a canteen and gave it a shake. The splashing was her undoing. Dirt still swam in her mouth from her struggle with Skeeter. Time to find out the true fool. After peeking down the road, she stood and made her way out of the trees.

The man stepped down from the wagon. She stopped and

bunched her fists. He was less scary sitting on the seat. The dress and bad leg would keep her from getting far, but at least she could say she put up a fight.

"Whoa there, little lady. No need to run off. I just felt like a scoundrel sitting up there with you down here. I'll climb back up if you'd like."

Not many men she knew would make such an offer. Maybe he was a decent fellow after all. Then again, it could all be an act. But he had water and she was thirsty. She trounced through the tall grass and stopped just shy of arm's reach. He pulled the cork, wiped the opening with a semiclean rag, and handed her the canteen. Without an ounce of hesitation, she took it and poured the water down her throat, relishing every drop.

"Whoa now. Don't want to overdo right off. Give yourself some time."

When he reached for the jug, she forced herself to quit drinking and held it out to him.

"No. You go ahead and keep it awhile. Just slow down is all. Don't want you getting sick." He held out his hand. "Name's Gabe Noell."

She eyed him before offering her own. He seemed a good sort. Hadn't done anything to make her feel otherwise. . .yet. "Emma." He raised his eyebrows. *All right.* "Pickett."

He smiled. "Pleased to meet you, Emma Pickett." He gestured to the wagon. "Don't suppose you'd like to ride awhile?"

He had no idea. "Where you headed?"

"Tremble."

Her heart skipped. Wasn't that near Woodville? This might turn out to be an easier trip than she thought. "I'll take that ride, Mr. Noell."

"Gabe." He held out the cork to the canteen. "And I'd be delighted to have your company."

She took one more swig of water before plugging the opening, then allowed Gabe to help her up to the seat. Once he'd settled beside her, he flicked the reins. Her mouth twitched. Maybe God was finally smiling down on her.

"Not that it's any of my business or anything—"

Oh, no. Gabe was a talker. And a nosy one at that.

"Why would you be out here all alone and on foot no less? That's mighty dangerous for a young lady. You running from someone?"

"No, sir. My mule ran off is all, rotten critter that he is."

Gabe chuckled, making the skin around his gray eyes crinkle like he'd been laughing for years. That very moment, she knew she liked him.

He clucked at his horse and shook the reins. "Mules aren't so bad. They take some getting used to, like most people you come across. A little patience and understanding goes a long way with stubbornness."

Emma took a good look at her companion. A gentle strength lined his face, and wisdom shone from his eyes.

"Yes, well, you haven't met Skeeter."

Gabe howled his amusement and slapped his knee. "You give him that name?"

She grinned. "No, Doc did, his first owner."

"I wonder if Doc got bit a few times to come up with that name."

Yep, God must have decided to smile on her again. She couldn't have asked for a more kind and tender person to save her from her miserable predicament. The dark hair sticking out from his hat was salted with enough gray to give away his age.

He turned just then to meet her gaze. Without a word, he pulled out the rag he'd used to wipe the canteen and handed it to her.

The memory of sprawling in the road made her shudder. She must look a sight. As she scrubbed, the sound of another set of hooves grew closer.

"Hey, Gabe." A man on a black horse rode up next to the wagon. "Look what I found." The man had yet to notice her, he was so engrossed in whatever was tied to the end of the rope in his hand. He gave a yank that almost jerked him from his saddle. "Get up here, you stubborn old fool."

Seconds later, Emma almost fell off the seat as Skeeter came into view. The man finally peered up with a grin on his face, which melted into shock when he spotted her.

Gabe reined the horse and wagon to a stop. "Well, look what I found. Only I think my find's a little better looking than yours." He patted her hand. "Miss Emma Pickett, I'd like you to meet my other companion, Caleb Kelley."

Emma gaped at the old man, silently accusing him of treachery, and not just because he thought her only a *little* better looking than Skeeter. Gabe could have mentioned traveling with someone. The man's intense eyes made her knees weak. They burned a hole through her, yet she couldn't look away. She'd never met a man who made her want to run and stand her ground at the same time. If only she could read his eyes well enough to know his thoughts.

What kind of creature did Gabe dig up? At least Caleb knew his mule was a mule. This girl looked like a raccoon. Remembering his manners, he tipped his hat.

"Miss Pickett."

He couldn't stop staring. And not just because of her filthy face. The bonnet on her head screamed its colors loud enough to be heard in the next state. What would possess a woman to buy such a thing?

"That's my mule."

She spoke, but he didn't like what he heard. "Pardon?" He frowned, daring her to restate her claim. The beast might be willful, but he'd be hanged before he'd let a dirty gypsy girl steal it from him.

"I said that's my mule."

Her statement sounded much more timid the second time, convincing him she spoke a lie. Then her jaw jutted.

"My mule, my saddle, and my belongings."

The creature being fought over yanked so hard, it spun Caleb's horse around. By the time Caleb managed to get both animals under control, his temper had flared. He glared at the woman.

"Prove it."

"What?"

"What's in the bag?"

She looked into the sky like she'd find the answers there. "Let's see. There's some changes of clothing, another bonnet, a diary, a brush and comb, a small mirror, hopefully not broken—" She ticked off each named item on her fingers, making his doubts of her honesty shrink and his impatience soar. "Oh, there's also some doctoring tools."

Now she'd gone too far. "You claiming to be a doctor?"

And why was Gabe sitting there like a mute? He'd been plenty talkative earlier.

"Oh no." While the corners of her mouth turned up, her eyes changed from challenging to sad. "They belonged to the man who raised me. When he died, I kept them as a reminder."

His displeasure dissolved into bewilderment. This girl didn't fit into the mold of any he'd known before. She'd gone from dazed to timid, then commanding to solemn. But he wouldn't let his confusion blind him to the fact this might be an act. She could be a swindler. She certainly looked the part.

After tying the rope to his saddle horn, Caleb dismounted and rummaged through the bag. Everything she'd mentioned lay inside along with a few she'd missed, including a pistol. Did she leave that off the list on purpose? Did she know how to use it?

What he had to do next didn't set well. He looked up to apologize and found Gabe wearing a wide grin. Much as he wanted to wipe it off the old wood-carver's face, Caleb knew he deserved more than a humiliating smile.

"My apologies, Miss Pickett. It's just that it's hard to give up this dunderheaded mule when he gave me fits trying to catch him."

Her laughter grated on him. "What's so funny?"

She raised her hand. "I'm sorry. I understand completely. He's the very reason I look a mess."

If she only knew. He reached into her bag, pulled out the mirror, and handed it to her. Her gasp shamed him further as he silently berated himself for being quick to judge. When her embarrassment changed the color of her face, he knew he should look away, but the blotches growing on her neck fascinated him. Only when she huffed and turned away did he alter his attention.

"I'll just, um, tie your mule to the back of the wagon."

The dirt on the road took the brunt of his exasperation when he couldn't kick himself. He'd never been at such a loss for words before. Worst of all, a woman made him feel this way. He peeled the hat off his head and slapped it against his leg. How could a slip of a girl manage to twist his tongue into a knot? If he were honest, his mind and stomach were in a bit of a tangle, too.

"Don't let it get to you, son."

Gabe's appearance forced Caleb to get ahold of himself. Without answering, he slammed his hat back in place and pulled the mule closer so he could tie the rope to the wagon.

"Some women just have that effect on men. Nothing unusual about that."

Caleb jerked the rope into a tight knot. "I don't know what you're talking about. She doesn't affect me."

Gabe chuckled. "Yep, I can see that." He leaned against the back of the wagon and scratched the mule between the eyes, then up between its ears.

Caleb recognized the look moving over the old man's face. The carver had talked a lot over the last few days, but every bit of his chatter proved filled with sage advice.

"I learned long ago that it's best not to judge people till you get to know them. I've met those who could make themselves sparkle on the outside but were rotten clean through. Then there are some who can't pretty themselves up no matter how hard they try, but their heart is pure gold." Gabe crossed his arms. "Near as I can tell, this little lady's as good as they come. I'd like to help her for however long she decides to stay with us."

Warmth radiated through Caleb's chest, as though just by standing near Gabe, his decency transferred into him. He'd never met a man like him and felt blessed to call him a friend.

He clapped Gabe on the back. "Then let's do just that. I think I owe it to her after almost stealing her mule."

A chuckle rumbled through Gabe. "I was right proud of her for standing up to you. I almost hated that you backed down. That would have made for one exciting tugging match."

Caleb laughed. "I didn't back down."

"Nope. You finally started showing good sense." He pushed from the wagon. "I think we'd best get more miles under our belt before dark, or we won't get to Tremble tomorrow. I'm going to need all the time I can get if you want that bedstead finished by Christmas."

Tremble. The thought of home brought a smile to Caleb's face. "Then let's get going."

Prepared to receive another scowl from the young lady, what he found instead when she stepped down from the wagon sucked the wind right out of him. The raccoon-eyed, straggle-haired girl he'd left minutes ago had transformed into a creamy-skinned beauty. The hideous bonnet had disappeared, too, revealing hair almost as dark as his horse.

A smile lit her face. "I'd begun to think you two had jumped on Skeeter's back and hightailed it out of here to escape the ugly hag you'd picked up."

"I—we—" Not only did she steal his breath, but his words were gone, too.

Gabe elbowed him as he walked past. "What our tongue-tied companion is trying to say is that we don't know what ugly hag you're talking about. But the little lady we found sure cleans up nice."

Pink tinged her cheeks as she dipped her head. "Thank you."

"We need to get moving. Isn't that right, Caleb? We'd like to make it to the river before stopping for the night."

"Yes, right." Caleb gestured down the road. "The river."

"All right. Let me just put the mirror back in the bag."

She moved past, a noticeable hitch to her step. Did she get hurt while tussling with that stubborn brute? He rushed to her side and grasped her arm.

"You all right, Miss Pickett? Are you hurt?"

She shook loose and sent him another scowl. Now what'd he say to earn her ire?

"I'm fine. Just a little stiff." She stopped and turned, her expression contrite. "Would you call me Emma? Miss Pickett makes me sound as old as I feel. And after all that walking today, I'm feeling mighty old."

Caleb tore his gaze from her and went to fetch his horse. He could hear his father now. *Better to focus on work than women.* Easy for him to say. He'd never laid eyes on Emma Pickett.

Chapter 2

Emma gaped at the huge iron archway. Centered at the top, an ornate *K* announced the owners. In the distance, a mansion sat atop a distant knoll surrounded by monstrous pines. Gabe's slack jaw mirrored her shock.

Emma leaned forward on the wagon seat in search of Caleb. "You're rich?" Caleb's mouth fell open, but she didn't let him respond. "All you talked about yesterday and today was how you toiled and sweated at the sawmill."

The leather of Caleb's saddle creaked as he urged his horse closer. "I'm not rich. My parents are."

"Same thing."

Emma eyed the large house. She didn't know many rich folk, but those she knew had only given her trouble. Same for Doc. Being a humble man, he accepted it and went on his way. She never learned the trait. At best, she stored up the hurt and anger and avoided them. Most times they reciprocated. Once they saw her shabby clothes, their noses went in the air with a sniff. If they noticed her limp, they couldn't get away fast enough, a good many of them imitating her gait while laughing.

"You have something against the rich?" Caleb's question pulled her attention back to him.

"I might."

He slumped. "Does that mean you won't stay and work for my mother like we agreed? You said you needed the money."

She looked around. No question, the location was beautiful. But was it worth putting up with the meanness and attitude she received from the well-to-do? Doubtful.

"I think I've got enough to get me where I'm going." She clambered to the ground. "I guess this is where we part ways."

Gabe jumped down beside her. "You sure you want to do this, little miss?" He grasped her elbow. "It's dangerous out there. I'd hate for something bad to happen."

The tremor in his voice stopped her. In such a short time, he'd become dear to her. He was so kind and wise. Maybe even more wise than Doc. On impulse, she hugged him around the neck.

"I'll be fine, Gabe. I've been on my own before."

"For how long? Doc's only been gone. . .what?"

She pulled back to see his eyes. "Two weeks." She tried to smile. "I can take care of myself. You'll see."

"How will I see? You coming back?"

This time she did smile. "I might do that, once I find the person I'm looking for."

"In Woodville?"

Caleb's question caught her off guard, and she spun around. She didn't realize he knew her destination. Gabe must have told him. "That's where I'm starting."

The scowl on his face deepened. "Must be a mighty important person to make you go off gallivanting by yourself."

Typical. Why was it when a man left, it was called traveling or seeking adventure, but a woman's trip was considered gallivanting? She tromped behind the wagon, lifted her bag from the back, and tied it to Skeeter's saddle. The action woke the critter from his snooze. The ornery brute snorted, tossed his head, and flung his hoof back, narrowly missing her. Rotten beast.

She shot a glance at Caleb. "The person isn't important. My business with him is."

Caleb's eyebrows rose. "Him?"

She refused to fill in the details and struggled to climb onto the saddle. Gabe helped get her leg and skirt over Skeeter's rump. Once finished, he placed his hand over hers.

"If I can't stop you from going, at least promise you'll be careful, little one. Promise you'll contact me if you need help."

She gave his hand a squeeze. "You've got my word. But I really will be fine." She leaned down and gave him one last hug. "Don't worry, Gabe."

"I'll be praying. Every day." His words barely made it to her ears as he turned to untie the reins then held them out to her.

"Thank you. And thank you both for your help." Her gaze encompassed Caleb. "You came along when I needed you most."

She reached out to shake his hand. He grasped hard and wouldn't let go. His intense eyes held hers. "How can I change your mind?"

Her heart lurched, and she almost gave in. Almost. She forced her pounding heart to settle. "You can't. I have to do this."

Emma reined Skeeter toward the road and thumped his ribs with the stirrups. A second kick got him moving, though his steps were stiff and jarring. No doubt his attempt to let her know of his discontent. She wasn't in much better shape. She'd enjoyed the company of the men and wasn't ready to say good-bye.

Don't look back. People who look back only find trouble. That's what Doc always told her.

Gabe's voice urging his horse on drifted past her. Skeeter must have heard it, too. He craned his neck. Emma pulled on the rein to keep him going straight. Rebellion, pure and simple, took hold. Skeeter yanked his head back around, almost wrenching the reins from her grasp. His body soon followed his head.

"Stop it, Skeeter."

He fought her every attempt to turn him.

"You're going the wrong way."

She jerked harder. He broke into a trot. She hauled back on the reins until they were up past her ears. His hind end pitched up, almost unseating her. The beast took off at a run toward Gabe and Caleb. Emma grabbed the pommel and wrapped her legs around Skeeter's belly for support. Skeeter veered around the wagon and kept running, head down, toward the house. Emma could only hang on for dear life so she wouldn't end up in a heap again, much like the bonnet that flew from her head.

Skeeter planted his feet and skidded to a stop in front of the house. Emma flew forward. The pommel shoved into her stomach while her face smacked against the mule's neck. Nose throbbing, Emma slid from the saddle and checked for blood.

Nothing. But there would be, after she skinned the hide off the willful mongrel.

She shook her finger at Skeeter. "You dirty, rotten, good-for-nothing mule."

Skeeter snorted and shook his head.

Emma propped her hands on her hips. "How did Doc ever put up with you?"

Skeeter's eyes closed halfway as if he were bored. Emma's temper rose further.

"Listen to me, you worthless animal. Doc deserved so much better than you."

With each word, Skeeter's head sank lower. Could it be? Was it possible he missed Doc, too? Was that why he acted so obstinate? Maybe he sought the man he'd served for so many years.

"Oh, Skeeter." Emma reached down to lift his head. "I'm sorry." She scratched between his eyes. "You poor old soul."

"Excuse me."

Emma gasped. Heat crept from her curled toes up into her face. How much did this person see and hear? Horrified, she peeked over her shoulder. A woman old enough to be her mother stood with her hands clasped in front of her, the slightest smile curving her lips. Her dress, though simple, was made with the finest material and lace. Had to be the owner's wife.

Emma dipped into a curtsy. "My deepest pardons, ma'am. I didn't mean to intrude."

The woman's full smile appeared. "Oh, you didn't—"

Rocks skittered as Caleb reined his horse to a stop. He dismounted and strode up to them. "Emma, are you hurt?"

"No. I'm fine."

He stared into her eyes as if seeking the truth. Then a slow smile spread across his face. "Glad you changed your mind about leaving."

He turned away before she could correct him.

"Mother!"

The woman wrapped him in her arms then held him away.

"Welcome home. You took your sweet time getting back." She frowned and swatted at him. "You know better than to worry your mother like that."

Caleb took her hands in his and kissed her cheek. "I apologize. But I have a good reason." He moved to his mother's side and motioned Gabe over. "I'd like you to meet our newest employee."

While the three got acquainted, Emma used the time to examine Caleb's mother. The same eyes that looked upon her son with love held a hollow, indefinable sorrow.

Their conversation finished, Gabe headed back to the wagon, pausing long enough to pull Emma's wayward bonnet from inside his coat. "You dropped this." He handed it to her. "Thought you'd want it back."

She made a face when he chuckled.

"And this"—Caleb spoke to his mother—"is Emma Pickett. I told her you might have some work for her. Maybe cooking or cleaning?"

"I'm sorry. Emma—?"

"Pickett."

Looking her over head to toe, a strange look passed over the older woman's face. Shock? Disgust?

Filled with dread, Emma's gaze dropped to the bonnet in

her hand. Fire roared to life from her neck to her hairline. No wonder Caleb's mother looked so horrified.

"I don't have to wear this. I have others. I only wore this because the wide brim provided more protection." The words poured out in a rush. "My guardian insisted I own it." *You can stop talking now.* She curled her lips inward and bit down with her teeth.

"Guardian?"

"The man who raised me. He said it looked just like me. . . all bright and bubbly." *Stop it.* This woman made her jittery.

Mrs. Kelley reached to touch her then drew back, her arms wrapping around her stomach. "It's fine."

"Mother?" Caleb peered into his mother's face. "Are you sick?"

She did look a bit peaked. More so now than earlier.

Mrs. Kelley patted her son's hand. "Just a bit. I think I'll go in and lie down."

She only made it a few steps before Caleb stopped her.

"Mother, what about Emma?"

She didn't turn. "Show her to the women's quarters. I'll think about a job and let you know later." She took two more steps before halting again. This time she turned, her hand at her throat. "It was nice to meet you, Emma. We'll talk more tomorrow."

"Yes, ma'am." Emma looked to Caleb when his mother continued to the house. Could she help the woman in some way?

Caleb held up a finger before chasing down his mother. Emma waited while they had a brief discussion. A helpless expression on his face, Caleb returned and motioned for her to follow.

"Caleb?"

He stopped when she called but never looked up. "My sister got married a short while back. The next day, she and her husband moved to Missouri." He turned his hat in his hands. "Mother misses them, almost like she's mourning."

And here Emma stood, most likely a stark reminder of her loss, upsetting the poor woman.

"Come." Caleb grabbed Skeeter's reins. "Let me get you to your quarters before it gets dark. I'll put your mule in our barn."

His voice was as sad as his mother's face. Maybe her job would put her in close contact with Mrs. Kelley. The two might offer each other some comfort. The Lord knew Emma wouldn't mind spending time with a mother figure. She hadn't had that since her mother died.

She followed Caleb with a lighter step. More time with Gabe and possibly a motherly employer. This job might be a blessing. It put off meeting the man she sought, allowing her more time to plan for that day. Emma eyed Caleb's broad back. The chance to meet up on occasion with a fine gentleman didn't hurt either. Skeeter's orneriness may have done her a favor.

Caleb tied Skeeter inside the barn and brushed the old brute from his ears to his hind legs. The beast deserved a thorough job. After all, he brought Emma back. But the meeting between her and his mother didn't go so well. With his sister married and gone, he'd hoped the two women would become close.

"Lord, forge a relationship between Mother and Emma."

"This trip so tough it got you talking to yourself?" Gabe grinned at him from the doorway.

"I thought you were getting settled at the men's quarters."

"Yeah, well," Gabe said, ambling into the barn and dropping his belongings in the hay, "that's what I'd like to talk to you about."

"Something wrong?"

"You could say that."

Caleb hung the brush on a nail. "Not exactly what you're used to?"

Gabe scratched the back of his neck. "Right. The place is. . .um. . ."

"Untidy?"

"Putting it mildly. You reckon I could hole up here in the barn till my job is done?"

Caleb clapped Gabe on the back. "Help yourself. The back corner of the loft is rather cozy. I used to go there when I needed a quiet place to think. I'll let everyone know that's your home for the next couple months."

"Appreciate it, young man. It'll make my stay much more pleasant."

"You're welcome. Get some rest. We'll pick out the logs you'll need for the bedstead first thing tomorrow."

With a quick good night, Caleb headed to the house, ready for a soft bed after too many nights spent on the ground. His mind dashed to Emma, wondering how well she'd settled in with four women already living in the cramped quarters. By the look on her face, he wouldn't be a bit surprised to find her gone in the morning. He hoped not. She probably needed to spend some time with women, his mother especially.

If he were honest, he wouldn't mind getting to know the feisty girl better. So many questions surrounded her, like what happened to her parents? Why did she have such a bad limp? What man was she looking for, and why? He hated to admit the last question bothered him the most. But that was one area where he dared not let his mind linger. If he did, he'd also have to admit that he cared.

Chapter 3

Water sloshed from the bucket Emma toted, soaking the right side of her dress. Her right shoe squished with each step, mocking her dream of working next to Mrs. Kelley. The matriarch found a job for Emma, all right. Scrubbing the men's living quarters.

The expressions on the other ladies' faces when they heard the task she'd been assigned still puzzled her. Groans or outright laughter she could have handled. But surprise and dismay swirled around the room before they all made excuses to leave, giving Emma the impression they thought her ridden with some awful disease.

She pondered the women as she balanced the pail, broom, and mop in her aching arms. Marie, daughter of the cook and close to Emma's age, was a talkative little thing. Emma felt certain the girl fell asleep midsentence and woke up completing the thought without missing a beat.

The men's quarters loomed ahead, much larger than the women's lodge. Made sense since Caleb had to hire so many men to chop down trees and work the mill. Cleaning the building would take at least a week. She shrugged. Staring wouldn't get the job done. Besides, it would feel good to put the bucket down.

Emma climbed the steps, propped the broom and mop against the doorframe, and knocked. No way did she want to surprise some unsuspecting man. Hearing nothing, she turned the knob, opened the door, and entered.

Sweat. Urine. Some odors defied description. The stench slammed into her nose and sprinted to her stomach, churning it into a roiling mess. Burning tears sprang to her eyes. The bucket dropped with a thud as she slapped her hand over her mouth and lurched for the door. Once outside, she sucked in great gulps of fresh air.

Holding her apron over her nose, she turned and stared at the revolting structure. Surely people didn't live in there. They couldn't. How could they breathe?

Did Mrs. Kelley have any idea just how disgusting men were? Emma didn't. . .until now. Her next thought weakened her knees. What if Mrs. Kelley knew the exact condition of this place and sent her here on purpose?

Determination set in. Her life had been one long challenge from the moment a stranger killed her father and shot her in the leg. This test wouldn't be any more difficult, just stinkier.

She took a deep breath, grabbed the mop, and headed back inside.

"You sure you want to do that?"

She gasped and spun. Gabe stood at the far end of the porch grinning. She shook her finger at him. "You should know better than to sneak up on a defenseless woman."

He laughed as he scaled the steps. "Oh, I don't know. That mop looks pretty dangerous."

"It'll be even more so after it's spent time in there." She jerked her thumb at the door. "Are you sleeping in there?"

"Not a chance. I pitched my bedroll in the barn." He glanced inside then back at her. "You can't seriously want to go in there."

"No, I don't, but I have to. It's the job I was given."

He stared at her for a moment. "By the look on your face, this isn't what you expected."

"Not even close." She shook her head. "You men are nasty creatures."

"Now, now. Don't go lumping us all together." He grabbed the broom. "Come on. I'll give you a hand."

"You can't do that. You have your own job to do."

"I know, but it can wait. I wouldn't be able to concentrate knowing I'd left you to this."

She stopped him from heading in by touching his arm. "Promise me something."

"What's that?"

"If I pass out, get me out of there fast. I just know something disgusting will start crawling on me the minute I hit the floor." A shudder ran through her from her neck to her toes.

He chuckled. "You've got my word."

She followed him in and bumped into him when he came to an abrupt stop. "What?"

"It's worse than I remembered." He leaned the broom against the wall. "First thing I'm going to do is open the windows. We need fresh air."

"I agree." She glanced at the bucket of water at her feet. "Is there a well or stream nearby? This won't be enough water to wash the windows, let alone the floor."

Gabe grunted as he struggled with the last window. "I think so. I'll round up more buckets and start hauling for you once I get this open."

Emma hung out the blankets from thirty-five beds, hoping to get rid of some of the smell since she didn't have time to wash them today. Gabe wrangled another five buckets and filled each one. He'd disappeared one more time in search of a second mop.

With the bedding out of the way, she picked everything up off the floor and started sweeping the thick layer of dirt toward the back door. Dust rose in a cloud that sent her into sneezing fits. But if she didn't sweep first, the water would turn the dirt into thick mud.

The mound of filth at the door grew to the point where she needed a shovel. Barring that, she decided to do her best by flinging it with the broom. She braced her feet, gripped the handle tight, and heaved as hard as she could.

"Gabe? You in th— Ack!"

Caleb lurched back, gagging and spitting. He pulled his kerchief from his pocket and swiped it across his face.

"Who in the world. . . ?" He sure sounded mad. "Gabe? You in there?"

She couldn't flee. Time to confess. "I'm sorry."

He flinched and turned. "Emma? You did that?" He glanced around. "What are you doing in here? This is the men's quarters."

"I know. And even if I didn't, my nose told me so." She shuddered. "Men are disgusting."

Caleb frowned. "Not all men. Besides, the most energy these fellas have after a full day is to eat and fall into bed."

"Maybe you shouldn't work them so hard."

Caleb looked fit to be tied as he squinted down at her. His bearing made her think of the geysers she and Doc had read about some time back. . .all hot and spewing. If the color of his ears was any indication, he was plenty warm and ready to blow.

He removed his hat and slapped it against his leg, sending more dust dancing through the air.

"Why are you here, Emma?"

She held out the broom. "Cleaning."

"Clean—" He glanced around. "This is the job Mother gave you?"

The words wouldn't come, so she nodded.

He scowled and slammed the hat back on his head. "What was she thinking?" He stomped toward the door. In a panic, Emma raced after him and grabbed his arm.

"Wait."

"Why?"

"Because. . ."

He crossed his arms again. "Yes?"

"Your mother must have thought it necessary, or she wouldn't have had me do it."

"Doesn't matter. I'm talking to her."

"No, wait."

He peered down at her without a word.

What was she supposed to say? No, she didn't want to be here, but something held her here. "I want to do it."

"What?"

"All right, maybe not *want*, but I'm doing it anyway. She gave me a job, and I'm going to do it." For some unknown reason she wanted to please Mrs. Kelley. "Just let me finish this, then I'll be on my way again." If that's what was wanted of her.

"But Emma—"

Ignoring his stare, she bent to the task of sweeping again. Nothing would stop her.

"Then I'll help you."

She stopped cold. "What?" She already had Gabe helping. Mrs. Kelley would fire her for sure if she found out her own son stooped to cleaning. "Oh no you're not."

"Then I'm going to talk to Mother." He spun around to leave.

"Wait." Hardheaded man. "All right. I'll let you help. Just don't tell your mother. She'll set me on Skeeter herself and show us the road."

A grin spread across Caleb's face. "Does that mean you want to stay?"

Confounded man. Thought he was so smart. She grabbed the mop, fought the desire to whop him upside the head, and handed it to him. She pointed at the water bucket, refusing to answer.

The pile of dirt still sat near the door, so she moved to finish sweeping it out. Seconds later, water washed across her feet. Caleb held the empty pail, his mouth hanging open.

"Ah, I'm sorry. I didn't think. . ." The shock on his face transformed to a struggle to hold back a laugh. "Maybe I should sweep."

Obviously the man had never cleaned a day in his life. "You

sure there's nothing else demanding your attention?"

Footsteps pounded across the porch and into the room. "I found another mop. . . ." Gabe skidded to a stop in a dirty puddle, his eyes large as he spotted Caleb. "Morning."

"Good morning, Gabe. I've been looking for you." Caleb let the bucket slide from his fingers and wiped his hands on his pants. "I thought we were going to look through the logs for my parents' bedstead."

"Um, yeah. I got a little sidetracked. I hated leaving Emma to this mess all by herself." He motioned to the water at Caleb's feet. "Appears you ran into the same predicament."

Time to stop this. "I told you both I can do it myself. Now go about your business, and leave me to mine."

The two men shared a long look, then Caleb smiled. "Whaddaya say we help with the floor and let her finish the rest?"

Gabe grinned. "Sounds good."

Before Emma could argue, they each picked up a bucket and flung the water across the floor. As if in a race against each other, the men grabbed their mops and started slinging them back and forth. Best thing Emma could do was stay out of their way. In a short time they reached the end and returned to dump two more buckets across the floor. She hoped they'd at least leave the last one for her so she wouldn't have to fetch another for the windows.

When they'd reached the end of the room for the second time, they turned and leaned on their mops, pride at their accomplishment evident by their smug expressions. She couldn't help but laugh.

"Thank you very much for your help." Oh, the floor would

have to be mopped again to get rid of the streaks of dirt they'd left behind, but she wasn't about to bring them down by mentioning that fact. "There's no telling how long it would have taken me to do the job you did in all of five minutes."

Their faces beamed at her praise. They reached to shake hands.

From the doorway, a man's desperate voice called, "Caleb? You in there, boss?"

Caleb ran out the door. "What's wrong?"

Gabe and Emma followed him outside. A man stood bent over, gasping for air.

"Accident. Down at the harvest site." He sucked in another breath. "It's bad, boss."

In a heartbeat, Caleb, Gabe, and the messenger sprinted away. Emma hesitated only a second before racing in the opposite direction toward her new quarters.

Chapter 4

Caleb glanced back to make sure Emma didn't follow. He needn't have worried. Last he saw of her was a glimpse of her skirts as she sped toward home.

He slowed to let the logger catch up. "What happened?" What was this man's name? He'd been working for them only a week. Wright. Martin Wright.

"A tree. . .fell. . .crushed two. . .men."

Martin looked ready to collapse. Better not ask more questions, or they'd end up carrying him to the accident site.

They arrived to find everyone clustered around one man. A quick glance at the other man revealed unseeing eyes staring at the sky and a gaping head wound. Alex—something. He, too, was new.

Caleb shoved through the group to find Tom Rustin, one of his best workers, on the ground. He dropped to his knees next to the unconscious man. One of his arms lay at an impossible angle. A search for a pulse came up successful though it was weak.

"Anyone gone for the doctor?"

"Yes, sir. Soon as it happened."

"Good." Caleb pulled the kerchief from his neck and pressed it against the scrape on his forehead. Gabe took over that job, allowing Caleb to look Tom over better. The broken arm was obvious. He prayed what he couldn't see was in better condition. "Don't quit on me, Tom. You're the toughest old duffer I know."

The nickname he'd given Tom almost from the time they started working together made his chest ache. Caleb learned everything he knew about logging from Tom. He wasn't ready to say good-bye.

Footsteps and crunching leaves rattled through the forest. The doctor must be here. The men parted, and Emma crashed through brush and branches right before she tripped and sprawled to the ground.

What is she doing here?

Caleb ran to her side and helped her up. "You shouldn't be here, Emma. It's not a pretty sight. Go back home."

She didn't answer but stooped to pick up a black bag then trotted the few steps to Alex's body. She lingered only long enough to check for a pulse before running to Tom to do the same. Then she opened the black bag.

"Someone find me some straight sticks about a foot long." She pulled out some scissors and started cutting Tom's sleeve. "And I'm going to need some strips of cloth."

After a quick glance at his arm, she gripped the front of Tom's shirt and jerked it open. The act broke Caleb out of his trance and propelled him to her side.

"What are you doing, Emma? You're not a doctor."

He grasped her wrist to stop her. By the look on her face one would have thought he'd slapped her.

"No, I'm not a doctor, but I helped one for years. Now please, let me work."

He stared her dead in the eyes and saw. . .confidence. The decision might be one he'd regret, but he let her go. If she could help, he'd let her.

Emma took care to be gentle as she examined the broken arm. Her fingers reminded Caleb of butterflies as they flitted along the swollen skin—light but thorough and skilled.

"Did anyone see what happened?" Emma stopped her examination to glance around. "Anyone? I'd like to know how this arm was broken."

Caleb wanted to know that himself. He looked at the man who'd worked for him the longest, his high climber. "Well?"

Seth scratched at the back of his head and on down his neck before shoving his hands in his pockets. "It's my fault, boss. I crowned the tree all right, but it fell on that other tree. Made widow makers of the branches. Tom saw and ran at Alex, probably to shove him out of the way." He motioned to the fallen treetop. "One of the branches whacked Tom, but Alex took the brunt. Crushed him as it rolled past."

The description made Caleb shudder. Such a dangerous job. No matter how careful they were, he lost men every year. Emma had returned to her work. She placed the fingers of her left hand on the break while slightly turning his arm with her right. Tom groaned and she stopped.

Emma glanced at him. "I need you at his shoulder."

He moved to do her bidding.

"Just hold his shoulder and upper arm to keep them from

moving." She looked him in the eyes. "Can you do that?"

Caleb reached for Tom. With careful movements, he grasped him tight. "Like this?"

"Perfect."

Emma clutched Tom's forearm and slowly leaned back, pulling his arm toward her. Not only could Caleb hear the quiet grind of bone on bone, but he could feel the tiny vibration through Tom's shoulder. He prayed Emma knew what she was doing. Tom wouldn't be happy without full use of his arm.

"There." With great care, Emma released Tom and once again ran her fingers along the break. She nodded. "That ought to do it. Where are those sticks I asked for?"

Several dropped beside her. She took her time picking out the ones she wanted. "And the strips of cloth?"

Seth peeled off his shirt and tore it into narrow shreds.

She smiled. "Thank you."

She hadn't even started with the splint when the doctor strode into the camp. He stopped next to Tom, his eyes taking in the sticks and bandages before sending a scowl toward Emma.

"What have you done?" Anger rumbled in his voice. He waved his hand. "Get back and let me check the damage."

Emma scrambled out of the way as the doctor knelt. Caleb wavered on whether he should stand up for Emma. Doubts of her abilities tore at his insides. What if she really did hurt Tom more than the tree limb? But still. . .

"I let her work on him, Dr. Haffey."

"Quiet, please." He took his time checking Tom's pulse and assessing the injuries. Eyebrows raised, the doctor peered at Emma. "You do all this?"

"Yes, sir."

She sounded scared, her eyes wider than those of a cornered cat.

The doctor nodded, one corner of his mouth curling. "Well done, young lady. You a nurse?"

"N–not exactly. I grew up with a doctor and learned a lot."

The doctor's smile faltered. "Yes, well, watch that head wound while I finish with this arm."

Emma's next breath came out in a rush. Caleb wondered how long she'd been holding it. She scooted toward Tom.

"Whenever you get tired of working for this young rooster" —Dr. Haffey gestured toward Caleb with his thumb—"maybe you'd consider working for me."

Emma's face flamed, though her smile revealed her pleasure. As she kept pressure on Tom's wound, Caleb's estimation of her rose faster than his high climber could scale a branchless tree. He already couldn't get her out of his mind. Now she'd be embedded deeper than the roots of the tallest pine.

Chapter 5

A week had passed since Tom's accident, and Emma still couldn't keep the smile from her face. She wasn't much for humming tunes like Doc always did, but a song escaped from time to time, especially now that she was working closer to the mansion. Granted, she wasn't in the house yet, but her new job of organizing the outside storage shed smelled better than the men's quarters.

Caleb caused the change by talking to his mother, something Emma still groused about. She'd rather have earned the change on her own, but she was grateful all the same. Caleb's thoughtfulness sent a thrill through her heart.

Best of all, almost everyone looked at her differently. Word had gotten out that she'd helped Caleb's employee, and for the first time, she felt appreciated by someone other than Doc. Everyone, that is, except Caleb's parents. It seemed they went out of their way to avoid her. If she could ever figure out why, she'd do her best to change that situation, too.

A door slammed. Emma stepped outside with another box

to add to the others and almost collided with Mr. Kelley. The look on his face made her choke on her apology.

Nostrils flaring, he tipped his hat. "Excuse me." Without a moment's waste, he was on his way again.

"Was there something. . .I. . .could. . .do for you?" The last three words trailed off in a whisper.

Why did he hate her so? She'd grown used to the rich looking down on her, so why did the Kelleys' abhorrence hurt more than the others? Her throat burned as she fought back tears. The desire to run set her feet in motion. She'd never been more annoyed with her limp, adding to the ache in her heart.

The barn door gaped in silent invitation. She rushed inside and headed straight for Skeeter's stall. That bonehead would leave with her today if she had to drag him by his tail.

The moment he saw her, Skeeter backed into a corner and put his head down, ears lowered. Not to be deterred, Emma grabbed his halter with both hands and pulled. He didn't budge.

"Move, Skeeter. I gotta leave." Her voice broke and dropped to a whisper. "I need you."

She tugged his halter one more time, to no avail. Defeated, Emma slumped against the wall and slid to a crouch. Gasping for breath in the dank stench, sobs fought for space in her tight chest. Try as she might, she couldn't stop the tears, berating herself as they fell. She'd vowed to never again let the rich make her feel like less of a person, and now she'd let herself down.

"Hey, now, little lady." Gabe squatted next to her and reached to wipe a tear from her cheek. "What's all this?"

His tender voice made her want to cry harder. That wouldn't

do. Time to buck up. She gulped in a deep breath and let it out in a slow puff. She paused a moment longer to make sure she could speak without her voice quivering.

"I'm all right. Just a bad moment."

Gabe helped her to her feet then motioned to a bench outside Skeeter's stall. They sat silent for a long minute. He bumped her shoulder with his.

"Wanna talk about it?"

No.

"My ears work great even if my mouth doesn't. Usually gets me into trouble."

Gabe's charm coaxed the smile she knew he wanted. Was it possible God was using Gabe to fill the hole Doc left?

"That's better. Now, how about you tell me what caused those tears. I may not be able to heal as well as you, but I know talking helps."

Emma wasn't so sure, but it couldn't hurt to try. She trusted Gabe, at least for now. "I'm a good person."

"You sure are."

"Just because I limp doesn't mean I'm less of a person."

"I agree."

Emma leaned away to see Gabe's face better. "So, why is it some people think otherwise?" She wanted a good reason for her problem but doubted Gabe had one.

"I take it you still can't get Caleb's parents to warm up to you."

Emma's mouth dropped open. "How did you know that?"

Gabe's chuckle made his shoulders bounce. "I'd have to be blind to miss the way you look at them with those pleading eyes and deaf not to hear your attempts to get them talking."

Was it that obvious? She cringed. No wonder they avoided her. Who'd want to be around a needy person? Not that she was one of those.

"Give them time, Emma. One day they'll see your sweet heart."

Doubtful. How could they when they wouldn't come near her?

Gabe bumped her again and motioned to her leg. "What happened, Emma? Do you mind talking about it?"

"Depends on who's asking." She bumped him back. "I reckon I can tell you, though."

She stared at the far wall and pondered the memory. Some things were fuzzy. Others could have happened yesterday.

"I was shot."

Gabe reared back. "What?"

She nodded. "Right after they killed Daddy."

Gabe sat silent. For once. Might as well finish the tale while he was still quiet.

"Mama had died not long before. She'd been sick awhile. Coughed herself to death." Emma could still hear the ragged sound in her mind. "Daddy was so upset it nearly killed him." She wouldn't tell Gabe of her own broken heart. "Not long after she was buried, Daddy loaded our belongings in the wagon. Never said where we were going. We just went."

"How old were you?"

Emma smiled. Gabe could only stay silent so long. "Seven, I think."

That's what Doc had guessed when he found her. Since she couldn't remember her birth date, they started celebrating her birthdays on the day her leg was declared healed.

"We spent a lot of nights sleeping under the wagon. Then one day we stopped at a town. Daddy told me to wait in the wagon, that he'd come right back. But he didn't. He was gone forever. So I went looking for him." She swallowed hard. She couldn't see faces, but she could see the event clearly. "I rounded a corner, saw a man pointing a gun at Daddy, and I screamed."

Gabe grasped her hand. "And that man shot you?"

Emma nodded as it played through her mind. "The pain was awful. I hit the ground hard. But I heard two more shots, then that man ran away." She took a shaky breath. "I saw Daddy in the dirt. I tried crawling to him but it hurt too bad." She shook her head. "Next thing I knew, Doc was standing over me."

"And he took care of you ever since." When she nodded, Gabe leaned forward and looked her in the eyes. "And the man you seek in Woodville?"

The anger returned. "The man who killed Daddy."

"How do you know he's in Woodville?"

She stood and paced. "I found Mama's diary in Daddy's things when Doc died. She mentioned his name, why they were meeting in Irontree, and where he'd planned to start a business. I'm gonna see if he's there."

Gabe leaned back and crossed his arms. "Why were they meeting?"

Emma's heart clenched. This was the part she didn't want to tell. She stopped pacing and faced him. "To split some stolen money from the war."

Gabe only nodded. Good. She couldn't explain anything else.

"And what do you plan to do when you find this man?"

Now, why did he have to go and ask that? She shrugged and looked away.

"Does that gun in your bag play a part in this?"

Shock spun her around to face him. How did he know about that?

He met her gaze. "Caleb told me he felt it when he looked through your things."

Men! Nosy rascals. She'd set Gabe straight right now. "I don't know what I intend to do, but at least I'll have some protection if he decides to finish the job he started."

Annoyance swept through her. That wasn't true. She knew what she intended. She'd seek justice for her father, maybe for herself. Peace wouldn't come until evil had been avenged.

Gabe stared at her face, then nodded. He reached into his pocket and pulled out a knife. From the shelf next to him he picked up a narrow piece of wood about a foot long. The corners had been cut out, making the piece look like a long plus sign. He made several notches then started whittling chunks out, letting the shavings drop to the ground.

"Do you believe in God, Emma?"

Where did that question come from? "Yes."

"Do you love Him?"

She frowned. "Of course."

"Then why don't you obey Him?" He never looked up but kept carving the wood. "You can't have it both ways, little one."

Her nails bit into her palms. "I don't understand."

More shavings fell. "You can't seek revenge then become obedient again. You can't pick and choose when you will and won't follow God. It's something that's done all the time or not at all."

An oval dangled from the piece of wood. Gabe continued whittling, his rough, scarred hands caressing the wood as he worked. "What if Christ had decided to disobey the Father just one time and not come to earth to die for us? If He'd not come to earth as a baby, we'd have no Christmas to celebrate." Gabe looked up. "And no redemption."

He went back to carving and soon another link dangled with the first. "We need to follow Christ's example and be obedient to the point of death." A third link fell. "All the time."

Emma puzzled over Gabe's words as he continued working with the wood. She never said she wanted to exact revenge, yet Gabe seemed to know and warned her against it, for her own sake, not that of the killer. Finally, Gabe stood and handed her the wood, now transformed into a chain. She'd never seen anything like it as she rubbed her thumb over the smooth links.

Gabe grasped the dangling end and pulled the chain taut. "We need to learn to be content in our circumstances, whatever they may be. The only person vengeance hurts is the one holding on to it." He placed the tip of his knife on one of the links and started gouging and flicking tiny pieces of the wood. "It eats away at you until—"

Emma placed her hand over the knife handle. "Stop. You're marring your beautiful creation."

Understanding dawned. Emma looked into Gabe's eyes. He winked and patted her hand. Whistling, he wandered back to his corner of the barn and began carving at the bedposts intended for Caleb's parents.

Left alone to deal with the sin damaging God's creation, Emma wondered if Gabe thought her marred beyond repair. Or was it just her who thought that of herself? It was too late to fill the holes vengeance had produced.

Chapter 6

C aleb followed his nose to the kitchen, pushed through the doors, then inhaled, long and deep. Ah, Thanksgiving.

Two things in this world bore a fragrance like no other. The scent of cut wood and the smell of turkey and dressing as they cooked. Both trees and meat held a faint aroma, but it wasn't until a blade or heat was applied that they revealed their essence. He smiled. Not exactly deep thinking, but they were two of his true loves.

Glancing around the kitchen, he spotted the other thing quickly adding itself to his list of loves. Not it, but who. He headed across the room and stopped next to her.

"Good morning, Emma."

He waited for her to turn and. . .there. That shy smile of hers warmed him every time. Best of all, it seemed reserved just for him. The last few weeks, he found every excuse possible to spend time with her. Her latest tasks of tending the flower beds, bushes, and fall garden allowed him plenty of chances to run into her and offer his help. Not that his efforts were appreciated every time. She shook a hoe at him once and flung a clump of dirt at him another when his clumsy attempts hindered rather than helped. But the time with her was never in vain. Not only did he get to know her better, but she showered him with those wonderful smiles.

"Mornin', Caleb." The head cook waddled over before Emma said a word. "I knew we'd see you long before dinner. It's become tradition for you to smell the food before you eat it."

Mabel had been their cook as long as he could remember. He grinned and gave her a hug. "And as usual, Mabel, it smells amazing."

"Oh. . .go on with yourself." She bumped his hip with hers. "You're just sweet-talking to get a sample."

As her cackle pierced his eardrums, she pulled one of her scrumptious bread rolls from her apron pocket. His mouth already salivating, Caleb wasted no time taking a bite. The light, yeasty roll melted into a warm taste of paradise, nearly making his eyes roll to the back of his head.

"Heavenly," was all he managed as he shoved the remainder in his mouth.

"Uh-huh. Well, it's all you get for now, so don't go begging for more."

Mabel wandered back to the stove to stir one of the pots. Surely she knew a small taste was sheer torture. But Caleb also knew she'd be good to her word. He'd receive a slap to the hand if he tried to sneak more.

About the only thing that would take his mind off the wonderful smell filling the kitchen was Emma. He wouldn't get a chance to spend time with her until tonight, if at all, so he'd have to steal a moment this morning.

He leaned close to whisper, "Happy Thanksgiving." There was that smile again.

"Thank you."

Oh, how he wished they could spend the day together. But his mother had other plans. In fact, it seemed she worked hard to keep him from Emma's side. Today she invited Mayor Peck, his wife, and their daughter to share not only their meal but the whole day. Caleb knew full well his mother hoped something would happen between him and Ruby Peck, and she found numerous ways to get them together. Ruby was pretty enough. Beautiful, actually. But there was nothing more to her. No flair or spunk. Not witty at all. . .like Emma.

With just the right prompt, Caleb could get a spirited statement from Emma that would make him smile for hours.

"If you wore your bonnet, you'd blend right in with the fall colors."

Emma held the tip of her knife under his nose, her face expressionless. "I've got a knife, and I'm quite good at using it." She stated each word slowly then returned to her task.

Caleb tried not to laugh but was unsuccessful. It burst out of him like a trigger had been pulled. He'd kiss her in a heartbeat if he didn't think it'd get him into trouble.

"Caleb!" Mabel shook her spoon at him. "You get on outta here before your blood is spilled all over my nice kitchen."

Though she sounded gruff, a smile tickled the corners of Mabel's mouth. Caleb gave a quick bow then sent Emma a hasty wink and rushed outside. He stood on the back porch appreciating the majestic pines standing sentinel. But he appreciated Emma so much more.

How did she manage to bury herself so deeply in his heart? Maybe her quiet dignity in the face of difficulties? Emma was a fighter struggling to do the right thing, no matter what. Caleb admired that quality. To lose her would be the worst thing he could imagine. Hopefully she'd learn to love Tremble and forget her desire to meet up with the man from Woodville, whatever the reason. Until now, Caleb never knew the feeling of hating a man he'd never met. But the defiance Caleb read in Emma's eyes made him nervous. What caused it, he didn't know, but he felt certain it would be the basis for her leaving.

As he proceeded indoors to greet their guests, he prayed Emma would understand his need to socialize with Ruby today. First thing tomorrow, he'd make sure Emma realized just where his thoughts spent the most hours each day. Harder yet would be making his mother accept his feelings for Emma, though he had yet to figure out why.

Emma focused on getting through the swinging door and into the kitchen without dropping everything. If she made it safely inside, she'd have survived serving the Kelleys and their guests without embarrassing anyone, especially herself. And she would no longer have to watch Caleb and his lady friend together. The day was sheer torture. She'd tried not to let the sight of them bother her, but she'd failed miserably. Caleb had managed to work his way into her heart, and she couldn't chop him loose no matter how hard she tried. She wanted to be the girl sitting next to him, smiling up into his charming face, not that wretchedly beautiful Ruby Peck.

She pushed through and set the tray on the counter. Done.

All that was left was to clean up. A quick look around told her the ladies had been busy. Except for the tray of dirty dishes she'd just brought in, almost everything was finished.

"We've got this, Em." Mabel headed her way. "Grab the linens from the table and take them to the washroom. We'll wash them tomorrow."

Arms full, Emma made her way down the hall. After she had been on her feet since early morning, her leg begged for rest. Just a few minutes would do wonders. The washroom would provide the perfect opportunity—

Emma gasped at the sight of Caleb and his pretty young guest ensconced in the washroom. The girl had her arms wound around his neck, her lips tilted toward his. With his hands on the girl's hips, Caleb didn't look like he minded. At least not until he caught sight of Emma. Then he pushed his lady friend away.

Embarrassment made Emma drop the linens. The ache in her heart made her run. Ignoring Caleb's calls for her to stop, Emma rushed outside and into the trees.

Chapter 7

Where did she go?

Caleb glanced from one side to the next. How did Emma manage to disappear so quickly? He had to find her. He pushed farther into the woods, desperate to let her know she didn't really see what she saw.

That sounded so dumb. Of course Emma saw Ruby trying to kiss him. Emma needed to know that he wanted no part of Ruby's interest. He wanted Emma. Where was she? If only she was wearing that gaudy bonnet. He'd spot her instantly.

"Emma!"

Please don't leave.

Skeeter. Emma was probably trying to get him out of the barn. Caleb raced that way. He broke into the clearing and slid to a stop. Hoe in hand, Emma chopped in the garden like she was after a snake. Most likely he was the snake. He approached, praying for the right words.

"Emma."

She ignored him. He crossed the tilled dirt and grasped

her elbow. She jerked free.

"I'm busy."

"It can wait." He caught both her arms and turned her to face him, allowing him to see her red-rimmed eyes. His heart constricted. "It can wait."

The hoe fell from her hands. "Then I'm sure something else needs my attention."

"That would be me."

Peering up at him, a grimace twisted her lips. "You've already got someone for that."

"I want it to be you."

She frowned. "Didn't look that way to me." Her face turned sad. "But I've got no claim on you. I just. . ."

He wanted her to finish, to say the words. "You just what?"

Emma shook her head. Her lips tightened. Caleb pulled her closer.

"You just what, Emma?"

Her mouth trembled. "I've enjoyed your friendship, that's all."

He wanted to kiss her. The time wasn't right. Not yet. "Is that really all?" She stared at his throat. He needed her to stare into his eyes. "Because I want to enjoy more than that."

He got his wish. A shade lighter than the pine needles, her eyes were so beautiful.

"With two women?"

What? Oh. Ruby. "No. What you saw was Ruby's desire, not mine. If you'd come in a minute earlier or stayed a second longer, you would have seen that she was the instigator, and I was the finisher." He bent down until their noses were mere inches apart. "It's not her I want."

He leaned back and inspected her hands. She did the

same, then looked at him again.

"What?"

He smiled. "I just wanted to make sure you didn't have a knife that you're quite good at using in your hands so you wouldn't hurt me when I did this."

He pulled her close and placed a quick, gentle kiss on her lips. She was as sweet as he expected.

"Caleb Kelley!"

At his mother's voice, he released Emma and turned.

"You have guests. Remember your manners."

His mother's red face could be seen across the yard. "I'll be right there." He touched Emma's shoulder. "We still need to talk. In the meantime, go get a coat on. It's chilly out here."

She nodded. He wanted to kiss her again, but it would have to wait. Besides, he didn't ask her permission the first time. As he headed to the house, he knew it was time to tell his parents of his feelings for Emma. They'd have to find some way to get past their opposition, whatever their reason for it, and accept her. He'd have it no other way.

"You cannot court that girl. I forbid it."

Caleb's mother glared at him with her arms crossed as she paced the sitting room. The minute Caleb mentioned Emma's name, she'd begun her march, her fingers tapping an angry drumbeat on her arms.

"Why? She's a wonderful young woman. You'd see that for yourself if you'd take the time to get to know her."

She paused her pacing. "She's a servant."

"Is that the reason, or is there more you're not telling me?"

His mother's mouth opened and closed before she shot a glance at his father, sitting quietly and staring at the floor. Her eyes narrowed and her lips tightened before she resumed her march.

"If that's your only problem with her, she can go work for the doctor."

"She's not good enough for you." His mother stopped in front of him. "Can't you see that? You need a lady with class."

"She has class. She just doesn't have much money."

"I don't want you spending time with her."

Caleb's heart ached. How would he get through to his mother? He loved her, but he was also falling for Emma. He wanted them both. "If you have no reason for me not to see Emma other than what you've stated, then I'm going to continue getting to know her."

"Against my wishes?"

"Give her a chance, Mother."

She speared his father with another look. "Are you going to continue sitting there mute or do you plan to support me?"

He lifted his head. He looked tired, sad even. Finally, he moved his hands in a helpless gesture, stood, and left the room. Once gone, his mother turned back to Caleb.

"How can I change your mind?"

"How can I change yours?"

Her shoulders slumped. Tears softened her expression. She cupped his cheek with a cold hand. "I love you, Caleb." Then she walked out.

Caleb stared at the doorway. Did that mean she conceded? Only time would tell.

Chapter 8

Emma tugged at the box of Christmas decorations. The rotten thing wouldn't budge. In fact, it nearly tore from her efforts. What on earth was so heavy?

She gave the box a kick, frustration eating at her heart. She wished she could kick Caleb, but he wasn't in sight. Hadn't been since he stole that kiss in the garden, and that was a week ago. The thought of his lips on hers warmed her all over again, but only for a moment. Doubts returned to chill her already-cool skin. Was her kiss so awful he couldn't bear to be near her? He said they needed to talk, so why was he avoiding her?

Aiming her irritation at the box, she stepped behind it and gave it a shove. It didn't move. What was in there? Rocks? Since she was in charge of setting out the decorations, she'd need to see inside eventually. No time like the present. Curiosity flaming, she squatted and lifted the lid.

Logs? Seriously? Who in their right mind would store logs for the next year? Especially when they owned a sawmill and all the trees in sight. Emma cast a look around, wondering if this was someone's idea of a prank.

Suddenly a mouse shot out the top of the box. Emma shrieked. Then when the whiskered intruder launched off Emma's arm and scurried into the room behind her, she screeched and scooted in the opposite direction, brushing frantically at her arm as though the varmint still sat there. That's when she noticed the hole chewed into the corner of the box.

Footsteps pounded up the stairs and down the hall. Caleb slid to a stop when he saw her, then he took the last few steps and knelt beside her.

"What happened, Emma? Are you hurt?"

Before she could answer Caleb's question, Marie appeared behind him, followed by a huffing Mabel and a wide-eyed Mrs. Kelley.

Caleb touched her hand. "Emma?"

"I'm fine." Tongue-tied at the sight of his mother, Emma stammered. "It was just a—"

"A what?"

She grimaced and swept at her sleeve again. "A mouse leaped out of that box."

Caleb's brows went up and his lips twitched.

"Don't you dare laugh, Caleb Kelley. That nasty creature jumped on me." She shuddered and pushed to her feet.

Caleb followed. With one arm across his chest, he propped his other elbow up with his hand covering his mouth. Emma knew full well he hid a grin. She sent him a scowl then turned it on Mabel and Marie when they snickered.

Mrs. Kelley pressed to her son's side. "Did she say a mouse?"

"Now, Mother."

"Caleb, you know I don't abide mice in my house. You've got to get it. I won't sleep until I know it's out." She gave him a slight push. "Please, Caleb."

He sighed. "All right. I'll get it. Go about your business. I'll let you know when I've found it."

The ladies scattered. All but Emma. She wanted an explanation for his absence even though her heart quivered with unease about his reason.

"I'll help."

Caleb grinned. "I can't imagine you running on tiptoes holding up your skirts would be much help." He looked thoughtful. "Then again, that might be an interesting sight."

She swatted at him but he leaned back, making her miss. Then he moved closer until she thought he planned to steal another kiss.

"Tell you what." His quiet voice sent a tingle across her skin. "You go on about your decorating. When I'm finished, I'll come find you. In fact, I was looking for you when I heard your scream."

"Why?" Her voice was just a whisper as she prayed it was for the reason she hoped.

"I'm on my way to find a tree to decorate for inside our house. I'd like you to come along."

For her opinion? Did he consider it one of her decorating duties? Disappointment nearly sent her running.

He leaned closer, his cheek nearly touching hers as his lips tickled her ear. "I can't think of a better way to spend the rest of the day."

His breath on her ear sent shivers all through her skin.

Then he moved back and looked into her eyes. "Besides, it looks like it might snow. I can't think of anything prettier than flakes falling around you."

Heart hammering, she could hardly speak. "I'd like that."

Smiling, he touched her cheek. "Dress warm."

Praying her legs would carry her, she made her way down the hall. How could his eyes make her knees so weak?

Caleb pitched the hairy nuisance outside. The rotten critter had wasted a good hour of his time. An hour he could have spent with Emma. He'd already lost a week working out a problem with the mill. He shoved into the kitchen, certain she'd be there. Only Mabel sat at the table.

"Your mama gonna sleep in peace tonight?"

Mabel's wide grin wiped away his irritation. "She will." He strode to the washbasin to clean up. "You know where she is?"

"Not right off, but it's my guess she's quietly overseeing Emma's work."

Caleb wasn't surprised Mabel noticed the tension. She rarely missed much. "If you see her, tell her the house is mouseless."

Without a doubt, more of them crept around the floors, but he wasn't about to mention that. . .to *any* of the women. Did he dare ask Mabel if she knew where to find Emma? Her all-seeing eyes had surely picked up on his interest, especially on Thanksgiving Day.

"She's in the den."

He turned. Mabel sat polishing the silver with a smile on her face, humming. Meddlesome old woman. He loved her like a second mother. He dropped a kiss on top of her head as he walked past.

"Thank you."

"Mm-hmm."

He found Emma where Mabel said he would. She knelt next to his mother's music box, engrossed in her examination. He sneaked up behind her.

"Want to hear it play?" He laughed at her shriek as she turned. "I didn't mean to scare you."

"Yes, you did. Twice in one day is more than I can handle."

He tried to look repentant, sure he'd failed. "Let me make it up to you. I'll take you on a nice, relaxing ride in the woods." He put his hand on her back and led her from the room. "Then I'll let you chop down our Christmas tree."

Her mouth dropped open. "Why, thank you, sir. Just don't stand close. I may mistake you for a trunk."

He burst into laughter, looking forward to the rest of the day more than ever. After retrieving Emma's coat and securing her on the wagon seat, he draped a blanket over her legs and clucked the sleepy horse into motion.

Caleb settled back next to Emma, close enough that their arms bumped as the wagon swayed. "Your job is to spot the perfect tree."

"What do you consider a perfect tree?"

"Whichever one you choose, as long as the base isn't so large it'll take all night to chop through." He paused a moment. "I'd hate to see you lose sleep because you can't get the tree to fall."

"Me? I thought you were just teasing."

He put on his best innocent look. "I'd never do that."

"Right. And Skeeter isn't lazy."

He roared with laughter. "Emma, I don't think I ever laughed so hard before you joined us."

She cast him a sideways glance. "I aim to please."

Caleb thought a moment to decide if he should ask the question most on his mind. Convinced it was the perfect opportunity since she couldn't run off, he said a silent prayer and stepped into the abyss.

"You didn't want to stay at first, yet you're still here. Does that mean you've changed your mind? That you're no longer looking for the man you sought?"

She sat quiet so long, he figured she refused to answer.

"I almost left one day."

His heart pitched. "What stopped you?"

She heaved a sigh as she stared at her mittened hands. "Gabe. He said something that made me think I should reconsider."

When she didn't say more, he thought he might bellow with frustration. Instead, he gripped the reins tighter. "And?"

"I'm still thinking, but I'm still here."

His smile moved all the way to his heart. "And I'm so glad. I'll have to thank Gabe."

He wanted to know more but decided not to push. Not today anyway. This was to be a day they'd both want to remember. A day they'd get to know each other better. Maybe even the day he'd be brave enough to say the words on his heart.

"Right there."

Emma's loud voice made his heart jump to his throat and even spooked the horse. He followed her pointing finger to a perfectly shaped cedar. They hadn't gone as far as he would have liked, wanting more time with her, but this would do. He stopped the wagon close to the tree then helped Emma down.

Standing next to the tree, he wondered if it would fit through their door. He looked at Emma with raised brows.

She shrugged. "It didn't look this big from back there."

He laughed. "It'll be fine. I'll just cut off some of the base if need be."

He grabbed a hatchet from the wagon bed, knelt next to the tree, and chopped off all the lower branches. Then he cut a notch at the base. Time for the big axe. He returned to the wagon, exchanged tools, and stopped beside Emma.

Straight-faced, he handed her the axe. "Your turn."

With a stunned expression, she took it, the axe head dipping before she grasped it with both hands. She glanced from the tool to the tree to his face. "You're serious?"

He sat next to a large oak and got comfortable. "Let me know if you need help. Oh. . .and you need to take off the mittens." He made the motion of chopping. "Better grip. Especially if you spit on your hands."

She made a face. "Spit on my hands?"

"Sure." He pretended to do just that, rubbed his hands together, then acted like he gripped the handle.

Emma gaped at him several moments longer then tromped to the cedar. Hefting the axe to her shoulder, she took another step closer, took aim at the notch he'd made, and chopped. Even with her loud grunt, she barely made a mark. She speared him with a look. Somehow he kept his face blank.

"If you put your right hand closer to the axe head, you'll have more control of each swing."

She held it out to him. "Show me."

He grinned. She was clever. Standing, he took the axe from her, showed her his grip, then swung. A chunk of wood fell. He chopped one more time, then handed her the tool and motioned for her to take over while he resumed his position against the oak tree.

Her next few swings did more damage than her first attempt, but not much. He had to give her credit, she was tenacious. But he already knew that about her. Determination was a way of life for Emma. He wanted to learn more.

He timed his question as she was about to swing again. "How many babies have you delivered?"

The axe head rested on the ground. "What?"

He shrugged. "I was just curious about the work you did with Doc."

She scowled, turned away, and chopped one more time. "Four." She glanced over her shoulder. "Four babies, two broken bones, countless stitches." She hefted the axe again. "And soon, one amputated leg." *Whack*. "And I don't mean mine."

Caleb rolled to the ground with laughter. Without a doubt, he loved this girl. A life with Emma would be filled with fun and joy. He stood and held out his hand for the axe. She gave it without a word and dropped on the spot he had vacated.

Say the words.

But he didn't know how she felt about him. Was he just a friend, or did she care for him as he did for her? He continued to stare, working up the courage.

She frowned and wiped at her face. "What? Are there wood chips sticking to my face?"

He smiled, doubting she managed to knock off one chip.

"You amaze me, Emma. Most women I know wouldn't have even tried."

"Don't give me too much credit. I didn't want to have to walk home."

He chuckled and shook his head, knowing full well that had nothing to do with her efforts. Still apprehensive, he turned and chopped at the tree as though he could kill the cowardice he fought. Chop. Fear of asking about her limp. Chop. Fear of revealing his feelings. Chop. Fear of going against his parents.

He hated the last one most of all. What kind of man was he? Chop. And the cedar fell. Puffing, he set the axe head on the ground and leaned on the handle.

"All right, you have to load the tree." At her exasperated face, he grinned. "You can at least help."

"Done." She stood and brushed the soil from her skirt then peered up at him with her head tilted. "You've never asked about my limp, but it doesn't seem to bother you."

"The only thing that bothers me about your limp is if it hurts you. But if you ever want to talk about it. . ."

Her answering smile looked pleased, but she didn't say a word as she grabbed hold of the top of the tree. That conversation would have to wait.

Shadows were lengthening quickly as they maneuvered the tree into the back of the wagon. Emma plucked at the branches. He held out his hand for hers. When she took it, he gasped at her icy fingers.

"Where are your mittens?"

Spotting them on the ground, he retrieved them, working up the nerve to tell her what was in his heart. Before he could utter a word, hurried footsteps and breaking branches caught his attention. He moved between the noise and Emma, not sure what came at them. One of his loggers appeared in the clearing.

"Come quick, boss. Your dad's bad sick."

Chapter 9

Emma held tightly to the seat as Caleb raced through the woods. Even the man who brought the news of Caleb's father had trouble staying in the back of the wagon.

Caleb glanced over his shoulder. "What happened?"

The man slipped and then knelt. "He collapsed. No warning. Just crumpled."

"Someone go for the doctor?"

"Benjamin."

The man grabbed his mouth and pulled away a bloody hand. Emma guessed he'd bitten his tongue during the last jolt.

"I'm walking," he hollered and launched over the side of the wagon.

Emma understood. She'd do the same given the chance. They stopped in front of the house, and Caleb helped her down. He ran toward the door then slowed.

"Aren't you coming?"

His mother wouldn't appreciate her arriving with Caleb. She was sure of that.

"I thought maybe you should check on him alone."

"You might be right. I'll find you later."

He disappeared inside. She walked around to the back of the house and entered the kitchen. The ladies moved quietly, working hard at doing nothing. The tension inside her matched that in the room. By the looks on their faces, she dared not break the silence.

Emma peeled off her coat and hung it by the door then moved to the washbasin, giving her something to do besides facing the stares of the other women. A door slammed followed by rushing footsteps, then more silence.

Oh, Lord, let Mr. Kelley be all right.

"Emma!"

Caleb's shout stopped her heart and made the hair on her scalp stand up. Mabel shoved a towel into her hands, took her by the shoulders, and pushed her from the kitchen.

"You best get a move on."

"Emma!"

The urgency in Caleb's voice made her run up the stairs. Caleb waved her into a room she'd never before entered. The Kelleys' master bedroom. She wanted to stop inside the door, but Caleb pushed at her back.

"We can't find the doctor. You've got to help my father."

Mr. Kelley lay against the white pillow looking almost as pale, covers pulled up to his chin. Beads of sweat dotted his face. As she reached to touch his forehead, Mrs. Kelley rushed into the room.

Lips tight, she stopped across the bed from Emma. "What

is she doing here? Get her out."

"Mother."

"I mean it. I want her out."

Emma moved to leave. Caleb put his hand out to stop her. "We need her. Dad needs her. Until we can find the doctor, Emma's all we've got."

"But—"

"Enough. Don't let your pride keep Dad from getting help."

Emma wasn't meant to hear the last part, but it still hurt. Forcing herself to look at Mrs. Kelley, she waited. She wouldn't do a thing until permitted. Finally, Mrs. Kelley nodded.

Mr. Kelley's forehead radiated heat like a low-burning cookstove. Emma flipped back the covers.

Mrs. Kelley grabbed them and tried to put them back. "What are you doing?"

Emma yanked the blankets from her grip and tossed them from the bed. She looked at Caleb. "Open the window."

Mrs. Kelley grabbed his arm. "That's absurd. She'll kill him. Caleb, get her out of here."

Caleb looked at her, panic in his eyes. "Emma?"

"You keep him covered with a fever like this, and you'll cook him to death." That was overstating, but she had to make them understand. "We've got to get his temperature down fast."

Mrs. Kelley gave a vehement shake of her head. "Everyone knows you sweat out a fever."

"Not all fevers. I promise I won't keep the window open long. Just enough to cool the room."

Caleb rushed to the window and shoved it open. "What else?"

Mind racing, Emma told herself to calm down. "A basin of cold water and some cloths. That'll help cool his skin."

"I'll get them." Mrs. Kelley's face softened. She caressed her husband's cheek before hurrying from the room.

Caleb took his mother's place across the bed from her, his eyes questioning, though he never said a word.

Her smile, though shaky, was meant to be reassuring. "I promise this is best. Your father's too hot. That's dangerous."

"I trust you. What can I do?"

"I need the doctor's bag. After that, you can rub your dad's skin with cool water."

"Done."

He ran from the room, leaving her alone with Mr. Kelley. She felt his forehead again as she examined his face. She'd never seen him like this before. He always appeared angry or worried, tall and strong. Now he looked so pale and weak. Old even. She lifted his lids to see his eyes rolled back. Fear that he would die in her care shook her.

Lord, please let the doctor be found. Keep this man alive.

Caleb returned carrying the water basin and set it on the stand next to the bed. His mother followed with several cloths in her hands.

"Marie's run to get your bag."

She reached for the buttons on his shirt. "All right, in the meantime, let's cool his skin with the water."

"Stop!" Mrs. Kelley pushed her hands away. "I'll do this. You don't need to see his. . ." She licked her lips. "I can do this."

Emma looked to Caleb. He stared at his mother a moment then nodded.

"Let us do this, Emma. Stay close. If we need you, I'll come for you."

"All right. I'll be right outside."

Feeling better about the temperature in the room, Emma stepped out and closed the door. Marie arrived with the medical bag, handed it over, and left. Emma paced, gazed over the hall banister, then paced again. Was Mr. Kelley's fever coming down? Was he conscious yet? Why did Mrs. Kelley hate her? And where was the doctor?

The front door opened, and the doctor's long strides carried him across the foyer and up the stairs two at a time. He paused when he saw her.

"Miss. . . ?"

"Pickett."

"Have you seen him?"

She nodded, twisting her hands together. "He has a high fever. I had them open the window and cool his skin with cold water."

He appraised her much like he did the first time, then gave one quick dip of the head and entered the bedroom. Emma heard Mrs. Kelley's words tumble over themselves as the doctor closed the door.

The waiting made her want to scream. Her nerves were already doing that very thing. Did she do right? Would the doctor scold her for her involvement? Half an hour crawled by, every torturous second ticked off by the large clock in the hall below. The door swung open. Caleb waved her inside. Her tension rose with each step. What would she find? Caleb moved aside and the first thing she saw was the doctor setting out his surgical instruments.

Chapter 10

Though the room was cool, Emma broke out in a sweat. The doctor motioned to a bottle next to the wash-basin. "Clean your hands, then help me with these instruments. Caleb, take your mother from the room and bring some fresh water and cloth."

Mrs. Kelley refused to budge when Caleb took her arm. "I want to stay."

"Mother."

"Mrs. Kelley, I'll do no more to help your husband until you leave."

The doctor's bushy brows nearly touched as he waited for her decision. She allowed Caleb to lead her out.

"Now then"—the doctor finished his task—"near as I can tell, Mr. Kelley still has an old bullet inside him." He opened the man's shirt and pointed to a scar. "No exit wound. Mrs. Kelley told me he's been having stomach pains. I intend to go in and look around. I need your help. Are you willing?"

No!

She swallowed hard. "Of course." *How'd he get shot? Better yet, why?*

The questions would have to wait. Time to mentally prepare for what lay ahead. She'd helped her mentor with surgery several times and never enjoyed it, but she'd also learned a doctor needed help to get the job done quickly. The faster an incision was closed, the better.

"Good. I'll have Caleb close the window when he returns. In the meantime, let's get started."

Caleb returned with the water, closed the window, then hovered while they cleaned the instruments and Mr. Kelley's incision area. The doctor tied a mask to his face and motioned Emma to use a large kerchief Caleb retrieved for them. Finally declaring them ready, the doctor ordered Caleb to light several lamps before making him leave. Pleading darkened his eyes as he looked into hers before closing the door.

Once a small amount of ether was applied to ensure Mr. Kelley wouldn't awaken, the doctor made his incision, and Emma dropped a veil over her mind. Donning a mental shroud helped her get through the process. Doc taught her that trick. If she spent much time thinking about what was happening, she'd run from the room.

Each move became instinctive. Swab. Retrieve and hand off instruments. Few words were spoken. Only those needed for direction. Time disappeared. Her shoulders ached. So did her lower back. Weariness set in.

Focus.

"There." The doctor moved some tissue. "See it?"

She handed him the abdominal forceps and took the probe to hold back the tissue. In seconds, he had the slug resting on a cloth on the side table. The doctor probed around a bit more. He grunted.

"Not sure that helped, but it certainly didn't hurt to get that out. Let's close."

After doing their best to clean the wound, they applied the last of the stitches. Emma swabbed the incision with iodine before layering bandages over the site. They both removed their masks, and the doctor dropped onto the chair behind him.

Emma eyed him. He looked exhausted. "Excellent work, Doctor. I wish you and my mentor could have met."

He raised his head. "He taught you well. I've not had such efficient help in many years."

She nodded her thanks and began cleaning the instruments. When finished, the doctor allowed Mrs. Kelley and Caleb to enter. Emma headed for the door.

"Miss Pickett?"

She turned at the doctor's call, wishing she could have escaped unnoticed.

"I'll need you to sit with Mr. Kelley tonight. The risk of infection. . ."

He didn't need to say more. Many died from that very thing after surgery. The Kelleys didn't need to know that.

She nodded. "I'll be right back."

When she'd returned, the doctor was gone, and Mrs. Kelley sat perched on the edge of the chair, staring at her husband. The lamplight flickered, making Mrs. Kelley appear to be shaking. Caleb entered with another chair and placed it opposite his mother. Then he took Emma's hands in his.

"Thank you for all you've done."

"I didn't—"

Caleb was already shaking his head. "I know better."

The intensity and fear in his eyes kept her from arguing. "You're welcome."

He motioned to the chair. "If you need anything else tonight, let me know. I'm in the room at the end of the hall." He turned to his mother. "I'll walk you to the guest room."

"I want to stay a little longer. I promise I'll go to bed soon." Her eyes implored him to understand.

He moved to her side and bent to kiss her cheek. "Very soon. You look tired."

He said his good nights, leaving the women alone. Nervous and not knowing what else to do, Emma checked Mr. Kelley's pulse and temperature. He still felt warm but better than earlier. She positioned the chair so she could see his face, then sat, hoping Mrs. Kelley would retire soon. And to think mere months ago, she'd hoped they'd become friends.

"Emma."

Emma's heart nearly leaped from her chest at Mrs. Kelley's voice, so soft and tender. . .and tired. She looked up, wary. "Yes?"

Mrs. Kelley's lips trembled. Her mouth opened and closed several times. Whatever she wanted to say, the words wouldn't come. She finally stood and headed for the door. Halfway there, she stopped.

"Thank you." Then she walked out.

Emma stared at the vacant doorway. It wasn't much, but it was a start. Too tired to contemplate the lack of warmth, she settled into the chair, glad for the armrests. They'd keep her from tumbling to the floor in case she fell asleep. This would be a long night.

The minutes ticked into hours, then into days as Mrs. Kelley, Caleb, and Emma took turns tending Mr. Kelley. The fever remained. After five days of trying to cool his skin with little change, Emma fought thoughts of Mr. Kelley dying with little success. She even read it in the doctor's eyes that morning before he left.

Emma always watched him at night along with a few hours in the afternoons, and it was wearing on her. Caleb arrived each evening to tend his father. She looked forward to relieving him each night as it gave them some time together, something they'd had little of since they cut down the Christmas tree. Her smile returned as she recalled his words before retiring.

"I know you're just as tired as the rest of us, Em, but you look as fresh as spring flowers."

The fact that he shortened her name established familiarity, a relationship, and she clung to that as the night wore on. Mopping Mr. Kelley's face and neck, trying to cool his fever, helped the time pass. She wouldn't be comfortable until the fever was gone. . .if ever. Once again, she mouthed a silent prayer for his recovery.

Elbow on the armrest and chin propped on her hand, Emma allowed herself to doze. This position would keep her from sleeping too long.

"Don't leave me alone, Daddy."

"I won't be long. Just sit tight, Em. I'll be right back."

Mama left and never came back. What if Daddy did the same? She wiggled on the wagon seat until she could stand it no longer. As she scrambled to the ground, her skirt tore. Daddy would be mad. That didn't stop her from looking for him.

Rounding the corner of the building, she saw a man pointing a gun. Daddy pulled his.

"No!"

Emma jerked upright. Dawn's fingers were just taking hold of the day. How long had she slept?

Mr. Kelley moaned. His hands rubbed at the covers as his head rocked back and forth. Emma felt his forehead. The fever had grown worse. She wrung out the cloth in the water and rubbed it over his face and neck. He moaned. She opened his shirt and placed the cloth on his chest before checking the incision. She dabbed on more iodine and placed fresh bandages over the wound.

"No!" Mr. Kelley's hand shot out, only to fall back on the bed. "No, Joe!"

"Shh." Emma dunked the cloth again and placed it on his forehead. "I'll get you through this." She went to open the window again.

"The money."

She turned.

"I didn't steal." His fingers scratched at the covers. "Split." He tossed his head. "Don't shoot."

Emma returned to the bed. This sounded all too familiar.

"No, Pick."

Emma's scalp tingled as her heart pumped double-time. Her father's name was Joe. Mama's diary said friends called him Pick. She sank onto the chair. Breathing grew difficult. This couldn't be. The man she sought was Charles Little. Mama wrote his name next to that of Leo Norris. Said she was afraid of meeting these men. She wrote of her fear they'd get greedy and kill Daddy for the money.

More mumbling drew Emma closer. Sweat poured down Mr. Kelley's face. His moaning grew more urgent, increasing in pitch and volume.

"Norris!" Mr. Kelley followed the name with a yell before going rigid, then limp.

Emma grabbed her chest as she stood, toppling the chair. Mama never mentioned Mr. Kelley's name. What was his first name? She'd never heard it said. Frantic, she caught his fevered face between her hands to make him stop flailing.

"What's your name?" A sob escaped. "What's your name?" She shook him, rage filling her. "Tell me your name."

Someone grasped Emma's arms and pulled her away from the bed. She fought to return. Hands held her back.

Caleb turned her to face him. "Emma?" His expression conveyed his confusion.

She shoved him away but Caleb refused to let go. Mind spinning, she grabbed his shirtfront. "What's your father's name?"

Caleb frowned. "Why?"

"What's his first name?"

Mrs. Kelley rushed into the room. "Caleb."

He ignored her. "Charles. Why?"

Her ears roared. Her chest tightened. "You changed your name?"

"What are you talking about, Emma?"

She shook her head, wishing she could think clearly. "You've been hiding behind a different name all this while."

Seething, she pushed with every ounce of strength in her body and freed herself from Caleb's grasp. She backed toward the door, looking at both Caleb and Mrs. Kelley. Numerous questions raced through her mind. Only one escaped.

"How could you?"

She ran down the steps and out the front door. Her stomach demanded relief and emptied itself at the first tree. Leaden footsteps carried her to the ladies' quarters. Betrayal carried her heart to desolation.

Chapter 11

Caleb started after Emma. His mother stepped in front of him.

"Don't go."

"What? Why not?" His mother's face was pale, sad. Worse, guilt hovered in her eyes. "You know what she was talking about?"

He stood in indecision. Should he stay and finish questioning his mother or should he go after Emma? Knowing she was probably packing to leave, he sidestepped his mother. He had to keep Emma here.

"Mae." His father's weak voice drifted from the bed.

"Charles." His mother rushed over and kissed his forehead and each cheek. "Oh, Charles, I thought we'd lost you."

His father tried to lift his hand. It fell back to the mattress. As badly as Caleb wanted to question his parents, now wasn't the time. He stood behind his mother. "Welcome back, Dad. You gave us a scare."

"Son." His throat worked to swallow. "Water."

His mother grabbed the glass on the bedside table. She lifted his head and helped him drink. He dropped back to the pillows.

"What happened?"

Yet another question that needed to be answered. When did his father get shot? Caleb remembered him being sick and in bed many years ago. Was that when he acquired and recovered from the bullet? Though he wanted to race after Emma, he waited for his mother's answer.

Please, God, keep Emma from leaving.

His mother took his father's hand in hers. "The doctor removed the bullet from your stomach."

Understanding came slowly. He glanced at Caleb then back at his wife. Caleb silently begged them to explain. If they didn't, he'd demand to know what happened.

Caleb's mother leaned forward. "It's time we tell him, Charles."

Suddenly Caleb's skin prickled. He wasn't sure he wanted to know their secret.

Emma dropped onto her bed and pulled her bag and things from the trunk next to her. This time Gabe wouldn't stop her from leaving. Not bothering to pack carefully, she flung items by the fistful into her bag. When her hand clasped the pistol, she stopped.

The only reason she carried the weapon was for justice. Her father deserved it, now more than ever. She'd met the people who killed him, lived with them, worked for them, knew them now for who they really were.

Just as she dropped a veil over her mind for surgeries, a new veil fell. She stood, the gun clasped in both hands, and walked out the door, across the yard, and back into the main house. The steps, now so familiar, brought her slowly to the bedroom. She moved unhindered to the foot of the bed.

"Emma?"

Caleb's voice called to her from a distance. She lifted the pistol and pointed it at Mr. Kelley.

"Emma! What are you doing?"

Caleb took a step toward her. She cocked the hammer.

"Stay back. This has to be done."

Was that her voice? She turned to Mr. Kelley. She'd thought about this moment for years, yet she still didn't know what to say. . .could never quite picture the man's face until now. There he lay, the murderer she'd despised all these years. All she had to do was pull the trigger. Her finger wouldn't move.

"You killed my father."

Mrs. Kelley stood. "No, he didn't."

Her daze gave way to anger. "You be quiet. I want him"—she shook the gun at Mr. Kelley—"to admit what he did."

"But—"

"Mae. Quiet." He touched her hand. "Like you said, it's time."

Mrs. Kelley sat on the side of the bed, still holding her husband's hand. "You couldn't do this when he's stronger?"

Emma hesitated. Then she pictured her father crumpling after the gunshot. "No." Caleb moved toward her. She took a step back and swung the barrel at him. "I mean it, Caleb. This is going to happen. He's going to confess. . .now."

Caleb shook his head, but she ignored him. She couldn't

trust him. He knew about the gunfight. She motioned to Mr. Kelley. "Tell me."

He struggled to lift his head. "It was an accident."

She waved the gun. "Try again."

"None of it was supposed to happen. I promise." He coughed and took a drink from the glass his wife offered. "Do you know about the money?"

She frowned. "Only what my mother wrote in her diary. She wrote that the war was over but skirmishes continued long afterward. You found a chest of money after one of those fights." He nodded. "She also said she didn't trust you or Norris. She was afraid of you both. With good reason."

"She shouldn't have been afraid of me. Your father and I were friends." He raised his hand when she tried to challenge his comment. "We thought it best to hide the money until we were certain no one could tie us to it. We put the money in a bank in Irontree. We didn't trust Norris, so we only put our names on the account. We figured if Norris had his name on the account, he'd go back and get it all for himself."

"Which is what you did."

"No. I did get the money out, but I waited until the day we decided on. I had every intention of finding your father before he went to the bank."

This was the part Emma knew very little about. From the time her father left her on the wagon to the time she saw him killed, what she knew she'd put together over the years by sheer guesswork. Her mother's diary stated they were to meet at the bank on a certain day and time, then split the money evenly. By all appearances, Mr. Kelley ended up with all the money. His plan worked.

"Keep going."

He took a deep, shaky breath. She wavered. Could she live with herself if he died because of her?

"As you probably guessed, I missed your father at the bank. He found me holding the bag of money at the edge of town and accused me of betraying our friendship."

Emma tossed a scornful look at Caleb. She knew that feeling all too well.

"His hand was on his gun. Before I could explain, Norris showed up and accused us of stealing his share of the money."

"Norris was there?" She didn't remember seeing him, but everything had happened so fast.

Mr. Kelley nodded. "He was standing between two buildings, closer to me than your father. He demanded I throw him the money bag, that he would split the money himself. I told him no and he pulled out his gun"—he pointed a trembling finger at Emma—"about the same time you came around the corner of the building behind your father."

She swallowed, trying to replay the memory she'd repeated in her dreams too many times. "But I saw the gun already in your hand when I rounded the corner."

"Right. I figured between your father and me, we could get the best of Norris." His eyes watered. He blinked several times. "But then you screamed. I heard a gunshot and fired without thinking." A tear ran down his cheek. "Your father shot Norris. Somehow Norris shot both me and your father, and"—he looked her in the eyes then turned away—"I shot you." He shook his head, more tears falling. "I'm so sorry."

Emma's heart thumped a slow, hard beat. Time stalled as her mind went back to that horrible day. She rounded the corner, saw Mr. Kelley holding a gun and also one in her father's hand. Her scream reverberated through her memory, loud and piercing. In the same instant, shots were fired and her father fell.

"It was my scream." She choked on a sob. "My scream killed my father."

Releasing the hammer, she lowered the pistol. She deserved the bullet, not Mr. Kelley. If she were honest, she'd known it all along. Unable to accept the blame, she had poured all her guilt and anger on someone else.

The gun slipped from her fingers and clattered to the floor as she ran from the room.

Chapter 12

The fact that his parents had lied to him, kept so much hidden all these years, scrambled Caleb's emotions into a lump of painful disbelief. The memory of racing out of a town when he was young came back. Gunshots, a man and girl lying on the ground, his parents not stopping to help. His father deathly sick for months. He stared at them now. Words wouldn't come. He needed time. Hearing the front door slam jolted him.

Emma!

He ran after her. Even his mother's call didn't stop him. Confronting his parents could wait. Keeping Emma from leaving couldn't.

Sobbing carried from Skeeter's stall. He found the mule scooting along the wall every time Emma tried to put the saddle on his back.

He stepped inside the pen. "Emma."

She held the saddle between them. "I'm leaving."

If only he could hold her, kiss away her tears. "Not like this. Please, Em."

Gabe arrived at the stall door. Emma slumped, defeat in her eyes. She let Caleb take the saddle and followed Gabe across the passageway. She dropped to the bench like her legs wouldn't hold her any longer. Gabe sat beside her.

"What's wrong, little one?"

Caleb placed the saddle on the rack and joined them. Emma's tears ran unheeded. She dropped her face into her hands.

"I killed my father."

Gabe's mouth dropped open. "What?"

Caleb shook his head, his heart aching for her obvious pain. "No, she didn't."

She looked at him. "I didn't pull the trigger, but I killed him all the same."

"You were a little girl, Em, scared for your father."

"My scream made them shoot."

"You don't know that."

"Your father said as much."

Caleb moved to sit next to Emma. She stood. He hated feeling helpless. "It was all an accident."

She peered into his eyes. "You knew."

"No."

"You recognized my name and, out of guilt, offered me a job."

He stepped toward her. She moved back. "That's not true. I didn't know." How could he make her believe him? "I love you, Em—"

She shook her head and turned her back.

Gabe stood. "Let me talk to her."

His whispered voice was full of emotion. Maybe he could help. He'd stopped her from leaving once before.

Caleb nodded. "Don't let her leave, Gabe. Come find me if she tries."

With each step, Caleb wished he could stay, but the need to confront his parents beckoned him. They'd destroyed lives. How had they lived with themselves all these years? Now that he knew, how could he live with them?

Emma lifted her chin. "I can't stay, Gabe, so don't try making me."

He sat on the bench and patted the spot next to him. "Convince me."

She sighed. There'd be no leaving without talking. She dropped beside him and stared at her hands. Self-loathing had a strong hold of her heart. A peaceful life was now an unreachable dream.

"You don't know what I've done."

"Caleb said you didn't do it."

She shook her head. "Not that." Her throat refused to swallow. "I pointed my gun at Mr. Kelley. I wanted to kill him." She brushed at the tears filling her eyes. "I couldn't handle taking the blame for my father's death, so I poured all my guilt and anger at the only other man I could accuse."

"You didn't know."

She nodded. "I think I did. I just refused to let myself remember that part."

Gabe took a deep breath. "So you've run all these years, and now you want to keep running." He patted her hand. "It won't work, Emma. You have to face this."

She didn't bother arguing. He was right, but she couldn't

go back in that house. She'd avoided the truth all these years. Would it be so bad to continue?

Gabe squeezed her hand. "God brought you here, Emma. Don't you see that? He knows it's time for this story to have an ending so a new one can begin. He put you on the same road at the same time as Caleb and me. He even used Skeeter to make sure you stayed."

Emma choked on her laugh. She'd had the same thought. But it didn't matter. She'd have to live with the truth of her guilt.

Gabe leaned away and reached into his pocket. When he pulled out his hand, a small chain hung from his fingers. A cradle dangled from one end and a cross from the other.

"I made this to remind me that God has a plan for each of us. We all have a beginning and an end. Each link in between is a phase of our life." He held out the chain. "Even Christ's life had a plan, a plan He never broke. His chain is complete." He looked her in the eyes. "You have a chain, too. Near as I can see, going back and facing the Kelley family to clear all this up is one of the links. You sure you want to break your chain by running away?"

"How can I be sure this is one of the links?"

He smiled but his eyes were sad. "Chains get intertwined with those of others. Yours linked with this family the day your father met Mr. Kelley. God had a purpose for you being here, Emma. You were here when Caleb's workman needed help, and you were here when Mr. Kelley fell sick." He leaned forward and peered into her eyes. "Near as I can tell, you're still needed here. Mr. Kelley isn't well yet and Caleb is hurting."

Gabe stood and held out his hand to help her up. "If you

feel you have to leave, I won't stop you. But I do ask that you pray about your decision first. A broken chain can be fixed, but it'll always be weaker than before. I'd like to see your chain remain complete."

He shuffled to the far corner of the barn without looking back. His sadness made her wonder if he felt his chain had been broken. She didn't want to feel that way when she reached his age.

As she watched him smooth the wood for the bedstead, Emma realized that even a rough log could become something beautiful but must first endure some painful shaving and carving. Gabe's wonderful chains were just a piece of wood before he applied his knife.

For years, she'd considered herself ugly and useless. Maybe she, in the care of God's loving, sculpting hands, could one day be a beautiful, useful servant. With a prayer in her heart, Emma wandered back to the house, fearing the cuts that were still needed to shape her.

Chapter 13

"You lied to me."

Caleb faced his mother in the guest room, needing answers to all his questions. He loved his parents dearly, but he'd never been so hurt.

Faceless memories trickled through his mind. "I remember seeing a man and girl on the ground." He moved closer to his mother. "And I remember Dad being sick for a long time. He was recovering from a gunshot, wasn't he? Why didn't you tell me?"

"You were young, Caleb. I didn't want to scare you."

He snorted and shook his head. She still hid behind lies. "When I introduced Emma to you, did you recognize her name?"

She looked down. "Yes."

At least she didn't lie about everything. "So you gave her awful jobs to get her to leave instead of taking the opportunity to make it right."

Her head hung lower. "Yes."

She sounded remorseful, but one more question remained. "Everything Dad told Emma about that day, was it true?"

She looked up. "It was an accident, Caleb. Your father never meant for Joe to die."

"But he meant to get all the money?"

"No. At least I don't think so."

"You don't think so?"

Her eyes pleaded with him. "Talk to your father when he's well, Caleb."

"You tell me. You're apparently of the same mind."

She took a deep breath. "We planned to find out if the girl lived so we could give her half the money."

Caleb snorted. "Do you ever get tired of lying, Mother?"

"It's true. That was our plan."

"So what happened?"

She shrugged, even looked a bit ashamed. "We got busy with the sawmill business and it just got easier. . .not to bother."

He groaned. "Unbelievable."

His heart ached for all that Emma had gone through. The fear, the pain, the anger. He couldn't fault her for pointing a gun at his father.

"And now?"

"I don't know. Talk to your father."

Anger still reigned inside him. "I'm through talking for a while. I need to think."

He walked out, ignoring his mother's pleading for him to come back.

The voices of Caleb and his mother drifted through the wall

of Mr. Kelley's bedroom, though Emma couldn't make out the words. Caleb was angry. That much she could tell. When he stomped away, she fought the urge to go after him. Instead, from the window she watched him ride toward the sawmill.

He said the words she'd dreamed of hearing. He loved her. Were the feelings sincere? Doubts and questions clamored in her mind and warred with her own feelings.

She'd started falling for Caleb almost from the moment she met him. The time they'd spent together over the last two months had made her love bloom. But now that she knew who he was, who his parents were, how could she trust him? He claimed he knew nothing about what had happened, but could she believe him? And if he did know, could she get past the deception and love him without reservation? Too many ifs.

Mr. Kelley stirred. She moved to the bed and checked his pulse and temperature. Though he was still warm, the fever had broken. She'd be able to leave with a clear conscience in the next few days. As she stared at his face, she realized she no longer hated him, though a strange longing still remained. Would that make leaving easier or more difficult?

She returned to the window and took in the view. She'd come to love this place, felt at home here even though the Kelleys had tried to keep that from happening. The tall pines looked like protective sentries, regal in their dark green garb.

Gabe raced across the clearing in a small wagon. He yanked back on the reins in front of the house. His haste made her skin prickle. A feeling of dread twisted through her.

The front door clanged open. "Emma!" Gabe's panicked voice bellowed. "Come quick. Someone's hurt at the mill."

Her knees went weak. Caleb was at the mill.

She sped down the stairs. "Is it Caleb? Is he hurt?"

Gabe took her arm and led her outside. "I don't know."

"What?"

He helped her into the wagon. "I was on my way here and was told to come for you. Nothing more."

Emma held on tight while the horses tore down the lane. All her doubts and questions no longer mattered. Caleb had become a large part of her heart, making it beat irregularly by a look, a smile. Without him, life would be a wasteland.

Please, God, let him be all right.

The moment Gabe stopped the wagon, Emma launched from the seat and ran into the mill. Emma waited for her eyes to adjust to the dim lighting, her chest heaving in fear. She scanned the large room. Men crowded one end of the building. None was the face she sought. Did she not see him because he was the man on the ground? Her nerves screamed.

Please, God!

Then he stood, looking strong and healthy.

"Caleb." She nearly fainted.

Caleb smiled. Emma stood in the doorway, the light behind her giving the appearance of a halo. But that didn't cause the smile. The relief on her face when she saw him was the most beautiful thing on earth. Whether she knew it or not, she loved him.

Gabe held Emma up until Caleb could get there to do it himself. He wrapped his arms around her and knew he wanted to spend the rest of his life doing this very thing. But now, he wanted to hear her say the words.

Love shone from her eyes as she peered up at him. "You scared me."

He laughed. Those words would do for now. He leaned down and received the kiss he'd craved since the first one he stole a lifetime ago. Her arms wound around his neck and held him there.

When he pulled back, cheers rang out from the men. Emma's face glowed red but didn't dim the smile on her face.

"Oh"—she pushed away—"wasn't someone hurt?"

Caleb pulled her back. "Doc's here. He was on his way to check on Dad. Perfect timing."

"And the man?"

He loved Emma's caring heart. "He'll be fine once the cut on his arm heals. An inch further and he might have lost the whole arm." He patted Gabe's back. "Thanks for your help, but I'll make sure Emma gets home."

Home. He knew in his heart this was where he belonged. But he'd leave with Emma if she wouldn't stay.

He turned Emma to face him. "We need to talk."

She placed her fingers over his lips. "I love you, and I'll marry you, and I'll live here with you. But first, you need to clear things with your parents. None of us will be at peace until we all give and receive forgiveness."

Stunned at her insight, Caleb thanked God for bringing Emma into his life. He kissed her fingers then held her hand over his heart. "How did you know?"

Her smile was the warmest he'd ever seen. "God spoke to my heart today, and for the first time, I really listened."

With those words, Caleb knew God had blessed them.

Chapter 14

Emma threw back her covers and nearly leaped from the bed. Christmas morning. She'd never looked forward to this day like she did today.

As she took extra care with her appearance, she thought back over the last two weeks. She and Caleb wasted no time speaking with his parents. The four of them gathered in Mr. Kelley's room. He confessed they'd changed their last name from Little to Kelley, his wife's maiden name, to keep from being arrested in case someone saw what had happened. They ran instead of staying to help for the same reason.

Emma smiled as she recalled what happened next. Speaking from the heart, tears falling, Mr. Kelley apologized for everything. Not only for what happened that day so many years ago, but also for how they treated her when she arrived. Emma hugged Mr. Kelley and promised she'd already forgiven him, bringing an onslaught of tears from everyone.

Without giving anyone a chance to recover, Caleb announced he and Emma were getting married. Emma scolded him later for his terrible timing, but she laughed about it now. When Mrs. Kelley asked if they'd chosen a date, Caleb shocked everyone, Emma included, by choosing the day after Christmas.

Tomorrow. She'd be Mrs. Caleb Kelley tomorrow. A grin spread across her face. He could be an impulsive man. Life as Caleb's wife would be exciting, to say the least.

She descended the staircase, fingering the decorations wrapped around the banister, remembering how she and Mrs. Kelley had spent the last two weeks throwing together wedding plans. A whirlwind would have been more fun, but it gave the two of them plenty of time to truly forgive one another. Her future mother-in-law had a caring heart. Eventually the two of them would be close.

Caleb met her at the base of the stairs, took her hand in his, and placed a warm kiss on her lips. She'd never get enough of those. Instead of leading her into the dining room for breakfast as expected, Caleb took her into the sitting room. The ladies had outdone themselves decorating the room for Christmas. The tree she and Caleb had cut down sat in the corner, decked out in beautiful ornaments.

But the most stunning thing of all was the sight of Mr. Kelley sitting in the large chair next to the tree. Smiling, Emma crossed to him and squeezed his hand.

"Merry Christmas, Mr. Kelley."

"And to you, my dear. I can't think of a better present than to have you here as part of our family today."

Caleb joined them, his eyebrows high. "Does that mean I don't need to give you my gift?"

Mrs. Kelley entered carrying a tray of coffee and cups.

"That's not what he said at all." Her sly smile made them all laugh. She motioned to the corner. "Besides, I'm dying to know what's under all those sheets. When did you bring that in?"

For the first time, Emma noticed a silent Gabe standing beside his hidden creation. She was just as curious as Caleb's mother. She knew what the gift was, but she wanted to see the engraving Gabe had carved into the headboard.

Wanting to give him a hug, she crossed the room. She'd come to love the man like a father and would miss him terribly when he left.

"Merry Christmas, Gabe."

He squeezed her hard. "Merry Christmas, little one." He held her longer, his cheek against hers. "You're lovely, Emma, inside and out."

Throat tight, keeping words from coming, she kissed his cheek. "Thank you for everything, Gabe."

Dishes clinked. "Join us for coffee, Mr. Noell."

Gabe released Emma, allowing her to see his red-rimmed eyes. He cleared his throat. "Maybe another time. I've got a few things that need my attention, but thank you, Mrs. Kelley." He bowed slightly and left.

They only managed a few sips before Caleb's mother set her cup down. "Time for gifts."

Mr. Kelley and Caleb roared with laughter. "We never open gifts this early, Mother."

She pursed her lips. "No time like the present for new traditions."

Caleb laughed, stood, and helped his mother to her feet. "Then help yourself."

Emma took her cup to the window, intending to watch

the unveiling from there. On the sill sat a box with hers and Caleb's names scrolled across the top.

Caleb joined her. "What's that?"

"I don't know, but it has our names on it."

He leaned down, placing his lips next to her ear, sending a shiver through her. "Open it," he whispered.

Together they tore off the paper and flipped open the lid. Inside sat a wooden chain. Emma smiled, knowing full well who had given it to them. She lifted it from the box and held it out to Caleb.

He fingered it, awe evident on his face. "There's no beginning or end. It's a complete circle."

Emma smiled. Gabe had given the perfect gift. Movement outside caught her attention. She looked out the window and saw Gabe's wagon heading down the lane and out the gate. Sadly, the time had come for him to move on. She missed him already. He'd played a huge part in her healing. She said a silent prayer that God would complete Gabe's chain. Then she turned to her future husband, ready to tell him the significance of their gift of the Christmas chain.

Born and raised in southern Minnesota, **Janelle Mowery** spent hours reading a great many books in her childhood years. Janelle now resides in Texas with her husband of twenty-one years and their two sons. Her love of history, mystery, and stories led her toward her dream of writing novels. She began writing her first story in 2001, became a member of American Christian Fiction Writers in 2002, and signed her first contract in 2006. When she's not writing, she loves reading, watching movies, researching history, and spending time in the great outdoors. To learn more about Janelle and her upcoming releases, visit her Web site at www.janellemowery.com.

LOVE CAME HOME
AT CHRISTMAS

by Tamela Hancock Murray

Dedication

To my daughter, Ann.
You make my life a brighter place to be.

Chapter 1

Standing near the welcome warmth of burning logs in the parlor fireplace, Gabriella Noell watched R. C. Sparks erect the newly felled pine tree he had just brought from a forest located near the outskirts of Houston.

"It's gorgeous, R.C." Staring at the tree, she clasped her hands and kept her voice to a low volume in consideration of her father resting in his nearby sickroom. "This is the most beautiful tree we have ever had. Thank you."

R.C. stepped back and admired the pine he had selected for Gabriella. "It is a fine specimen."

She took in a breath, relishing the sweet, crisp scent. "It smells so good. You really have brought Christmas into the house." Wanting him to know how much his gesture meant, she looked unflinchingly into his deep brown eyes. "Without you, we wouldn't have had a tree this year. Thank you."

"Aw, it was nothing." His handsome features, always glowing with ruddy health, lit with modesty.

She couldn't suppress a smile, since he reminded her of a

schoolboy who'd just brought an apple to the teacher. "Come with me into the kitchen and let me give you some of the cookies I baked earlier this morning."

"You don't have to share with me." Despite his protests, he followed her. "I don't want to disfurnish you."

"You won't. I made plenty." She threw him a reassuring smile as they entered the clean, spacious kitchen. Rolls warming for lunch on the wood-burning stove offered a yeasty aroma.

R.C. took in a breath. "Smells mighty good. You baking bread?"

"Just keeping the rolls warm. Care for one?"

"No, I couldn't."

Gabriella fetched a tin from a drawer and packed a dozen cookies. "Perhaps Fern would enjoy a few as well."

"Yes, she would. But that's mighty generous of you. Too generous."

"Not at all. While I'm at it, why don't I send a couple of rolls home for your lunch? Although I'm sure Fern's rolls are much better than mine."

"No!" He cleared his throat. "I mean, that would be mighty kind of you."

She included the bread and handed him the tin.

Unwilling to wait until after lunch, he opened the tin and popped a cookie in his mouth. "Mmm. Delicious." He shut his eyes. "Much better than our cook's. Fern will be lucky to get even one of these. I doubt they'll last until I get home."

Gabriella laughed. "I'm glad you like them. I can always bake more sometime."

"I wouldn't mind that one bit." He closed the tin and

glanced out the window, framed with white cotton curtains. "It's getting late. I'd better go."

She wished she could invite him to stay for lunch, but since she'd baked the cookies and even added rolls, an additional reward seemed too forward. "I understand. Again, thank you."

As he departed, passing the pecan tree that marked their yard, she made a point of not observing him from the parlor's oversize window. She didn't have to watch. An image of his fine features and dark, wavy hair was etched forever in her mind. R.C. had just come into her life thanks to her father's recent illness, when he'd started checking in on them every day. But R.C. would never look to her as a wife. According to Gabriella's friends, he'd spent a decade avoiding marriage to eligible young women in town, and even a well-fixed older widow or two. Why would he look twice at her?

Still, she wished she could have detained him so he could help her decorate the tree. What would it be like to have a husband with whom to share household pleasures? Sighing, she chose an ornament from the Christmas box. Pondering the shape of the wooden star, meant to represent the guiding light the shepherds saw on the night of Christ's birth, she thought about the grandfather who carved it for her fifteen years ago, when she was just a child. The wooden surface felt so smooth, so perfect. Just as her family had seemed perfect back then, before Grandfather left. Unwilling to let a stray tear deter her from decorating the well-shaped, fragrant pine, she placed the star in a prominent spot. She stood back and admired it.

"Thank the Lord for R.C." She wondered why a man so handsome and wealthy displayed no interest in marriage. He seemed to be considerate, even anticipating her wants without her needing to state them. She hadn't been able to bring herself to ask R.C. for a tree. He had thought of surprising her on his own. Smiling, she chose a dove-shaped ornament from the box. Grandfather had carved that one long ago for her parents, when they were newlyweds.

"Gabriella!" Father's voice, in the past so strong, rasped.

An unpleasant shiver ran through her. "Yes?"

"Come here. Now." He coughed.

"Yes, Father." She hovered a moment, wishing she didn't have to abandon her pleasant daydream to tend to her parent. A surge of guilt immediately followed the thought. Father, for all his brusqueness, had been good to her, and she owed him whatever comfort she could give him in his last days.

"Gabriella! Now!"

Stepping up her stride, she prayed his summons didn't spell an emergency as she rushed through the sickroom door. The pine scent gave way to the revitalizing aroma of menthol. Gabriella made a mental note to hang a small wreath inside the sickroom window so Father could enjoy a little Christmas. "I'm here."

"You are a poke." He reached for a kerchief and coughed into it.

Gabriella patted him on the back. "There, there, Father. I'm sorry. I didn't mean to delay." She guided him back onto his fluffy goose down pillow.

"You were never meant to be a nurse. If only Maggie were here. She'd take care of me." He looked heavenward, his eyes misting.

"I miss Mama, too."

"How can you miss her? You don't even remember her."

His frown matched his sharp tone of voice.

Gabriella swallowed. True, she barely had hazy memories of the mother who passed before she was four. But she did miss her. She missed having a mother to nurture and comfort her. If only she could feel the gentle touch of a mother's hand, a hand that would care for her when sadness visited, a hand that would brush her hair and help her style it in ringlets atop her head. A mother who would help her fasten lace to her dresses. A woman she could admire, who would tell her how much she favored her and share memories of her own youth.

Gabriella touched her hand to his and said a silent prayer. *Lord, I realize Father's sickness has made him even more angry. Grant me patience, please. In the name of Thy Son.*

When she spoke aloud, her voice came out as a whisper. "I'm sorry, Father."

His expression softened with memory. "If only the Lord hadn't taken Maggie away. Things would have been so different."

"We've had our happy times. And we have never been in want. The Lord has seen to it that we had more than enough and could share generously with those in need." As soon as she uttered the praises, she wished she could take them back. Her sentiments were sure to upset Father.

"The Lord indeed. I go to church because I have to, not because attending is my desire." He sniffed.

"Oh, Father, please don't say such a thing."

"No one has ever given me a satisfactory answer as to why my heavenly Father gave me an earthly father who abandoned us, leaving us with nothing." He crossed his arms.

"Yes, I know how you feel, Father. But you are a great success on your own. You should be proud." To emphasize her sincerity, she placed a firm hand on his shoulder, a shoulder that had become bony in recent weeks. "Please, don't think about that now."

"I am going to think about it. You won't tell me what to do." He frowned. "Anyhow, that's why I called you in here just now."

"What do you mean?" She withdrew her hand.

"I called to talk to you about your grandpa."

"Now?" She clasped her hands and wondered why the topic had taken on such urgency.

He nodded. "I can hear you shuffling around in the parlor, decorating that monstrosity R.C. brought in here. I can even smell it."

"If the scent bothers you, I can—"

He waved her comment aside. "No, it's not that. You decorating the tree out there makes me think of him all the more. All those ornaments he made, you know."

"I know." Not only had Grandfather fashioned ornaments, but years ago he had found time to make Gabriella a dollhouse, complete with furniture. She had long outgrown the years when she could play, but she'd never found the heart to remove it from her bedroom. Its presence reminded her of him every day. The house also reminded her father, but he responded with resentment when he saw it, whereas to Gabriella the gift represented love.

Father's voice cut into the atmosphere. "Why are you bothering with a tree this year? I don't know if I'll even be able to walk into the parlor long enough to see it."

"Maybe R.C. will help me bring you into the parlor, just long enough to see the tree. Would you like that?" She sat on the side of the bed next to her father, settling into the wool blanket woven from threads devoid of dye.

"I would." For the first time that day, Father's features melted into something like approval. "R. C. Sparks is a fine man. You should look at him twice, you know."

"He'd never look at me twice except as a little sister. Or with pity." She decided not to mention that whether R.C. gave her a thought in the world or not, Gabriella sneaked looks at him from the corners of her eyes whenever he was nearby. With strong, manly features and wavy dark hair, plus dark, flashing eyes, his presence overtook any room whenever he entered. When he left, the place felt vacant no matter how many others might be present. She decided conversation had best remain on their original topic. "So what is it about Grandfather?"

"Your grandfather. Yes. He had his faults, but he loved you. He loved that you're his namesake."

Gabriella had always treasured the idea that she'd been named after her grandfather. When he lived in Houston, Gabe Noell was a man both envied and admired. Always dressed in a black suit and smelling of spicy shaving lotion, he sported a pleasant paunch and a confident attitude that marked his status. She suspected in his prime he'd been quite the hard-nosed businessman, but she never saw that side of him. He only had a soft spirit toward his granddaughter. "Why do you think he liked to carve wood, Father?"

"He learned it as a boy, from his father. I suppose when he grew older, the act of making wood take shape brought back memories of a simpler time." Father let out a burdened sigh. "He worked hard but never seemed to appreciate the luxuries his success afforded. I never understood that about him."

Gabriella decided not to comment on her father's love of fine things. Even the gout he suffered didn't curb his cravings for rich food. "Maybe he wanted you to know more about simple pleasures. He tried to teach you how to carve, didn't he?"

Father nodded. "I just never had the knack for it. Guess that's another reason we never got along."

Try as he might to hide behind a self-evident reason, Gabriella knew better. The final rift came when Gabe decided to relinquish his riches to the poor. Since no one considered Father poor, that meant his—and Gabriella's—inheritance never materialized for them. With his business acumen and determination, Father made his own fortune, but he never let go of his resentment of his own father for his change of heart, and life. After Gabe made his announcement that his son and granddaughter would never see a penny of his fortune, father and son never again spoke to one another. Gabriella wished things were different. With no mother, the emotional support of a loving grandfather would have been welcome.

Father's cough brought her back to the present. His increasing discomfort made her all the more distressed and uneasy.

"May I fetch you a glass of water, Father?"

He shook his head, coughing all the while. "No, but there is something else you can do for me. You can find your grandfather."

She paused, too shocked to respond right away. "Find Grandfather?"

He nodded. "I have a few things I want to say to him before I. . ."

Gabriella stood and looked away from the sickbed. "Don't

say it, Father. I can't bear it."

Father's touch upon her hand turned her back to him. "I know you haven't had an easy life. Oh, some would say it's been too easy, considering our money and position. But you haven't had it easy in the ways that matter most. And that's partially my fault. I don't suppose I should have been so hard on your grandfather."

Remembering his earlier expressions of resentment, this new admission came to Gabriella as a surprise. A surge of sympathy visited her. "Please don't blame yourself. Grandfather was determined to give away his fortune. Nothing could have changed his mind."

"True, but my response could have been different. I—I shouldn't have turned from the Lord when I learned about my father's plans to disinherit us."

"He didn't disinherit us from anything except money."

"Except money. What else is there?" Father snorted.

"He didn't take away the real gifts you got from him. Such as his intelligence and his determination. Without such qualities, you never would have succeeded."

"Yes, I'm afraid I do possess some of his traits."

"All the good ones, I'm sure." Gabriella turned her teasing tone serious. Now that her father had begun to reveal his secrets, she didn't want the opportunity to talk about the Lord to slip away. His illness precluded him from returning to church, so for the time being, she was his only witness. "So, you want things to be better between you and the Lord?"

He pondered her question before responding. "I still don't understand everything the Lord does, but I know I'd be better off with Him than without Him. I hope it's not too late."

"It's never too late, until you pass from this earth."

"You sound like the pastor."

"I'm glad to hear it." She paused. "So you wanting me to find Grandfather is your way of reconciling with God?"

"Part of it. I don't want to leave this earth without saying good-bye to him. If he's still living, that is."

Gabriella felt a catch in her throat. Much as she hated to admit it, Father was right. Grandfather may have gone home to the Lord by now. And if he had, then what? She didn't want to consider the possibility. "What do you want me to do, Father?"

"I want you to find him, of course. And bring him here."

Gabriella pondered the possibility and came up wanting. How could she begin a quest for someone she hadn't seen in years?

As if he heard her question, Father responded. "There's a letter in the top left-hand compartment of my desk. Bring it to me."

Gabriella never ventured into her father's desk. Even sick as he was, that was his domain, and she respected the fact that the papers were none of her affair.

She could tell by Father's demeanor that the letter was important. Curiosity quickening her footsteps, she retrieved the letter and brought it to him.

"It's from your aunt Minnie."

"Aunt Minnie? But she—"

"I know she died. And we didn't go to her funeral. She wouldn't have wanted us there."

Gabriella flinched.

"But the letter is still valuable. Read it."

With sadness at all that had been lost in their family thanks to the bitterness of a few, she opened the letter:

Dear Henry:

I know this letter will come as a shock to you, but I felt I could not remain silent and still sleep nights. I know your father and you are not on the best of terms, but I feel you must know that in recent times, a man moved here. I never would have thought to connect an itinerant wood-carver to the Noell family, but this man looks all the world like Gabe. The same sharp gray eyes—the ones you and your daughter have—and that determined spirit—make me think he must be Gabe. It's quite clear by the way he conducts himself that he doesn't want me to reveal his secret. I can discern that he realizes that I know who he is. It is clear to me that he wants to keep to his new identity, although only the good Lord knows why. You wouldn't believe how he lives, Henry. He accepts alms from people who love his wood carvings. The place he calls home is a hole of a room in a hovel rented out by a woman of questionable reputation. He's so thin that one has an immediate desire to give him something to eat. Yet he seems happier than he ever did when he was flush with money and could buy any number of goods and services. I really don't understand how he could give up everything to live in such squalor, but he has. I buy the occasional carved trinket from him, just to keep my conscience clear, but I have the distinct impression most of my money goes to street urchins and other types of undesirable people. You do realize, of course, that our brother Frank would be quite vexed if he knew, so don't say a word.

Don't trouble yourself in answering. I am well as ever and you have no need to worry about me. I trust you will be discreet and not mention this little missive to anyone. I just feel better knowing that I have told you that your father is alive—barely—here in Dallas.

Yours,
Minnie

Gabriella envisioned her grandfather as this new, strange man. The image left her feeling a number of emotions, not all pleasant. "So you know where Grandfather is, and you didn't tell me?"

"I didn't have a reason to tell you because I wasn't going to look for him. Besides, he moves from place to place. Who knows if he's still there or not? Or if he ever was."

Thoughts of what could have happened to her beloved grandfather came unbidden into Gabriella's mind. She urged them away with such force that her head shook. "If only we'd been closer to Aunt Minnie. Then we could have written back and learned more."

"Perhaps, but I was lucky she wrote even then. As you can see, she told me not to write back, and I never dared go against her request." The pained look on Father's face as a response made her wish she'd remained silent. Father had alienated almost everyone in his family, including Gabriella's aunts and Uncle Frank, who all sided with Grandfather. "She never forgave me, you know. And neither did your aunt Dorcas. For your sake, I wish they had. Perhaps they could have been a substitute of sorts for your mother."

The thought had crossed Gabriella's mind over the years, but what would be accomplished by whipping a frail man on his deathbed about past errors? She reached for practicalities to console him with. "Oh, Father. You know Aunt Minnie was happiest with her cats, and Aunt Dorcas would never leave Arkansas."

A faint smile was her reward. "How right you are. I must say, I'm surprised you remember so much."

"They were both formidable. And who could forget Grandfather." Gabriella's thoughts returned to her mysterious grandfather. Thinking of his possible death, she cast her gaze to her father's nightstand. She noticed the Bible, a book he had seldom consulted until recent times.

"I know what you're thinking, and I hope it's not too late. I'm praying he's still there."

"How will we find out? We have no address."

"There is only one way. You will have to go to Dallas and find him."

Chapter 2

Fern's shrill voice sounded from the kitchen. "Come to dinner, R.C."

R.C. moved with no urgency to comply. Cook's night off was his least favorite of the week. His sister's meals didn't please him. Thankfully, they could save money by hiring a maid only three days a week, so he could eat well most nights.

He wished he could keep a full household staff and afford to host elaborate dinner parties to attract eligible bachelors for Fern. Her plain looks and lack of ladylike tact made most potential suitors shy, but she deserved to marry well, and if she did, he would need to fend only for himself. His inheritance money wouldn't last forever, especially not after he made that bad loan earlier in the year, which wiped out more of his bank shares than he cared to contemplate. He had new deals cooking around the Houston area, but the real estate venture in Dallas was a once-in-a-lifetime opportunity sure to shore up his remaining nest egg. With the city attracting new people, he hoped to sell whatever land he could snap up to another speculator for a healthy profit.

"R.C.!" Fern's voice sounded more insistent.

"Coming!" He stuffed his copy of *The Houston Post* in the wooden container beside the leather chair and headed toward the kitchen. The scent of something burnt floated in the air, although Fern had managed to salvage enough for a meal. Awaiting him was a plate of mashed potatoes with visible lumps and a piece of beef that looked tough and dry as shoe leather, along with a hard roll. He thought of Gabriella and wished she had included more bread along with the delicious cookies.

R.C. strengthened his voice to make his blessing ring with genuine gratitude for the repast, afterward resolving to ask Cook to leave two portions of her vegetable stew the following week for Fern to reheat—if she could even manage that. He cut into the beef and discovered he needed to saw with his knife to make a dent.

Fern observed his struggle. "Sorry I scorched the gravy, but nobody ever died from dry meat."

"This too shall pass." With the heart of an adventurer, he placed the beef in his mouth.

She buttered a roll. "I've been meaning to ask you a question. You can wait until after the start of the new year to go to Dallas, can't you?"

He wondered what prompted her to query. "I doubt it. That land deal won't wait forever. Thompson says some others are looking mighty hard at it. I'm taking a chance to wait at all. Just be glad we can celebrate Christmas Day here before we have to head on out."

"Oh, what's so special about Dallas, anyway?"

"It's growing by leaps and bounds. I expect the population will hit ten thousand before we know it. I think land near the city will only grow more valuable as time passes."

"So the land deal will be your Christmas gift, I suppose." Fern sighed. "I've been waiting to see what you might put under the tree for me. I hope it's better than the casserole dish you gave me last year."

He didn't conceal his surprise at her evident disappointment. "But you needed a fresh dish. You broke ours, remember?"

"As though you would let me forget."

"I'll try not to mention it again. But as for this year, I didn't put your present under the tree yet because you'll be able to guess what it is as soon as you pick up the package, no matter how thick the tissue paper I use to conceal it. I splurged on a special item that, I assure you, was not easy for me to acquire." When Mrs. Matthews decided to rid her house of several old volumes, R.C. had purchased her copy of *The American Frugal Housewife: Dedicated to Those Who Are Not Ashamed of Economy*. He had been proud of himself for scooping up such a rare find. Surely reading the book and following its advice would improve Fern's life.

A knowing smile crossed her lips. "I saw that the gold locket I wanted is missing now from the store window. It wouldn't happen that a certain brother of mine plans to surprise me, would it?"

His pleasure evaporated. So his sister had wanted a frivolous trinket instead of an informative book. He searched for a preemptive way to mitigate her disappointment. "But you have so many nice necklaces. Mother left you more than one for every day of the week."

"I know, and I treasure them all. Too much, in fact. I fear that if I wear them every day, they'll get damaged, and I'll never forgive myself." She fingered the cameo she wore on a gold chain, a favorite carved from precious ivory.

He weighed his words. "I can't promise a necklace, but I do hope you'll like what I did choose. I suppose you'll have to find a husband who'll buy you trinkets."

She stared at her coffee. "You're right. I can't expect my brother to be sentimental. At least I know now, so I won't be terribly vexed on Christmas Day." She came close to batting her eyelashes at him. "So as a consolation, might we wait until after the New Year to leave?"

"Why?" He used the opportunity of waiting for her to answer to try a forkful of potatoes. As expected, lumps abounded.

Fern pouted. "I want to go to the cantata, and Margaret Owens told me she's hosting a big meal the first week of January for all of us in Mrs. Harper's Sunday school class. That includes you, of course. And I think she might be inviting a few of her other friends. It should be quite the soiree. We may meet lots of new people. Doesn't that sound exciting?"

R.C. couldn't have cared less. Not that he minded their friends, but staying home by the fire with a good book fascinated him more than forcing himself to make idle talk with a bunch of silly womenfolk—all hoping for marriage and a chance at his fortune—fluttering in his midst. None of them appealed to him as did Gabriella Noell.

Letters from solicitors, land dealers, and bankers had

awaited his responses that morning, but what had he done? Swayed by Gabriella's wistful observations about Christmas trees, he had spent the morning chopping the finest one on the Millers' property. With their permission, of course. And to think he never would have made Gabriella's acquaintance if Tyler Boswell, who did business with him and Henry Noell, hadn't asked R.C. to check in on them now and again.

He felt sorry for Gabriella. A beauty indeed with rich golden hair and gray eyes, she stayed cooped up in the house with her crotchety father. She dressed in a manner befitting her father's wealth, suggesting to R.C. that she was just as spoiled and demanding as Fern. Yet she possessed a spirit that made him want to draw closer. "I don't suppose Gabriella Noell is invited."

"Gabriella? Why, she's never invited to anything, she's such a recluse."

"I think she'd be popular if she went to more parties. From the looks of her dresses, her father spends at least as much money as I do on female attire."

"There you go again, fussing about my clothing allowance. I might have known you had an ulterior motive for asking about Gabriella. No wonder you're still a bachelor. No woman in her right mind would marry a skinflint like you. Although she doesn't know you're so cheap, does she? She just thinks you're her knight in shining armor, running over there to help her every day. So do you want me to get her on the list of invitees?"

"Oh no, don't do that." He never wanted Gabriella to think he was pursuing her. "No, I was just wondering."

"Wonder away, but I want to stay here long enough to

go to all the festivities. No need for me to be a social outcast all my life. It's high time for me to set my cap for one of the bachelors. I just haven't decided which one yet."

Since they had moved to Texas from the river bluff town of Lexington, Missouri, to better their business and personal prospects, R.C. knew his sister had set her cap for more than one bachelor, but so far she hadn't had any takers. If only their mother had lived, perhaps she could have taught her daughter the finer points of etiquette. But as it was, R.C. did well to keep his business prospects humming. He had no time or money for extras. Except for Gabriella's Christmas tree. "Are any of those sugar cookies left?"

"The ones Gabriella gave you for putting up the tree?"

"Are there any others?"

"You know I'm terrible at baking. And anyway, I ate the last one. I thought you saved it for me. Sorry."

So much for a dessert to redeem the dreadful meal. He held back a groan.

"So we can stay here until after the New Year?" She cocked her head in anticipation of a favorable response.

Cookie deprivation had soured his mood. "I'm sorry, but I don't think I can wait."

She pouted. "Can't I stay home, then?"

He wished she could. "No, I don't think a lady should be alone."

"I could stay with Alma."

"No, we will not impose on her family. Besides, we won't be gone long."

"I'll be so bored." She stirred her potatoes with her fork.

"I'm sorry, but that's the way it has to be." He was sorry.

Sorry he felt compelled to take his sister with him. She would indeed be bored, and be a handful. He vowed to make the trip as short as he could.

Gabriella heard her father yelp. She ran to him and found him gasping for air, red-faced. She struck him on the back, trying not to show her panic. "Father, are you all right?"

He shook his head before collapsing onto the pillow. Ragged breaths escaped his lips, convulsing his whole body.

Seeing him struggle panicked Gabriella. "What shall I do?"

"Fetch. . .Dr. . . .Snow."

Dr. Snow stopped by often to check on Father, but not because Father asked. Gabriella had made certain the doctor's visits were regular. For Father to make the request, this couldn't be good. "Yes. Of course."

Having no choice but to disregard Father's past admonition that ladies should not wander the streets of Houston alone, she grabbed her lightweight morning coat from the front hall closet, slid into it, and rushed several blocks through chilly, sunny weather to the doctor's white clapboard house. Winded with exertion by the time she reached the front porch, she pulled the heavy brass door knocker to summon him.

"Please, Lord, I beg Thee to let him be home."

No sooner did the prayer leave her lips than the doctor, a familiar figure with white hair and a mustache to match, answered.

She eyed the black medical bag he held and noticed he wore his hat. "Oh. I caught you at an inopportune time. An emergency?" That would mean her father would have to wait.

"Judging from your red cheeks, you hurried to see me. You must be the one with an emergency. Your father?"

She nodded. "He's had another spell. This one's worse than the last. He asked me to fetch you."

"That's not like him at all." He looked up the street, in the opposite direction of the Noell house. "Mrs. Smith just went into labor. She can wait a spell. Come on, let's go." He shut the front door behind him. The motion made the door knocker *clank*.

"Thank you." Relieved though she was, she couldn't help but feel a bit guilty about delaying the doctor's arrival to Mrs. Smith's bedside. She said a silent prayer for the expectant mother.

Once they were at the house, Gabriella didn't have to direct the doctor to the sickroom. He'd been a visitor too many times.

Anxious, Gabriella stood in the parlor by the tree. She clasped her hands, shut her eyes, and prayed for a miracle. "Heavenly Father, I beg Thee to heal him."

After a few moments alone with her father, the doctor returned to her, shaking his head. "This spell seems to be worse than the last."

Her stomach clenched. She knew he spoke the truth, but she had hoped for better news.

"Gabriella, I think you'd better sit here on the sofa."

Her stomach clenched another degree as she obeyed. "What is it?"

The doctor joined her on the sofa. "I have seen many men at the end of their life's journey. Your father is strong, and he has a will of iron, but even with those factors in his favor, it's not looking good for him. I think you have no choice but to prepare yourself for your father to depart this life."

Gabriella's throat closed. She never deluded herself into thinking Father would regain full vigor, but hearing the doctor utter such a grim prognosis left her chilled. "Are you sure?"

"I believe in the power of Providence, and Providence may speak by granting your father many more years here on this earth. But barring the intervention of Providence, I am quite certain your father's time is short."

Gabriella was too stunned to cry the tears she wanted to shed. Sniffling, she reached for her cotton handkerchief hidden in her skirt pocket.

"I'm sorry to deliver such news." He cleared his throat. "Has he gotten his affairs in order?"

At least the practical question gave her a concrete matter to divert her attention. "Yes. Our lawyer assures me all is well. Only, I have to do something. I—I have to leave for Dallas." As though she could depart that moment, she rose and started toward her room. She stopped herself and swirled back toward the doctor. "Oh—but it's too late now." Her wail made her sound like a babe, but she couldn't help herself.

"Too late for what?"

"For me to find Grandfather. I must go to Dallas right away. Father wants to reconcile with him after all this time."

A look of understanding lit the doctor's eyes. "Not an uncommon deathbed wish. That's a time when we reassess and visit our regrets."

"I must find a way to go to Dallas, but I know Father won't let me make the trip unescorted, no matter how dire the situation."

The doctor grasped his chin, his forehead wrinkled in thought. "Providence may be on your side in this matter. Just the other day R. C. Sparks told me he's heading out that way to investigate some business venture of his."

She twisted her lips. "R.C. and his ventures. Some say he's always chasing rainbows, but from what I hear, he's quite the businessman."

At that moment, the front door opened with a *creak*. Pamela Evitts, their next-door neighbor, had felt welcome to enter without knocking for as long as Gabriella could remember. "Who's this that's always chasing rainbows?"

Miss Pamela's manners left Gabriella conflicted. On the one hand, the older woman did care about Gabriella and her father, and her advanced age demanded that they respect her. On the other hand, Miss Pamela didn't mind taking advantage of her considerable years to speak her unedited mind and not conceal her busybody tendencies. Gabriella decided not to respond.

"Howdy, Miss Pamela." Dr. Snow stood in acknowledgment of the entrance of a lady into the room. "How is your rheumatism today?"

The older woman rubbed the small of her back as though she just remembered her condition. "That liniment you gave me helps some, but it doesn't stop it entirely. I'll manage as best as I can. At least it's not raining today." She looked straight into the doctor's eyes. "So who's chasing rainbows? It sure can't be Henry." She nodded in the direction of Father's room.

"R. C. Sparks, that's the one," Dr. Snow said.

Gabriella held back a grimace.

Miss Pamela cackled. "Oh, that one's a sourpuss. Too sour

for a man as rich as he is. And he's going to get richer, too, what with going off to buy up more land."

"So that's his plan." Dr. Snow rubbed his chin once more.

"Real estate speculation, yes sirree. Takes money to make money." She clucked her tongue. "That inheritance he got can't last forever, I don't imagine. Surely he's trying to shore up whatever's left."

Dr. Snow lifted his index finger. "No amount of money can last forever once one starts on a spending spree, but I understand R.C.'s got plenty of land and railroad interests to keep him afloat."

Miss Pamela nodded once. "Yes, he's been successful ever since he came out here from Missouri River country."

Irritated by the exchange, Gabriella couldn't resist intervening. "Perhaps, but I don't understand what any of R.C.'s ambitions have to do with me."

Dr. Snow's bushy eyebrows rose, reminding Gabriella of doves in flight. "I merely have the notion that you can accompany him on his trip."

She gasped. "Doctor, I could never do that, even for a mission of mercy."

Miss Pamela cocked an eyebrow. "What's all this?"

Dr. Snow was all too eager to bring Miss Pamela up-to-date.

"You—you mean you know where your grandfather is?" Miss Pamela wore shock on her pale face. "Why didn't you do something about it?"

"Father wasn't ready. He revealed his desire to me only two hours ago, as his mortality finally trumped his pride."

"Oh my." Miss Pamela's expression changed to that of a person reminiscing.

"Are you quite all right?"

Miss Pamela ignored the question. "Why, I remember Gabe well. He was such a handsome man." When she spoke, years rolled off her face, and Gabriella could visualize her as a comely woman, decades younger. "He used to walk me to church, you know."

"I remember that," Dr. Snow said. "For a while people thought the two of you were courting."

Miss Pamela blushed. "My, my, I wouldn't presume to call it such a thing. But we did have many a pleasant conversation. I missed him when he left. And I think of him from time to time now. Imagine, seeing him again."

"If. . ." Gabriella couldn't bring herself to complete her sentence.

"If what?"

"We don't know he's still alive, or if we can find him. My aunt didn't seem to think he was in very good health."

"Oh. Well, I'm certain he is. I can feel it in my bones. You do need to take Dr. Snow's advice to fetch him and bring him back here."

Gabriella suppressed a groan. She knew as soon as Dr. Snow presented his side of the story, Miss Pamela would agree. She reached for the most logical argument. "I told Dr. Snow before you dropped by that I can't make such a trip unescorted, but going with a man would be even worse for my reputation."

Dr. Snow's mouth dropped open in surprise. "But my dear girl, you won't be without a chaperone. I am shocked that you'd think I'd suggest such a thing. The two of you wouldn't be alone. He's taking Miss Fern."

"Fern?" She suppressed a giggle. Known for her contrary

nature and impatience for inconvenience, Fern wouldn't enjoy traveling across the state. "I don't imagine they would be happy companions."

"All the more reason for you to join them. You would be a great source of company and comfort for Fern." Miss Pamela looked to Dr. Snow. "Don't you agree?"

"Yes, I think you should go and keep Miss Fern company." He winked. "And I'll wager R.C. might like to have a pretty face come along, too."

Gabriella felt heat rise to her cheeks in spite of herself. True, R.C. had done nothing but shown kindness to her, especially since Father became ill. But the doctor exaggerated his interest, surely. "Oh, he's been kind to me in the name of Christian charity. That's all. Please don't read too much into it." Her gaze flew to the Christmas tree R.C. had chopped for her. Catching herself, she returned her gaze to the good doctor.

He responded with an argument. "Nevertheless, I think it's the only way you'll find your grandfather, at least in time to bring him back here for reconciliation."

"But what about Father? I can't abandon him now." Her gaze fell upon the door to the sickroom. This time, she let it linger.

"You have a cook and laundress, and my wife can come in twice a day to tend to him."

Gabriella calculated the hours of the day. "Yes, I think someone would be with him almost all the time with a schedule like that. Maybe I can leave, after all."

Chapter 3

R.C. knocked on the burnished front door of the pristine white Noell house. Though he was always welcome and was arriving at his usual afternoon time, he didn't want to be intrusive.

When Gabriella opened the door, her smile looked brighter than usual. Then again, any time the blond beauty graced him with her presence, the room brightened.

"Your father must be feeling better today." He tipped his hat.

Her eyes widened. "Oh?" She stepped aside and allowed him to enter.

"You look so cheerful."

"Oh." Her averted eyes, followed by her blush, made him wonder if she was glad to see him. "I—I wish I could say he's better. In fact, he's worse."

He watched her close the door. "I'm sorry to hear that. I won't linger, then, unless there's something you need."

"I don't have any immediate needs, but I'd be happy for you

to share a cup of coffee with me. Offering a little bit of liquid warmth in this December weather is the least I can do to show my gratitude for how well you look after us."

"I don't mind." He followed her into the kitchen. Watching her pour coffee from a pot waiting on the stove, R.C. thought back over the past three months, when he first started taking an interest in the Noells. Henry Noell's reputation as a hard man left him with few friends. Little was known about his daughter, Gabriella. He was aware she'd been named after the father who abandoned Henry and that Henry protected her like a precious jewel. Rarely did he grant her permission to leave the house except to attend church. R.C. and Fern had lived not far from them since they moved from Missouri. In those few months, he'd had no reason to think much about them until he'd become their guardian of sorts.

Gabriella sat in the chair next to his at the table in the nook. "A penny for your thoughts."

"Oh, I was just thinking about how much I like coming by here. Hope I'm not too much of a bother."

"Of course not. Although what I'm about to ask might cause you to think I'm a bother to you." As if to distract herself, she poured milk into her coffee and stirred.

He couldn't imagine how someone so beautiful could ever be a bother to anyone, much less himself. "So what is your request?"

She took in a breath. "I would like to accompany you and Fern on your trip to Dallas. Dr. Snow told me you plan to leave soon."

What possessed her? Had she suddenly decided she wanted adventure? He thought about the sick man resting just steps away from them. "I must confess my surprise. Surely this is not the time to take a trip, though no doubt you feel the need for adventure."

"I'm not going for pleasure. I will be on a mission. I promised Father I would try to find Grandfather so they can reconcile before Father passes."

Reconciliation. R.C. could understand why Gabriella thought the matter urgent. The War Between the States had torn asunder R.C.'s family. His father and uncle had once been close, but when Father fought for the Confederacy and Uncle Norton chose to wear the Union's blue uniform, the two men never reconciled. Both perished in battle, and never would they have a chance to mend their relationship this side of heaven.

Gabriella's voice brought him to the present. "I have reason to believe Grandfather is in the Dallas area. I must find him. Please, R.C., you have to take me with you."

Asking for help no doubt chagrined her. The look of an innocent begging for mercy did have its appeal, but to take her on such a journey would be burdensome. "Because I have two meetings planned along the way, I will be traveling by personal conveyance, so the trip promises to be tiring. Taking my sister along is trouble enough without adding another female." He grimaced. "I won't be around much to see to you ladies, and certainly not around often enough to provide you with entertainment. As you know, I'll be tending to business much of the time."

"All the more reason for me to go. I can offer excellent company and conversation for your sister. I know we haven't always been on the most intimate terms, but we get along well enough. In fact, I'd enjoy the chance to get to know her better."

"Is that so?" He couldn't imagine what his spoiled sister and this self-sacrificing young woman would have in common.

She put on a winning smile. "And besides, I'd love to learn more about business. I find it fascinating."

He noticed her fine housedress. "Do you, now? Most women of my acquaintance care only about the results of sound business practices. That is, having enough money to buy a dress and bottle of rose water."

Her face darkened. "Considering my father's recent illness, dresses and rose water have been the least of my worries."

"I'm sorry. I reckon you've had a rough time."

"No, I shouldn't have been so sour. At least I still have my father. And hopefully now, a grandfather, too." Not willing to listen to any more protests, she hurried to change the topic. "I was named after him."

"I heard that. His name is Gabe, right?"

"That's right. Gabriel Noell. But he goes by Gabe." The corners of her mouth turned downward. "I'll never forgive myself if I don't find him."

"It's that important, is it?"

"Very. It's Father's dying wish. And I'm afraid I don't have long. I just need to visit every boardinghouse in Dallas until I find him. I hope."

The task sounded daunting. "And your father has agreed you should make this journey?"

"Yes. I don't think he would under normal circumstances, but he—he realizes his condition is dire."

Pity pulled at R.C. What must it feel like to know you're at death's door and there's not a thing you can do about it? How could he turn down a dying man's request? "Well, I suppose

I can do that much. I'm afraid you'll be mighty bored, though. And I don't promise we'll be staying in the best accommodations. The journey promises to be difficult and dusty."

"Fern will be miserable along with me, I suppose. We can take comfort in one another. Oh, and as for accommodations, I will pay more than my fair share of expenses."

R.C. wished he were in a position to decline her offer, but with his coffers dwindling, he couldn't afford to take on an extra mouth to feed without financial consideration. "Very well."

She took in a breath and rewarded him with a beaming smile. "Do you really mean it? You'll allow me to join you?"

"Yes, I mean it."

"When will we leave?" She cast a worried look in the direction of the sickroom. "The sooner the better."

At that moment, R.C.'s plans changed. "Be ready tomorrow at dawn."

Chapter 4

A t the appointed time, the coupe carriage started toward Dallas. Once they left the Houston vicinity, the road became bumpy and unpredictable. Sharing enclosed space with Fern while R.C. drove them perched in front, Gabriella forced herself to be cheerful despite the high emotion and anticipation the trip meant for her. With eagerness, she peered out the window. "Aren't we blessed that the Lord gave us such good weather for our trip? Why, I hardly need my morning coat."

Fern shrugged. "I wish it were spring, so we could see bluebonnets in the fields."

"Maybe we can make the trip again then." Gabriella smiled to display more enthusiasm than she felt by the suggestion. The landscape was more brown than green this time of year.

"Are you always this cheerful?"

"I try to look on the bright side, yes."

Fern turned and knocked on the window to get R.C.'s attention. "I'm bored! When will we stop to eat?"

"You just ate," R.C. snapped.

"I'm hungry." Fern crossed her arms.

"You can't be hungry. You aren't doing a thing but sitting there."

Gabriella didn't want to say it aloud, but she had to agree. They weren't exerting themselves to sit, even though they bumped along over roads that in some places were little more than old trails.

Fern pouted and looked out the window.

"Maybe we can play a game to keep us from being so bored." Gabriella looked outside for inspiration. "Perhaps we can see who can spot the most different breeds of birds. Or we can look for one in particular. Maybe a mockingbird. Or we can listen for their calls and songs."

Fern snorted. "That doesn't sound like much fun to me."

"I have a backgammon game packed in my trunk. I'll bring it out tomorrow so we can play."

"I'm not sure I know how to play backgammon."

"I can teach you. Father and I used to play all the time."

"Why did you waste all your time playing games with your father?" Fern gave her a quizzical look. "You're lovely. Too lovely to sit around the house with an old man."

Gabriella wasn't sure how to respond. She felt complimented by Fern's observation. And knowing Fern's reputation for bluntness, she knew Fern spoke the truth as she saw it. On the other hand, she didn't like that Fern said she wasted time with her father, and the unflattering reference to her father's age. "I don't feel that any time spent with my father was ever wasted."

"Well, aren't you the self-righteous one."

She flinched. Perhaps her snappish attitude with Fern did seem self-righteous. "I'm sorry if I sounded arrogant, but I meant what I said. I treasure the times I spent with Father."

"Even if he's known to be rather vexing?"

The coupe came to a halt, and R.C. disembarked to help the women exit the coach.

Gabriella noted that the rough-hewn way station promised no luxury, but no doubt R.C. did well to locate accommodations of any description along this road.

Fern sniffed. "I wish we could show you better hospitality than this sorry ride, Gabriella. Not to mention, what type of food will a questionable place like this have?"

"No matter what it is, you'll eat it and like it." Seeming to regret snapping at his sister, R.C. softened his tone. "This way station is the only place we can stop for a prepared meal in this region."

"That can't be right," Fern argued.

R.C. stopped her cold. "I have an appointment to keep between here and there."

The roadside shanty was as promising on the inside as it had been on the outside. Dressed in a stylish traveling suit, Gabriella looked out of place amid the ruffians, as did Fern, though to a lesser degree. Gabriella couldn't help but notice that several men looked her way. Fewer surveyed Fern with such interest.

R.C. took Gabriella's arm and escorted her to a table, keeping Fern close all the while. "Sorry this is a bit rough." When he whispered in her ear, she noticed his breath felt warm, inviting.

"That's quite all right. I'm not on this trip to be treated like a queen."

A bulky man with a missing front tooth interjected, "You sure look like a queen, all dressed up like that." His tone mocked her.

"Now you listen here." R.C. narrowed his dark eyes and leaned into the man's face. Gabriella could only imagine the stench of breath R.C. had to endure. "We are only here to have a meal. We're not looking for trouble, and I'll thank you to keep your observations about this fine lady to yourself."

"What about the other one?" The new inquiry came from a short, bearded fellow. "Can we talk about her?"

R.C.'s glare deepened. "I'll thank you to keep your opinion about my sister to yourself as well."

"Yer sister? How's about that? You'll thank us or what?" An ominous glint entered his eyes.

R.C. looked him in the face without flinching. "As I said, we are not here to cause you trouble. We're just weary travelers, looking for a quick meal, after which we'll be on our way."

Though R.C. made no threat, his stance and manner told everyone in the room that he meant business. Gabriella couldn't imagine what it would be like to be a man threatened by another man, but she knew she wouldn't want to tangle with R.C. at that moment. She didn't know when she'd ever felt more proud of him.

The men made no more trouble, and as R.C. promised, their party didn't dawdle over their meal. Gabriella noticed that R.C.'s demeanor seemed as relaxed as if he were in his own dining room. Fern didn't indicate nervousness, either. Gabriella tried not to seem too jumpy.

She held on to R.C.'s arm for dear life as they departed. As soon as they were out of earshot of the bullies, she felt free to speak. "You were brave to face that man like that."

"Brave, nothing. We have just as much right to be there as anyone else. Besides, I promised your father I wouldn't let anything happen to you. And I won't."

Gabriella couldn't help but feel a little disappointed. But why? Did she really hope she had touched R.C. in some way, beyond being a responsibility to her father? Was she merely a paying passenger?

Sitting in her seat, she sighed in spite of herself.

"Tired?" Fern asked.

"A little, maybe."

"Maybe later we can play that game you suggested. You know, the one where we watch for birds. I didn't realize before you got me started on looking for birds how fun it could be to spot a red cardinal."

"Not to mention the woodpecker. Wasn't he gorgeous?"

"He was. Maybe I'll invest in a pair of binoculars for the future."

"Perhaps the two of us can go bird-watching sometime."

Fern smiled, giving Gabriella hope that maybe a friendship between them could develop.

After a long afternoon of travel, filled in part with bird sightings and waiting for R.C. to meet with a businessman, they stopped for the night at a town with a small hotel. These accommodations looked more friendly than any other they'd seen but not much more friendly. Eating a tender piece of beef and sweet potatoes, plus rolls with preserves, they could relax and look forward to what they hoped would be a restful evening. The table that the party of three shared gave them enough room that they could engage in some conversation.

"I'm sure your father will be grateful when you find your grandfather." Fern slid her fork into a slice of pecan pie.

Gabriella pictured the grandfather she remembered. "I'm looking forward to seeing him. I miss him terribly."

"How can you? He left when you were a little girl."

"I know. But I have the Christmas tree ornaments he carved for me. And a beautiful dollhouse. You'll have to come over and see it."

"I've never seen the dollhouse, but you'd like the ornaments, Fern," R.C. noted between bites of his own slice of pecan pie. "They're all fine examples of expert wood carving. I can see why Gabriella's aunt said he makes a living from his artwork."

"Finding him will be only part of the excitement of being in Dallas." Fern looked beyond their table, skyward, as if dreaming.

"What's so exciting about Dallas?" Gabriella couldn't resist asking.

Fern nearly dropped her fork. "Haven't you heard? Terrible outlaws ride through Dallas all the time."

R.C. set down his napkin in an abrupt manner. "Fern, must you vex Gabriella?"

"I'm not vexed." Gabriella had been so intent on finding her grandfather that she hadn't considered there could be more danger than what they had encountered at lunch. Besides, she was with R.C., and he'd made it clear he'd protect her. "Uh, outlaws?"

Fern became animated. "Yes. They are quite desperate. Did you know Belle Starr was arrested for robbing a bank while she was dressed as a man?"

"Belle Starr? Who's she?"

Fern gasped. "You don't know who Belle Starr is? Why, she's only one of the most notorious outlaws around Dallas."

"Now, Fern, not everyone is as fascinated by the darker side of life as you are. Besides, you're scaring Gabriella. We don't want her to think she's not safe with us." R.C.'s eyes spoke a mixture of concern and protection.

"I think the idea of outlaws swarming all over Dallas is terribly exciting." Fern grinned.

"Terribly exciting until you get shot." R.C. snorted. "Now enough of this talk. We all need to turn in for the night. Fern and Gabriella, I have arranged for the two of you to share a room. I hope that suits."

"Really? I was hoping for some privacy." Fern looked to the ceiling and back. "Leave it to my cheap brother to try to save a few dimes any way he can."

Gabriella felt disappointed that the prospect of sharing a room with her was so distasteful to Fern. "I don't mind paying for my own room, and if necessary, half of yours as well."

"You'll do no such thing, Gabriella," R.C. admonished. "What has gotten into you, Fern? Have you forgotten every trace of manners you learned?"

"But—"

"No buts." A thought seemed to cross R.C.'s mind. "Unless, of course, you don't want to share a room, Gabriella."

"I—I don't mind. Why, I was looking forward to it." Gabriella patted Fern's hand. "We can get to know one another better, Fern. But really, if need be I can sleep on my own."

"No, it's settled. You'll room together."

Gabriella was sorry to see the meal end, since it meant that R.C. would separate from them. The innkeeper showed the women to a modest room. Twin iron beds had clean sheets but the mattresses sported indentations from previous patrons.

"Looks as though George Washington slept here."

Glad to hear Fern joke, Gabriella played along. "Maybe even Saint Paul."

The women snickered, a good sign that the night would pass if not in complete comfort, at least in developing friendship.

Not ready to sleep despite the long trip, Gabriella sat on the unclaimed bed. "I'm sorry R.C. made us stay together since you'd rather be alone. I'll try to convince him to make other arrangements for the duration of the trip."

"No, that's all right. I don't suppose I should have complained." Unpacking her night shift, Fern's tone indicated she still wasn't happy. "I'm amazed by you, Gabriella."

"Amazed? Why?"

"It's been a terrible day, but you've never said a word of complaint."

"Complaining won't make things better. It might even make things seem worse."

"I suppose that's the best attitude to take. How can you maintain such a kind disposition, especially with your father being known for his hard personality?"

That hurt. "His hard personality?"

"Why, yes. Everyone knows him as crotchety and difficult."

Perhaps Father's reputation was deserved, but why did Fern feel compelled to share the news of everyone's negative opinion with Gabriella? After all, she was his daughter.

Obviously unaware that she had made any blunder, Fern

slipped on her night shift. "At least you are nothing like him. Perhaps you are like your mother."

"I—I don't remember Mother. I wish I did. At least you remember your mother."

"Yes. She was a plain woman. R.C. inherited Papa's fine physique and handsome face, but I got Mama's face and form, I'm sorry to say."

Gabriella couldn't deny that Fern would never win a contest to be a model in the Montgomery Ward catalog, but she looked for something positive to say. "I wouldn't be sorry. You are blessed with thick hair and a clear complexion. Not every girl can say that."

"Really?" Fern regarded her image in the mirror over the basin. Her nose boasted plenty of length, and her irises seemed so colorless they melted into the rest of her sallow face. "I suppose you have a point." A glimmer of a smile crossed her lips then faded. "R.C. says I'll die a spinster because of my plain looks and my way of speaking my mind."

As for Fern's blunt speech, Gabriella didn't want to emphasize how much she agreed with R.C. "I know you don't mean any harm."

"No, I don't." Her eyes didn't meet Gabriella's. "I didn't say anything to offend you, did I?"

"Well, you were a bit rough on my father just now."

"Oh." Fern shrugged. "It's no secret. You mean to say you didn't know his reputation?"

"I don't suppose it comes as a complete surprise, but you might have exercised more sensitivity. He is on his deathbed, you know." Verbalizing the unwelcome thought gave Gabriella the impulse to do something with her hands. She searched for the pins that held her hair in place so she could brush and then braid it.

"Maybe R.C. is right. Maybe I will die a spinster. I don't want that. I want my own home and family. I don't want to live with my brother the rest of my life."

"Isn't he kind to you?"

"Yes, even though he's cheap."

Gabriella chuckled. "I think he's aware of your opinion."

"If he'd be more free with his money, I'd be happier."

"Would you? I don't think so. I think you were right the first time. You want your own home and family. And I surmise you'd like the same for him." Rising, she found the purse where she kept her boar bristle brush. "Doesn't he want a home and family, too? A home where his sister isn't his hostess?"

"With the right wife, yes. Someone with a nice disposition. And that brings me back to my question. How do you keep such a nice disposition about yourself? You have a depressing life. Your father is old and sick—dying, even. Your mother is dead. Your grandfather has disappeared, and you may go all this way with us only to discover he's dead, too. You have no husband. How do you stay cheerful?"

"I was more cheerful until you told me how terrible my life is." Gabriella looked to the ceiling and back in an exaggerated manner to show Fern she joked.

"I'm sorry. But it's true."

"I try not to look at my life as one long rain shower. I look to the Lord as the source of my joy. Each day I pray for His strength, and then I rededicate my life to Him." Gabriella took the brush to her hair and made a mental note to thank the Lord that their carriage had been enclosed. Otherwise, the dirt and dust from the road would have been impossible to remove.

"I love the Lord, too, but R.C. still thinks I'll be a spinster."

"The Lord hasn't promised me a husband. I'm far from perfect as a maiden, and I'll be a far-from-perfect wife. But I'll do my best. Remembering the One I really serve helps me to be my best."

"Maybe I should do the same. But I don't want to be one of the sugarcoated Christians that puts on an act when everything is terrible. I see the world as it is."

"Fern, I don't think there's much danger of you ever being too sugary."

"What's that supposed to mean?"

"I mean no harm. I only mean that you shouldn't lose your honesty. Just be more cautious in the way you express yourself. Jesus' commandment that we are to love our neighbor means we must consider others' feelings when we speak or act. That's all."

"I'll never get it right."

"Neither will I. But we can practice with each other. This trip will give us plenty of chances." Gabriella tugged on her hair to set it into a braid.

Fern grimaced. "That's for certain. We'll have more than enough reason to complain. If only R.C.'s meetings along the way hadn't precluded us from taking the train."

The next day, R.C. looked in wonder at the two women who joined him for the next leg of the trip. His sister seemed more relaxed than usual, less combative. He'd been so engrossed in his business meetings the previous day that he hadn't noticed how Gabriella's hair dazzled when the sun picked up the lighter strands in her lush mane. She'd curled all her hair up in one of those complicated styles the women liked of late. The same sun that played with feminine hair proved unforgiving to their skin, too. He'd noticed many a member of the fairer sex who looked beautiful in candlelight were trapped into revealing pock marks and blemishes when harsh sunlight beckoned. Not Gabriella. He imagined he could run his fingers over her cheek without encountering the first dip or bump.

"What's the holdup, R.C.?" Fern placed her hands on her hips.

"Holdup?"

"You're standing there like you've got all day."

"Oh, I'm sorry. Just daydreaming."

"That's not like you."

Caught, he searched for another excuse. "That's what a successful journey will do for a man. Now if my contact in Dallas goes just as well, I'll be whistling all the way home."

"I'd like to see that."

"So would I." Gabriella smiled.

R.C. consulted his pocket watch. "I wish the stableboy would hurry with our horse."

"Looks like we've got someone else ahead of us in line, too." Fern nodded toward a fellow traveler standing nearby.

In spite of Fern's lowered voice, the man overheard her and didn't mind striking up a conversation. "Yep, it sure is a shame how long they're making us wait. Seems everybody wants to get out of here all at once."

"So it seems." R.C. hoped his disinterest would be enough to brush off the man's attentions.

"I couldn't help but overhear y'all earlier. So what are y'all looking for in Dallas? I'm headed that way myself."

R.C. bristled at the fellow's nosiness but didn't want to be rude in front of the ladies. Boredom probably spurred him to tend to their affairs. "I am on business, and one of the ladies here hopes to find her grandfather."

"Is that so? Does her grandfather live near here? If he does, I might know him."

R.C. hesitated, especially since two more men joined the first one. But he reasoned it might be a good idea to grasp at any straw, no matter how bent. "We think he lives in a boardinghouse in Dallas, but we can't be sure."

The youngest of the trio answered. "I'm from Dallas. Do you know the name of the boardinghouse?"

"No, but I understand it's not the most luxurious." R.C. sensed the boardinghouse lead wouldn't be of much help, so he added another clue. "He's an itinerant wood-carver."

The first traveler brightened. "A wood-carver? Why, I think I might know who you're talking about. The wood-carver I know preaches excellent sermons and gives carvings of Christmas ornaments and figurines to the children. Sometimes he shares his talent with the adults as well. He makes beautiful chairs and tables for people who order them. He doesn't seem to keep the money for himself, though. At least, not more than it takes to keep body and soul together. You ought to see the clothes he wears. Rags, nearly. But he won't buy anything new for himself."

Gabriella gasped at the description, sounding so close to Aunt Minnie's letter.

R.C. threw her a look of caution to let her know he was to

handle the conversation. "Do you know where we might find such a man in Dallas?"

"I don't rightly know. I do know he lives on the outskirts of town, all to himself. Hermitlike."

R.C. pressed. "When did you last see him?"

The man scratched his chin. "It's been a few months. He didn't look so well at the time."

Gabriella blurted, "You—you don't think there's reason to think. . ."

"Of course not." R.C. patted her shoulder. "By all accounts, your grandfather was a force to be reckoned with. If he was alive a few months ago, I have no doubt he fought off whatever sickness he had."

At that moment the stableboy appeared with the men's ride.

"Have a good trip, now. Hope you find him." The stranger doffed his hat, as did his companions.

As soon as they were in relative privacy, Fern didn't waste any time posing a query to Gabriella. "Doesn't that bother you?"

"What?"

"Those terrible descriptions of your grandfather."

R.C. wished his sister could hold her tongue. "I'm sure it's not as awful as they depict."

"Perhaps they do tell the truth." Gabriella's eyes took on a sad light. "I am sorry he's living in poverty, but it's by choice. I'm not surprised he inspires people. That's just the type of spirit he has. When I was a little girl, he always made me feel special."

"It's a shame your father and he had to argue."

R.C. suppressed a groan. At least Fern didn't come right

out and ask about the dispute.

Gabriella didn't seem upset about answering. "They argued over money. My grandfather found the Lord and spent what would have been my father's inheritance—and therefore mine—on the poor. Father never forgave him."

R.C. admired the lack of rancor in her voice. "But you can."

"Of course she can," Fern scoffed. "She's got plenty of money thanks to her father."

"Please forgive my sister." R.C. reached for a teasing remark. "You can see why she's an old maid."

"That's quite all right, Fern. You do have a point. Why should I be bitter over money? Father has made fortune for himself. I don't know all the details, since I'm a woman and he won't share much along those lines with me, but I do know I'll be comfortable financially all of my days."

"So you're not bitter at all." Fern tilted her head in a doubtful manner.

"I try not to be bitter, but I do regret that their dispute caused me to miss out on the loving relationship I could have had with them both. Instead, I had to deal with my father's hurt feelings and pain. I hope I don't seem the worse for it, though."

"No, your disposition is very sweet." At once, R.C. was both glad and sorry he'd blurted the observation. Gabriella's purpose was to find her grandfather, not a husband. Still, she blushed prettily.

"Father was bitter over the money because he felt his father left him in a bind he didn't need to be in. But you know what? I think Father is proud of all he was able to accomplish on his own. If Grandfather hadn't left him without an inheritance, then he never would have had the chance to see what all he could do for himself. I think Grandfather did him a favor in that respect. And he's just now seeing that."

"Yes, a man wants to feel a sense of accomplishment, as though he's done something with his life," R.C. agreed.

"Like marry off your old maid sister?" Fern quipped.

"No, I think you can accomplish that on your own, if you really want to be married." R.C. remembered his sister as a sweet baby, and his brotherly instincts surfaced. "If you don't, I'll take care of you."

Gabriella placed her hand on Fern's shoulder. "How blessed you are to have a brother who cares so much about you, Fern. That's priceless."

Fern showed no sentimentality. "What will you do once your father dies?"

R.C. groaned.

"I'm sorry." Fern blushed. "Gabriella is trying to teach me tact, but I'm a slow learner."

"As the expression goes, 'Rome wasn't built in a day.'" Gabriella smiled at them both. "As for where I'd live, I have family. I am on very good terms with my aunt in Arkansas. She could use an extra pair of hands around the house."

"Arkansas. That's down the road a mighty long piece." R.C.'s voice sounded regretful, revealing more than he wanted to admit.

Chapter 5

With rested steeds, they made better time than R.C. anticipated, and before they knew it, the city of Dallas, dangerous and promising, rose upon the horizon. R.C. knew of a reputable hotel, and after getting the ladies and himself checked into their respective rooms— the women again agreeing to share quarters—he met them in the lobby so they could find a place to eat. He didn't know about the ladies, but a big, thick steak seared on the outside and deep pink in the center sounded good to him. He reasoned that he deserved the splurge since his new business prospects looked promising.

The women descended the stairs, and R.C. had to keep from letting out a breath of admiration. Gabriella had looked stunning in her plain but fashionable traveling suit, but in the high-necked green dinner dress she wore, she appeared to be an artist's rendering of the perfect woman. Her glance caught his for an instant, and he sensed her approval of his appearance as well. He was glad he'd taken extra time to rid himself of his five-o'clock shadow with a fresh shave. He found himself hoping she would draw close enough to him to notice the enticing aroma the shaving cream left on his face and the scent of lavender soap the laundress had used on his shirt.

As they neared, he could feel their anticipation. Fern grabbed Gabriella's hand. "Isn't this exciting! Oh, I do hope we see some outlaws. Maybe even a shoot-out."

R.C. tried not to look embarrassed. The hotel was among the best in town, but what if the wrong person overheard her remarks? "Don't be ridiculous. Besides, you don't want to get caught up in the cross fire of a shoot-out."

"I didn't say I wanted to die an old maid, brother dear. I just said I wanted to see a shoot-out." Fern glanced to the ceiling and returned her gaze to their female companion. "Oh imagine, Gabriella, if one of the outlaws saw us in a crowd, took us on his horse, and rode away. . . ." She sighed. "I wonder what an outlaw's hideout is like?"

"If an outlaw took you on his horse, it would be to steal your jewels and to ask for a ransom."

"Oh, how romantic!"

He eyed Fern's lace collar. "There's nothing romantic about losing your ruby brooch and making me pay a ransom to get you back. If you think it's so romantic, I'll let the outlaw keep you."

"R.C.!" Gabriella's tone was scolding, but she smiled.

"Aren't you glad you don't have a big brother to spoil all the fun?" Fern's wry expression told them she was chastised well enough.

Gabriella didn't respond to Fern but cut her gaze to R.C. ever so briefly. How did she feel about him? What was she thinking? Oh, why did he bother to speculate? She couldn't be feeling anything about him. She had too many other things to vex her—her grandfather, her father, and the real possibility of being alone all too soon. She had no time to think of marriage, even if she'd been so inclined.

Marriage? Since when had he thought about marriage?

That evening he had to meet with the landowner and his lawyer to discuss terms of sale. An event that under normal circumstances would have sent his heart racing seemed dull in comparison to what a future with Gabriella might hold.

Over the next hour, he caught himself only half listening to the others. Flashes of future romance and family life came to mind an astounding number of times. Fern still had a ways to go as far as developing tact, but Gabriella's lessons seemed to be doing her some good. He wanted marriage for his sister not only because it was her desire, but she would make a sensible mother who would rear sturdy children. A Christian man would find in her a devoted wife.

But if Fern did manage to make a match, that would leave him alone. He hadn't thought about the prospect of true solitude until he witnessed Fern and Gabriella exchanging pleasant conversation. R.C. would miss Fern if she were to marry.

His thoughts turned to Gabriella. He could imagine himself dining with her for every meal. Her flashing gray eyes, her lovely hair that he imagined would be pleasing to the touch, her lilting laugh—all made him want to be with her more. From time to time she would look at him with—was it longing? He found himself hoping so.

Chapter 6

The next day, R.C. could see the distress in Gabriella's face as he escorted her around the city. First they tried a pharmacy, then an insurance office, then a dry-goods store, only to turn up nothing. None of the tradesmen could help them, either.

They looked to a gorgeous church on Floyd Street. "Perhaps the pastor here knows something. After all, your grandfather is reputed to be quite the preacher."

"Yes, let's."

They entered but found no one in the building. Still, the stop wasn't wasted since it allowed them time to pray in the empty sanctuary. From the corner of his eye, R.C. observed that Gabriella appeared as an angel as she petitioned the Lord. He hoped their prayers would be answered.

As the three exited, he searched for words to comfort her. "I've been thinking how everyone says the wood-carver they knew moves from place to place. Do you reckon he might have moved on by now?"

"I've thought of that, but I'm praying he hasn't gone far."

A surge of generosity filled him. "I'll be willing to take you anywhere you think he might be."

Her grateful look filled his heart with joy. "Thank you for that. I don't want to take advantage. And besides, I don't know how much time I have before. . ."

He wanted to embrace her, to comfort her, to let her bury her face in his shoulder. He wanted to take her burdens onto himself. But he couldn't. He had to content himself with patting her hand. "I don't believe the Lord will take your father before he can reconcile with your grandfather. I just don't believe that."

"He had so many years, and he let them slip through his fingers."

"Time moves much too quickly, doesn't it?" Fern's tone displayed pensiveness.

As they walked, R.C.'s mind went to unwelcome thoughts. He wasn't getting any younger himself. Marriage was something he'd always planned on but had never taken the time to court a girl toward that end. He'd had a few opportunities but had always put making the next business deal over and above romance. Could it be that the Lord had wanted him to wait for Gabriella?

"I'm so discouraged. I'll never find Grandfather. Maybe we should just go home."

"Look, we have one more place to try." He tipped his head toward a saloon on Elm Street. How could he in good conscience take two young women into such a place? "I wish we could have found out something before having to resort to a saloon." He thought for a moment. "Tell you what. Let me take you two ladies back to the hotel, and I'll go in alone."

"Must I wait another moment?" Gabriella's impatience showed. "Everyone is sure to know we're respectable as long as we stay near you."

Because he wanted to please Gabriella, the idea tempted him. Then an image of leering, drunken men entered his mind. The idea of their gazes touching upon Gabriella—not to mention his own sister—made him clench his fists. "It's been a tough road, and I do mean that in the strictest sense of the word, but I want to protect you ladies. I'll not have a whiff of scandal associated with you by allowing you to go there. I'll make my errand as quick as possible."

Seeing she had lost the argument, Gabriella turned agreeable. "Whatever you say, R.C. I do thank you for asking on my behalf. Not that I think there's any hope."

He prayed, for her sake, that there was.

Gabriella made an attempt to concentrate on her knitting, but her position on the maple bed didn't lend itself to craftwork. Even worse, time dragged while she and Fern awaited R.C.'s return. "He's taking forever. I wish he'd let me go with him."

"He was only trying to protect you. He would never forgive himself if anything happened to you. And I wouldn't forgive him, either." Fern returned to her book.

Gabriella supposed Fern had a point. Based on Aunt Minnie's letter, Grandfather hadn't lived in a savory part of town. She wondered if it would be dangerous for her to visit Grandfather. At least R.C. had promised to bring him to the hotel once he was found.

Finally they heard a knock on the door. Gabriella felt her heart race. This was it! Surely he had news of her grandfather's whereabouts.

She rushed to place her knitting in her bag, out of sight, as Fern answered. "Oh, it's just you."

"Yes, it's just me."

Gabriella hastened to stand beside Fern. Her heartbeat increased. "You—you don't have Grandfather with you." Tears threatened.

"Please don't be alarmed." R.C. touched her on the arm with a quick motion. He didn't come into the room but remained outside in the hall, keeping his voice low so as not to disturb others or to be overheard. "I have some news. I found your grandfather's last landlady, and she says he left only a couple of weeks ago."

Gabriella gasped. "Praise the Lord. He's alive, then."

"I have every reason to believe so."

Her concern turned to excitement. "So where is he? Here in town? Please, take me to him quickly."

"I will, but he's not here in town."

"Oh." Her shoulders slumped.

"He's not so very far from here. They seem to think he might be living near Camp Ford."

Fern's eyes widened. "You mean the old Confederate prison camp?"

"That's the one." R.C. looked at the floor, his mouth set in a sad line. "Hard to believe there were once six thousand men there."

"Not all were Union prisoners, surely."

"No. There were slaves and, of course, the guards."

"I remember Father talking about that camp. Not that he liked to speak about the war." Sadness tugged at Gabriella's heart. "He was there both as a recruit and, later, as one of the prison guards." She shuddered. "Why would my grandfather be somewhere like that?"

"Hard to say, but I'd venture that perhaps that's one place where people will let him live without bothering him too much."

"He's not actually living in the camp, is he?" Fern asked.

"I hope not." The idea of her beloved grandfather living in a place where so much heartache and death had taken place left Gabriella cold.

"The only way we can find out anything is to see for ourselves. I figure it will take us about two days to get there. We can stay in Tyler since that's the nearest town, and hopefully we'll find a place to stay along the way the first night."

The inconvenience didn't bother Gabriella. She only wanted to find her grandfather. "Let's leave as early as possible. I don't think I'll be able to sleep tonight anyway."

The night did prove restless. Gabriella tossed and turned, and she could hear Fern do the same. The next morning they were up bright and early.

"I feel terrible that you're taking us all this way, R.C." Gabriella tugged at the sleeves of her traveling suit, trying to make herself as comfortable as possible before boarding the carriage. "I know this wasn't in your plans. Believe me, I'll compensate you handsomely for your time and trouble."

"It's no trouble. And I'm not worried about compensation."

His strong voice and the look in R.C.'s eyes told her he meant it.

"That's a new twist." Fern's mouth curved as though to illustrate. "You must have my brother's heart, to make him not consider money."

Fern's observation took her by surprise. Had her growing fondness of R.C. been that obvious? And could it be so? Could she have captured his attention?

"Oh, pshaw! Please don't embarrass your brother." Gabriella cut a glance to him and noticed he didn't protest but hoisted himself into the driver's seat.

Situated in her own seat, Gabriella averted her eyes. . .and her thoughts. She didn't want her heart to be anywhere but on her mission.

The trip seemed both fast and slow. Fast because the mild temperature and sunshine helped them along the way. Slow because she was eager to learn the truth about her grandfather— whether he was dead or alive, and, if alive, if he wanted to return to Houston and reconcile with her father.

On the second day of their journey, they neared the old Confederate camp but saw no sign of a wood-carver, or any dwelling where he might live. Gabriella's eyes misted in distress at not finding Grandfather right away, and in thinking of the suffering soldiers, both sides fighting for what they believed to be right. The contemplation moved her to say a silent prayer. *Lord, let brother not fight against brother in this country ever again.*

They journeyed down a rough road. Hitting rocky places and holes caused the women to be jostled, but Gabriella ignored the discomfort. She was too busy looking for any sign of life. They rode the next four miles to Tyler without seeing anything promising. By that time, Gabriella wanted to cry.

Fern placed her hand on Gabriella's shaking shoulder. "There's time, and we haven't even begun to ask around here in Tyler yet."

Gabriella responded with a grateful smile. She could never reward Fern or R.C. enough for their patience and friendship. Even as she thought about her grandfather, she couldn't help but think about R.C. and what might happen once they returned to Houston. Was R.C. being nice to her because he felt sorry for her? She sensed deeper feelings, that she had touched his heart in some way. She knew he had touched hers with gentle compassion she didn't realize he possessed.

They disembarked in front of a hotel. Fern looked toward the Smith County Courthouse. "This is a bustling place."

"I'll have to agree." R.C. adjusted his hat. "The population is growing by leaps and bounds. Cotton is king in these parts, but on the way here, I was thinking about something else. A fruit orchard, maybe."

"R.C. always has his dreams." Fern shook her head.

Gabriella breathed in the mild air. "Why, I think this is a fine climate for growing fruit. People always need to eat, and who doesn't love fresh fruit?"

"I might look into acquiring some land here while I'm in town." R.C.'s interest seemed ignited by Gabriella's positive response. "You could take lessons from Gabriella, my dear sister. She is an encourager, whereas you always tell me things cannot be done."

"As if he has anyone to tend to an orchard here," Fern muttered in Gabriella's direction.

"I heard that," R.C. snapped. "I know people in more places than you think."

"Let's not argue. I think the best thing for us to do is try to get some sleep." Gabriella made the suggestion for the benefit of her companions, expecting once again a restless night for herself.

The next day they repeated what they had done in Dallas, with the women waiting while R.C. asked anyone who'd answer if they'd seen a man matching Gabe's description. Gabriella held out little hope. The old tintype she had lent R.C. showed them an image that, by all accounts, looked nothing like the man as he appeared at present.

As the women waited in the room, Gabriella worked on knitting a red scarf as a gift for R.C., a fact Fern promised she wouldn't reveal. Because R.C. had been so kind to her and her father, she had begun knitting it a couple of weeks before they embarked on the trip. If she didn't dawdle, the gift would be ready for presentation sometime during the Christmas season. Meanwhile, Fern sewed the finishing touches on a Sunday handkerchief for her brother, stitching his initials using the satin stitch. The blue thread looked striking against the white cotton.

Every five minutes, Gabriella looked at the little clock locket she wore, but Fern relented first. "I'm hungry. I suggest we find a place to have a bite to eat."

"But what about R.C.? Shouldn't we wait for him?"

Fern took her silver thimble off her thumb and placed it in her sewing bag. "He probably got involved in the search and isn't even thinking about eating. Who knows when we'll have lunch if we wait for him?"

Gabriella wasn't hungry, but she had reached the end of a row so she stopped for Fern's sake. The women checked their appearances in the mirror before heading downstairs to the lobby.

An older woman standing behind the desk looked up at them as they approached. "May I help you?"

"We were hoping you could recommend a good place nearby where the two of us could enjoy a light luncheon." Gabriella didn't listen to the answer. Instead, a wood rendition of Albrecht Dürer's *Praying Hands* image entranced her. "That carving. It's beautiful."

The woman looked at it as though she were seeing it for the first time. "Yes, it is. I bought it from an old wood-carver just a couple of weeks ago. I'm sure if you stay here long enough, you'll see him. He cuts quite a strange figure even for these parts."

Gabriella's heart beat faster and she heard Fern gasp. "Really?"

The woman nodded. "He's too thin for his own good and wears cast-off clothing. But I must say, he keeps himself clean and his hair and beard are always groomed."

That sounded like her grandfather. "He's an older man?"

"I'd say so. In his seventies, I would guess. And he has wisdom to go along with his years. He told me to remember that I should always pray without ceasing. The carving is a reminder."

"So he's a preacher?" Fern asked.

"Not so much. I mean, he preaches, but in a way that makes you know he cares about you. He doesn't preach at you or threaten you. When people are around him, they feel God's love. He's touched a lot of people here. I hope you have a chance to see him before he moves on." The woman looked the young ladies up and down. "You two have plenty of money. Be sure to buy one or two of his carvings for yourselves. He lives off the alms he receives for his carvings. He never charges anyone a set price. They give out of love, and in exchange for his encouragement and wisdom. You know, he's wise but never critical. That's not something you find every day."

Moved by sentiment, Gabriella placed her hands on her chest. To think that her grandfather had touched so many lives in such a positive way made her realize that if she ever held a trace of resentment toward him, it had to be released at that moment. Surely Grandfather was doing the work God called him to do. "Where does he live? Do you know?"

"The last I heard, he was living on the outskirts of town, in a rickety old house that was abandoned after the war of northern aggression." She clucked. "A lot of us folks saw mighty hard times after that terrible war. We're just getting back on our feet now, it seems. You know, we're mighty kind around these parts. Some of the men offered to fix up the house for him, but he wouldn't have it. I don't know why he wants to live like that. His wood carvings are popular and bring him fine prices."

Gabriella could understand what was incomprehensible to others. "Ma'am, we are waiting for Miss Sparks's brother to join us. When he arrives, do you think someone would take us to the place where the wood-carver lives? I'm afraid we might struggle to find it by ourselves. I'll pay well."

"If it means that much to you, I can get my son to show you the place." She paused, seeming to regret her eagerness to make the offer. "I don't mean any disrespect, but are you sure he wants to see you? I'd hate to invade his privacy."

"Oh, he'll want to see me. I'm his granddaughter from Houston."

"What? His granddaughter? I had no idea he had any family at all. He never mentioned anyone." She squinted at Gabriella.

That admission hurt, but Gabriella wasn't surprised.

"Why, I do believe I see the resemblance."

Her heart lightened. "I'm his namesake. Gabriella."

"How about that? Well, let's not waste another moment. Let me get my boy now."

R.C. could feel Gabriella's nervousness as they made their way to Tyler. He had already discovered from a blacksmith that a man matching Gabe's description lived on the outskirts of town, and the women's information matched his. Thankfully the innkeeper's son knew where Gabe—or at least the man they believed to be Gabe—lived.

"This is it." He nodded toward a wooden structure about a quarter mile from the old camp.

Gabriella gasped. She'd been warned that her grandfather lived in a poor state, but reality still shocked her. The one-room house barely stood against the wind. Its roof sagged, and yellowed newspaper covered a square hole where a window should have been. Warped wood had never seen paint. She speculated that the house had been built as a makeshift shelter, or perhaps as a guardhouse. She supposed no one anticipated it would be used this long, especially without upkeep.

R.C. clasped her hand. Grateful for the surprise gesture, she squeezed back, out of growing affection and a desire to hold on to an anchor.

"Is everything all right, ma'am?" Their boy guide wrinkled his brow.

She nodded too quickly. The grandfather she remembered would never have lived in such a place. If anything, he might have brought food and clothing to the occupants out of pity for their obviously distressed state. "I—I don't think we should bother. Grandfather couldn't be in there. There's been a mistake. I just know it."

"We've come too far not to find out for certain." R.C.'s voice was gentle but encouraging. "To tell the truth, from what you told me about your grandfather, I find this state of affairs hard to believe myself. Let me walk with you. We can face this together."

"*Together.*" Just what she wanted to hear. She hadn't realized until that moment how much she wanted a man to walk beside her in life.

She sent a silent prayer to the Lord so that she could cope with whatever lay behind the weathered door.

Their guide remained in the carriage, but Fern and R.C. stood behind Gabriella as she knocked.

Silence.

Her heart dipped. In spite of her disappointment over the sorry state of the dwelling, they hadn't come all this way just for him not to be home. Who couldn't have heard a knock on a house so small?

As though he could read her mind, R.C. knocked a second time, with force. The summons produced the sound of shuffling feet. They didn't have much longer to wait. Gabriella held her breath.

An elderly man answered. Despite the warnings that her richly dressed, paunchy grandfather had lost weight and taken to wearing cast-off clothing, she still wasn't prepared for the reedy man standing before her. Instead of wavy, dark hair and large mutton chops, this man's salt-and-pepper tufts barely covered his head, although a long beard concealed a large part of his face. But his gray eyes were unmistakable.

"Grandfather!" She ran into his arms.

His face lit into a smile. "Gabriella? Gabriella? Is that you?"

She stood back, taking in his countenance. "It is."

"What are you doing here?"

"I wanted to find you."

It was his turn to regard her. "Yes, I do believe you're my Gabriella. I wouldn't have believed it if I didn't see the family resemblance with my own eyes." He looked beyond her to R.C. and Fern. "And who are your friends?"

She made the introductions, and he invited them all inside the house. As he spoke, the sound of his voice, with its true cadence, proved to her once and for all she had indeed found her grandfather. The sentiment was just as she imagined their greeting would be. She looked around the tiny room, bare except for a table covered with finished carvings along with a work in progress, a chair, plus a sideboard with a portion of a loaf of bread. She shuddered.

Determined not to let him see her distress, she walked to the table so she could examine his handiwork. "You still have such a knack for carving. Your work is still beautiful." She shared the story of spotting the praying hands carving in the hotel lobby, and the innkeeper's glowing words about him.

Grandfather picked up a sheep and rubbed the bumps in

the facsimile of wool with his index finger. "I give my work over to the Lord and let Him decide what people will be blessed by it." He handed the sheep to his granddaughter. "Here. Will you accept this as a blessing from me?"

The sheep still felt warm from his touch. Gabriella would cherish the moment, and its memento, forever. "Of course. Thank you, Grandfather."

"Remember that you are one of the Lord's sheep."

"I will." Her eyes misted.

Grandfather looked toward R.C. and Fern, then gifted each of them with an angel figurine to represent the Lord's guardianship. Gabriella could see emotion on R.C.'s face, and Fern's eyes teared.

"Thank you, Grandfather, for showing my friends such generosity of spirit. We have heard all sorts of wonderful things about you on our way here. People have been touched by your carvings and your wise words."

"I take no credit for any wisdom I share. It's all from the Lord. He has been good to me."

"Good to you?" Gabriella blurted without thinking. Caught in her own truth, she confessed. "I don't understand this place."

"It's humble to be sure, but no one's laid claim to it, and the landowner gave his permission for me to live here as long as I like. With the money I save on rent I'd pay to a boardinghouse, I can give more food to the poor."

"But must you go to such extremes?"

He turned stern. "If you've just come here to chastise me, just like your father before you, I'll have none of it. Even though you are my namesake."

The prospect of losing his approval, even for a moment, was enough to make her retreat. "No, Grandfather. I don't mean to vex you. I know you are doing the Lord's work. The people in town have told us so."

"It must be hard for a pretty young woman such as yourself to understand, but it's not hard for me. I want to help others. And this is the way I want to do it. I am a happy man. Can you make yourself understand?"

Gabriella wasn't sure.

"Remember how Christ made Himself poor to come down to earth for us? He gave up anything any soul could want up in heaven and lived as a humble preacher."

"Of course I remember."

"That's what I'm trying to do. Not that I'm the perfect example. Far from it. Only Jesus is the perfect example. But I want to try." A faraway look lingered in his eyes. "I'm sorry I couldn't make your father understand. Jesus said the gospel message would separate families."

Gabriella felt led to recite aloud a passage from the book of Matthew that she had learned in Sunday school class years ago. She had held the passage in her heart because its words touched her all too closely. " 'For I am come to set a man at variance against his father, and the daughter against her mother, and the daughter in law against her mother in law. And a man's foes shall be they of his own household. He that loveth father or mother more than me is not worthy of me: and he that loveth son or daughter more than me is not worthy of me. And he that taketh not his cross, and followeth after me, is not worthy of me. He that findeth his life shall lose it: and he that loseth his life for my sake shall find it.' "

"That's it. I'm only sorry that the part about family division turned out to be the literal truth for me."

"I know." Sadness washed over Gabriella.

"Do you resent the fact that I took away part of your earthly inheritance to pursue the path I think God laid out for me?"

She thought before she answered. "This trip has shown me that I had to let go of any trace of resentment I may have felt. I have learned much in the past few days. For that, and for R.C. and Fern, I am grateful."

He scanned her clothing. "I see you hardly live in poverty."

"Father is very proud of the fact he made his own fortune after you abandoned us." She tightened her lips, sorry she blurted such a candid comment. Perhaps Fern's blunt way of speaking had rubbed off on her. "I'm sorry. I didn't mean that."

"Yes, you did, and it's true. I'm sorry that I left you alone." He touched his hand to hers. She noticed calloused fingers, a result of years of carving life into wood.

"I'm sorry to see you living in such squalor."

"I don't have to, you know. I have given away yet another fortune."

"Have you?"

"Yes. Wealthy patrons value my work. They pay me well."

"Of course. You are so talented."

"My talent is not why I am rewarded. I am rewarded because I am doing the Lord's work."

Sniffles from Fern caught Gabriella's attention. She dabbed her lace handkerchief to her eyes. "I'm sorry. You just touched me."

"And me, too, if you don't think me less of a man for admitting it," R.C. said. "Sir, you have inspired me to be less concerned about all the real estate deals I can make and more concerned about my family and friends."

"Are you as unfeeling as all that? I don't believe it. You have a heart, you do. And you are strong."

"How right you are, Grandfather. You would have been so proud if you could have seen R.C. protecting me on this trip. We had to travel through some mighty wild country, you know."

"Aw, I didn't do anything." R.C. shuffled his feet in the familiar way that always endeared him to Gabriella.

"And you're right in that R.C. does care about other people." Gabriella hoped he cared about her especially. "I can see now why people credit you with compassion and wisdom."

"My brother has a heart, but he's never shown it the way I've seen since he met Gabriella." Fern shot R.C. a knowing look.

The motion made Gabriella's heart do a little skip.

Grandfather's eyes took on a kind light as he studied Fern. "You, my girl, are honest and true. I have a feeling you'll make some man a good wife in the Lord's time."

"That's what I hope." Fern didn't seem embarrassed to make such an admission.

"Now, we didn't come all this way to talk about Fern and me." R.C. turned his attention to Gabriella. "Tell him why you really came."

Gabriella took in a breath. "It's Father."

"Yes. I was wondering when you would bring up my son. He doesn't realize it, but I pray for him every day. And of course I pray for you as well. Why do I get the distinct feeling that you have bad news to share?" Grandfather paled. "Is your father ill?"

Gabriella swallowed. "Yes. I'm afraid he is."

"I'm sorry, but there is nothing I can do but to keep praying. He won't see me, you know."

"If you had said that only a few days ago, I wouldn't have argued," Gabriella said. "But he's changed. He is sorry for the years the two of you lost, and he wants your forgiveness before the Lord takes him. I can't help but think your faithful prayers have something to do with his change of heart."

"Then he knows you're here?"

"Yes, he does."

"He asked her to come," R.C. confirmed.

Sadness deepened on Grandfather's expression. "His anger has eaten away at him all these years, hasn't it?"

"I'm afraid he is a bitter man. And he has been for years."

"He was bitter when I left, and I'm sorry his disposition never improved. That must have been difficult for you. If I could have changed that, I would have." Grandfather looked away, as if hoping to see something elusive.

"I know. But I know Father loves me."

"I think in his way, he does. And you certainly love him, to come all this way to ask me to forgive him."

"Yes, I do. It is his dying wish to reconcile with you in person. So will you come home with me?" She took Grandfather's thin but strong hands in hers.

"*Home.* That's such a funny word. I haven't considered the old place home in a number of years. But I will come with you, my dear."

"Oh, Grandfather, I am so happy." She hugged him.

Chapter 7

R.C. barely remembered the long ride back to Houston. For him, it was a fuzzy haze of joy. Gabriella had all but told him she admired him, right in front of her grandfather. He loved listening to Gabriella chatter with her grandfather, picking up right where they left off, it seemed. He could see that in the older man's eyes, Gabriella would always be the adorable little girl he left all those years ago. He sensed that Gabe Noell regretted missing out on her early years but could also see that the man had followed his heart and the leading he felt from the Lord. So few men had the courage to do that. Obsessed with making a good living, they sacrificed everything else. R.C. assessed his own way of living. He'd always loved the deal, and real estate was his passion. But it seemed hollow when he witnessed the love between Gabriella and her long-lost relative. And his faith seemed heartless in comparison to the faith of the itinerant preacher he had just met.

Thy will, Lord, Thy will.

They pulled into town early on Christmas morning. R.C. couldn't remember when he was so excited about the day, and his emotions had nothing to do with gifts. As quickly as possible, he dropped his sister off at their home, not wanting to delay her rest. Soon thereafter, as he escorted Gabe and Gabriella to the Noell home, he could feel Gabriella's excitement and Gabe's trepidation.

Gabriella bounded in the front door, with R.C. and Gabe following. "Father! I'm home!"

R.C. sent up a silent prayer that her father hadn't become increasingly ill in their absence.

"Is that you, Gabriella?" His voice sounded strong as ever. R.C. breathed a sigh of relief and thanked God.

"Yes, Father. I brought you the best Christmas present in the world." Gabriella took her grandfather's gnarled hand in her young fingers. She looked back at R.C. and nodded to let him know he was welcome to follow. Keeping a slow step with him, she escorted Gabe Noell into the sickroom. When the two men saw one another, R.C. could read their range of emotions. Their eyes registered surprise, first that they were there at all, then shock at each other's appearance, then fear at what might follow, then a softening of their stance toward each other.

"It's all right, Father. Grandfather is happy to see you. Aren't you, Grandfather?"

The old man nodded. "Henry." His voice registered just above a whisper.

Gabriella let go of her grandfather's hand, then hesitated.

Henry's cough made R.C.'s own throat ache in sympathy.

"Now take it easy, boy." Gabe moved closer to Henry, showing he was unperturbed by the prospect of becoming sick himself.

Henry's smile formed a half *C.* "I haven't had anybody say that to me in years. You haven't changed a bit."

"But I have."

R.C. looked at Gabriella. Both of them knew it was time to leave, to let the men right past wrongs and to reconcile. The men didn't seem to notice their departure from the room.

As she shut the door, Gabriella's eyes misted. R.C. couldn't help but put a comforting arm around her shoulders. She looked up at him in a way that he wished she would forever. "I couldn't have done any of this without you, R.C. Thank you."

"So you think they'll come to an understanding?"

"Yes, though much too late in life. They wasted far too many years."

R.C. thought about the path that each man took. "They are alike, yet different. Though it was painful for them to be on poor terms with one another, I don't think your grandfather would have touched as many lives if he had stayed here. God used him. It was obvious from all the talk we heard on our trip. You have a lot to be proud of, Gabriella, and thankful for." Never had Gabriella seemed so appealing. He wanted to kiss her full lips, to feel their softness against his. If he could, he would need no other Christmas gift. But he couldn't take advantage of her vulnerability, when there was so much other emotion. He had to wait.

Judging from her wistful expression, Gabriella seemed to be going through a similar battle with herself and was trying mightily to win. "I'm sorry I delayed the trip so we couldn't be home in time to celebrate today with a party. Perhaps you would agree to come to an Epiphany party instead."

"Indeed. I wouldn't miss it." He couldn't remember when he anticipated a celebration more.

Gabriella wrapped green tissue paper around the scarf she planned to give R.C. at the party. Tying a red bow on top, she hoped he liked it. She was sure the robust red color would look well against his handsome face, bringing out the ruddiness in his complexion and making him glow even more with the health he obviously possessed. She didn't know if he'd remember her with a gift or not. She didn't care. She just wanted to thank him for being kind to her, a tagalong on a business trip. She had also remembered Fern.

"Whatcha got there?" Entering from the back bedroom, smelling of bay rum, Gabe was hardly recognizable as the itinerant wood-carver she had found living near Tyler.

"The scarf I knitted for R.C. I showed you yesterday, didn't I?"

"That you did. Any man with sense would like that."

Gabriella chuckled.

"You always seem to be living proof of one of my favorite proverbs in scripture." He smiled. " 'A merry heart maketh a cheerful countenance.' "

"Yes, I am merry today. Especially now that you and Father have reconciled." She decided not to add that the prospect of seeing R.C. again kept her mood light.

She had tied the ribbon onto Fern's present when Miss

Pamela, this time as an invited guest, let herself in and yoo-hooed.

Gabriella turned and saw the older woman dressed in the blue velvet Christmas dress she had worn for the past couple of Christmas celebrations. "So nice to see you."

She heard Grandfather take in a breath. Miss Pamela's expression melted from happy party anticipation to the softness of a babe when she saw him.

Gabriella looked from one to the other. If she didn't know better, she'd think love brewed as sure as the pot of tea she had simmering on the stove.

Watching his reaction to Miss Pamela over the past few days, Gabriella saw a side of her grandfather she hadn't known. When she was near him, his enthusiasm matched any young suitor's. This was neither the wealthy gentleman of long-ago memory nor the wood-carver with whom she had just become acquainted.

"You look charming today, Pamela."

"Aren't you the bold one?" Though she teased, Miss Pamela's pleasure was evident.

Then, as if realizing he had an audience, Grandfather turned to Gabriella. "You're too young to remember this, but after your grandmother passed, Miss Evitts and I would see each other from time to time."

"But I wasn't enough to keep him here." The older woman's voice held no rancor.

"I'm sorry," Grandfather was quick to say. "If anyone or anything, except Gabriella, could have kept me here, it would have been you. But you see, I felt called to give up everything and live much as Jesus lived while He was here on the earth.

I couldn't live as I was and feel I was true to my calling, and I couldn't ask you to give up your life for me."

"I know. And I understand."

At that moment, Gabriella's admiration for Miss Evitts increased a hundredfold. She had never thought she could be that understanding. Certainly her father hadn't.

Before long the house bustled with a small but celebratory band of friends. Reconciliation helped Father rebound enough that he could make a brief appearance in the parlor, holding court in his favorite chair for all of a half hour. Gabriella hadn't seen him so happy in recent memory.

Spotting Douglas Tizdale, Gabriella remembered an errand she'd made a mental note to do. "Oh, Fern, come with me a moment." She took her friend by the hand.

"Something exciting?" Fern looked well. She had chosen a flattering pink party frock, the likes of which Gabriella could hardly believe she owned. "Yes, I have someone I want you to meet."

During introductions, the couple's gazes met, and when Gabriella pointed out Fern's new hobby of bird-watching, a passion of Douglas's, their faces reflected a natural bond.

R.C. came up behind her. "You certainly are a wonderful hostess. I am astounded that you were able to put on this extraordinary celebration so soon after returning from such a dramatic trip."

"Oh, it was nothing." Gabriella's modesty was both false and reflexive. Wishing she had thought of a more witty reply, she hurried to the next topic. "I have something for you. Could you take a moment with me in the kitchen? I'm afraid all the seats are taken elsewhere in the house."

"Your kitchen is always a pleasant place to while away the time."

The kitchen seemed particularly homey that day, with scents of cookies, candy, and wassail lingering in the air. After they were seated, R.C. handed a shocked Gabriella a box wrapped in white tissue paper with a paper lace tag.

She read aloud the handwritten words. "Merry Christmas with love from R.C." The reference to love made her blush.

"I hope you don't think me too bold."

Her heart beat faster. "No." Deliberately not looking at him, she tore open the paper with ladylike precision to reveal a bottle of *Fleur d'Italie* perfume from Guerlain. "French perfume! How exotic and exquisite!"

"I understand from my sister that women like this sort of thing instead of books such as the one I got her for Christmas."

"I believe she mentioned it. You're learning."

"I hope so." Nervous, he took in a breath. "Do you think I have a lot to learn about women?"

She laughed in spite of herself. "I wouldn't know."

"Maybe you would like to discover for yourself?" His voice wasn't coy or teasing.

Her heart beat faster. "I—I would like that."

"That's just what I wanted to hear." He took her by the hand until they were both standing, embracing one another. He gazed into her face. At that moment, she realized the kiss she had awaited was about to be hers. Half closing her eyes, she looked upon his lips, the lips she had been dreaming of kissing.

They drew closer, and then touched her, warmly and softly,

with ease at first, then becoming more urgent, filled with passion and longing. "How I have dreamed of this moment," he whispered in between kisses.

She drew him to herself more tightly, with an awakened passion she didn't know she possessed. If only the kisses didn't have to end. But finally, unwillingly, they drew apart from one another, yet remained in each other's arms.

"You were there all along for me, only I didn't know it. Praise the Lord for opening my eyes to see the real you." R.C.'s eyes glimmered.

"And I, the real you. May our eyes and hearts be open to one another forever."

Epilogue

December 25, the following year

Hurry! Everyone's waiting." Dressed in green finery, Fern, Gabriella's maid of honor, touched her shoulder for emphasis.

"They can't start without me," Gabriella teased.

"When I marry this spring, I won't be late for my wedding." Fern fingered the modest diamond ring on her left ring finger. "I'll never keep Douglas waiting."

Gabriella's mood was too light for her to resist another jest. Knowing Douglas would be escorting Fern as R.C.'s groomsman, she asked, "But isn't he waiting for you now?"

"Not any longer than I can help!"

Gabriella grew more pensive as she recognized her father waiting for her in the narthex. By the grace of God, through the power of forgiveness and reconciliation, he had slowly regained enough health to see her through this day. Gabriella took his arm and looked down the church aisle sprinkled with rose petals and saw R.C. waiting for her. Her friends and family stood in honor of her and of the day she would wed the one she loved. Even Grandfather, escorting Miss Pamela, stood to see her greet her groom.

Gabriella couldn't have asked for more. She was home, and would always be home, with those she loved. Indeed, love had come home for Christmas.

Tamela Hancock Murray, a Virginia native, is a bestselling, award-winning author of over twenty fiction and nonfiction books and many novellas. Her writing appears in several compilations as well. Tamela seeks to provide other Christians with edifying, entertaining works. She enjoys living in Northern Virginia with her husband of over twenty-five years. They are the proud parents of a daughter in high school and another who has already left the nest. In her spare time, Tamela enjoys volunteering, traveling, entertaining and of course, reading! Learn more about Tamela at www.tamelahancockmurray.com. She loves to hear from readers through her Web site or through e-mail at Tamela@tamelahancockmurray.com.

A Letter to Our Readers

Dear Readers:

In order that we might better contribute to your reading enjoyment, we would appreciate you taking a few minutes to respond to the following questions. When completed, please return to the following: Fiction Editor, Barbour Publishing, Inc., P.O. Box 719, Uhrichsville, OH 44683.

1. Did you enjoy reading *A Woodland Christmas*?
   ❑ Very much. I would like to see more books like this.
   ❑ Moderately—I would have enjoyed it more if _____
   _____
   _____

2. What influenced your decision to purchase this book?
   (Check those that apply.)
   ❑ Cover   ❑ Back cover copy   ❑ Title   ❑ Price
   ❑ Friends   ❑ Publicity   ❑ Other

3. Which story was your favorite?
   ❑ *To Hear Angels Sing*   ❑ *The Christmas Chain*
   ❑ *The Face of Mary*   ❑ *Love Came Home at Christmas*

4. Please check your age range:
   ❑ Under 18   ❑ 18–24   ❑ 25–34
   ❑ 35–45   ❑ 46–55   ❑ Over 55

5. How many hours per week do you read? _____

Name _____

Occupation _____

Address _____

City_____ State _____ Zip _____

E-mail _____

If you enjoyed

A WOODLAND CHRISTMAS

then read

A DOOR COUNTY CHRISTMAS

If you enjoyed

A WOODLAND CHRISTMAS

then read

A RIVERWALK CHRISTMAS